When the Drama Has Ceased

a novel by

J. Monique Gambles

It's BOLD Publishing
Published by It's BOLD Publishing
P.O. BOX 914
Desoto Texas 75123-0914

© Copy Right 2010

Also by J. Monique Gambles

Saturday's Epiphany: Reflections

For Peggy and Junney

You will always live within me.

$\mathbf{F}$oreword

Without a past
one would have no future.
Without accepting the past
and knowing when to let go of it, your past will eat you alive
and destroy your future.
The best thing you can do with the past is
to embrace it,
learn from it,
and let it go, if you want to make it.

Author's Note

This is a work of fiction. Any references to actual people, living or dead, events, or locales are intended to give the novel a sense of authenticity. Other names, characters, places, and incidents are either a product of the author's imagination or are used fictitiously, and their resemblance, if any, to real life counterparts is absolutely coincidental.

PART I
SEEDS PLANTED

Chapter One

Born Mackenzie Kennedy to proud parents Jun and Pat, Mackenzie was brought into a world filled with calamity. Her father, Jun, the pusher, pimp, and social user, and her mother, Pat, the battered and often misunderstood drunkard, formed the make-up of Mackenzie's genealogy. All that they were in some way or another would affect who Mackenzie would become.

By the time Mackenzie was six, her father had left her, her two brothers, two sisters, and Pat to be on the streets and live life by his own rules.

Stricken with extreme poverty, and a mother who began drinking heavier to heal her aching heart, Mackenzie wondered what would become of her and her family now that Jun had gone.

As fate would have it Mackenzie and her family would have to move from place to place and jump from school to school, trying to survive off of welfare and scraps from old family friends until Pat finally found an apartment on Nostrand Ave. The tiny, roach and mouse infested, one-bedroom apartment with peeling ceiling paint, and cracked, wooded floors would be home for the six of them.

After moving all that they had, Pat enrolled Mackenzie and her brothers and sisters into Public School Two Fifty-Six on Kosciusko Street.

With no male supervision except her brothers to keep her in line, Mackenzie resorted to being a tomboy to survive her early childhood, which was filled with physical, sexual, and emotional abuse.

Like any ol' tomboy, Mackenzie wanted to be just like her brothers. She'd often steal some of her brothers' clothes and wear them around the house, until she went to school one day with those clothes, and her brother saw her and gave her the meanest look she had ever seen.

When they made it home from school that day, Eric never said anything about her stealing their clothes, but it was obvious that he was extremely upset.

Eric was the quietest out of the five of them, unlike his twin, Erica, who displayed her emotions easily, and if you made her upset, she was sure to let you know several times for that matter.

From that day on, it was known that Mackenzie was banned from playing with the boys in the family and their clothes. In fact, on several occasions following the dungaree incident, Eric made Mackenzie cry by pushing her down when she tried to play with the boys in the family.

Mackenzie idolized her brothers and all the fun they had when they played their games and did things like make go-carts or race matchbox cars. To her, the things they did were far more exciting than what her sisters did.

Like many younger sisters, Mackenzie believed that her two older sisters were weird. Nothing they did interested her. When they all got together with their other girl cousins, Mackenzie wanted to die from boredom and all the girly things they did. Playing in her mother's clothes, playing with dolls, and mimicking the Sister Sledge group was definitely something Mackenzie had no interest in.

Only on occasion would Mackenzie be forced to be one of Sister Sledge's cohorts, but she was quickly booted out because of her lack of hip movement, which was fine with her. She would rather sit with her brothers cracking up laughing at them than trying to memorize the song, "We are Family."

It wasn't very easy living in the tiny one-bedroom apartment and trying to survive with no steady income. Mackenzie and her brothers and sisters ranged from ages six to eleven, and Pat did her best to provide for them in between heavy drinking and hanging out with her many male friends.

Even after all of this, Pat was still beautiful and a magnet for men. Pat was a fair-complexioned woman, with eyes that reflected Asian ancestry, and she had a pretty smile and skin that glowed when she entered the room. She sported a small, natural afro, and was slightly full figured; she was a true reminder of Flo from the Supremes and Cindy from En Vogue.

Pat enjoyed her kids, and she laughed and told them funny stories and jokes to keep them happy during these hard times. Mackenzie was always underneath her mother, and, in her eyes, her mother could do no wrong.

Some days, with no food to eat or clean clothes to wear to school, Mackenzie still hung close to her mother, blaming her father for their misfortune.

When Mackenzie and her brothers and sisters would come home from school hungry, and Pat was passed out from drinking all day, Mackenzie would play in her hair until she woke up angry at everyone in the house. While some of them cried, Mackenzie would tag along behind her mother in whatever way she could, helping her with whatever she could.

Grandma C would come by and scold Pat for not doing better for her children, Mackenzie always sided with her mother, trying to make excuses for why there was no food in the house.

After living on Nostrand Avenue for almost a year, starving some days and scrounging to get by, they all had to leave their apartment and move in with their Aunt Laura on their father's side.

While they stayed there for a few months, playing with their cousins and missing school, Pat went away. No one was more hurt than little seven-year-old Mackenzie. She wanted to tell Pat that things weren't going so well anymore. Twice some man had asked her if he could put his penis inside her. But Pat was so consumed with the temptations of heroine floating in and out of the house, and being forced to sign divorce papers from Jun, that she had no idea what Mackenzie or any of her other children were going through. She had gone away without ever knowing.

After about a week of staying there without Pat, they all moved to Cooper Park with their grandmother on their father's side. Then, out of nowhere, Jun showed up. The tall, dark-skinned, attractive man with deep eyes (so deep that when you looked at them long enough, they appeared blue) sported a low afro, was dressed in fine clothing and clean, puma sneakers, and was all smiles as if nothing had ever happened.

He was newly married with a family living in a two-story high rise in Coney Island, which overlooked the beach on Surf Avenue.

He'd come back for Mackenzie and her siblings. Mackenzie wasn't too happy with the new family setup. Her heart ached for her mother, who was nowhere to be found.

The new lady her father had married was mean. She didn't look at Mackenzie the way Pat did. In fact, Vi looked at Mackenzie like something was wrong with her. She always had something to say about Mackenzie and her high yellow complexion. Mackenzie was bright yellow, while the rest of her siblings were caramel to dark chocolate like their father Jun.

In her new home, Mackenzie felt alone and kept to herself. Vi had a younger son, so Eric shared a room with him, and Mackenzie shared a room with Lauren and Erica. Sean was lucky enough to be allowed to move in with their paternal grandfather in upstate New York.

Their new home in Coney Island was filled with traffic every weekend, starting on Thursday. And for the most part, Jun was always tending to his business during the week anyhow, never having time for his kids. His step-son, however, did manage to get some attention and even called him "*Daddy.*"

Whatever his business was, it kept many people coming in and out and passing around some instrument to each other, and they took turns sucking on it and coughing and carrying on afterwards. The laughter, noise, and many arguments that followed echoed throughout their apartment to the late hours of the night.

All the people that came to their high rise seemed to gravitate to Mackenzie's father like he was some god. Mackenzie usually snuck to the bottom of the stairs and watched while her sisters played with their Barbies. Watching the women and men needing to be close to her father, Mackenzie saw why Pat had fallen for him.

As they passed that instrument around, all Mackenzie could think was *"I hope none of them have a cold."* She turned up her nose in disgust and partial jealousy because their house-quests, always had Junes attention.

Aside from the many guests and all the noise they kept up happy to see each other and start their ritual home was more like living in a dungeon. There was no affection in that apartment except on some Friday's, when Jun would include Mackenzie and her siblings in his happiness and let Erica go down to the pizza shop and buy pizza and soda. And on some Saturdays, depending on how their Fridays had gone, Vi would get up, stumbling most of the time, to fix waffles, eggs, bacon, and cheese grits after making everyone, except her son, clean everything from their rooms to the walls.

Mackenzie endured a great deal of pain in that apartment while her father tended to his business. There was the black eye Vi had given her, (and then lied about to Jun, saying she had fallen) and the many names she called her for being too yellow. The teasing; telling her Jun wasn't her father "because she was too damn yellow"; and the time when she'd taped her panties to her nose because Mackenzie had accidentally urinated on her-self trying to walk up seventeen flights of stairs when the elevator was broken. Her brothers and sisters were happy, or so it appeared, but Mackenzie was visibly miserable.

Vi was the epitome of evil and executed her evilness on no one but Mackenzie. When they had their parties though, she would be so happy that she would dab her finger in the white, powdered substance on the table and suck on her finger like it was a piece of candy, shaking her head like bells were dancing around up there. That's when her whole personae would change.

By the time Mackenzie was about to turn eight, her imagination was wild; it was all she had in that apartment, because every other weekend, she was on punishment for something or another.

During school hours on her birthday, Mackenzie daydreamed that she would go home to a huge surprise birthday party, and all of her classmates would be there. But it was just the first of many let-downs to come her way. Mackenzie turned eight with as much excitement as a freshly painted wall waiting to dry.

After her birthday, Jun gathered the four of them together in the living room and told them that Pat had a new apartment in Brooklyn down on Bedford Ave. Sean would be living with her and her new fiancé, Ray. Mackenzie couldn't believe her ears. Part of her wanted to be so mad at Pat for leaving her here with these people and running off to find happiness without her. But more than anything, she was happy. She was going to be with Pat again. That was the best news she had heard since being there. It also helped her get through the disappointment of not having had a huge surprise birthday party.

Jun said Pat's wedding would be in two weeks, and they were all going except him. He had to go out of town that weekend. "Ya'll start visiting Pat every weekend from now on," he said, not showing any emotion. Mackenzie was a step ahead though; she was planning on moving back with Pat.

Chapter Two

Two weeks later, Jun sent them to the wedding. It was held in a big building with walls that were all the same color and smelled funny. The people all looked like they were moving in slow motion, and they had hazy eyes, scaring Mackenzie and her siblings.

Pat suffered a nervous breakdown while at Aunt Laura's after someone gave her some heroin. She had been in the G building at Kings County Hospital, and this had been her home for quite some time. All the strange people were her friends. Pat wasn't herself anymore, giving half hugs and seeming preoccupied to her children.

Feeling left out, Lauren and Mackenzie went outside, to get away from the chaotic atmosphere that included a big, black, over-bearing Ray who was going to be Pat's new husband. They walked up to the park area to swing for a while before they were chased back by a pack of stray dogs.

Out of breath and holding each other's hands to make sure the pack of mangy, wild dogs, with saliva and hanging tongues didn't get them, they ran as if their life depended on it. As though it were symbolic to the union of Pat and Ray, or Jun and Vi; they wanted to get away. With their now ripped dresses and subdued hearts, they went back into the reception, teary-eyed and fearful, and sat with their other siblings until everything ended.

When it was finally over, Sean just shook his head, and the rest of them caught the train back to Coney Island. They did not say much, just wondered what was happening to their mother. Walking down the long streets of Coney Island's Surf-Avenue and seeing the many faces that walked the streets as well, did nothing to ease the trouble that ran across their minds. The prostitutes, children sucking on candy apples, the aroma from Nathan's, and the reflection of the amusement park were usually hot topics for conversation, but not today. A change was coming, and it was one that Mackenzie and her sisters and brother were not too happy with.

They made it back home. Jun was surrounded by his company and ignored them as they went single file upstairs to their rooms, except Mackenzie, who stared at her father while he sucked on his pipe. Twisting her lips and squinting, her eyes even smaller, she looked at him like she wanted to knock his head off.

Mumbling to herself, Mackenzie stomped upstairs. "How could he leave her and make her marry some big, black man like that? Big eyes, big lips, and talking in slow motion?" She stomped all the way upstairs and didn't hear Jun coming behind her. He snatched her up in one swoop by the back of her dirty, torn dress. "Listen, you little maggot."

"Daddy, Stop." That was Erica coming out of the room, trying to get Mackenzie out of the air. "Daddy, put her down. She doesn't know any better. Put her down." Jun looked at Erica and realized what she was saying, then put Mackenzie down, plucking her on the back of her ear and going into his room, slamming the door.

Erica hugged Mackenzie and wiped her tears as Eric and Lauren watched, then she ran Mackenzie a bath so she could get cleaned up for bed. From that moment on, Mackenzie vowed that she hated her father, and she would never forgive him for destroying their family, or for destroying Pat.

The following weekend, they were all scheduled to go to Pat's new apartment on Bedford Avenue. Jun said he would ride them over there only this first time, but afterwards they would be doing it alone. Mackenzie sat as far away as she could from Jun, who kept asking her if she was talking to herself.

"No. Just mumbling mean things about you," she would say, and he would have to hold in everything so he wouldn't slap her across the train.

When they finally made it to the stop on the train, Jun walked them up the steps to the street, and that was it. He gave hugs to everyone except Mackenzie, who was already walking up the street, and then disappeared.

Catching up to her, they all walked down Bedford Avenue, past Dekalb Avenue, and the church on the corner, to a burgundy building. Nine thirty-five Bedford Avenue.

Pat came down to let them in. She was all smiles and happy today. They were happy, too, until Ray appeared, whisking away their mother and leaving her with barely any time that weekend to talk to them or question the bruise underneath her eye. Sean wasn't saying much either. For the most part, they all stayed outside on the stoop and met other kids on the block.

The next weekend, they took the trip alone. They called Pat from the stoop, anxiously waiting for her to come down the stairs because this weekend would be better. When the door swung open, Pat was standing there, smiling cheek to cheek with no front teeth. Mackenzie and her siblings gasped and opened their mouths in shock. Eric sucked his teeth, Lauren began to cry, and Mackenzie was frozen with fear. They saw beauty robbed from their one and only mother.

Once Pat closed the door behind them, sounds of crying filled the tiny hallway. As Pat tried to hush them, they all sung in unison a hurtful protest.

"Oh, I'm okay," Pat said, holding back her tears. "I'm fine. I promise." She offered no explanation about her teeth; she just guided them up the squeaky staircase and sat them down on the couch.

With tears streaming down their little faces, they were surely plotting how they could send Ray to an early grave.

Every weekend that followed, there was something new. A bruised neck, another black eye, a swollen face, you name it, Pat had it.

By the time summer arrived, they all watched the beginning of Pat falling apart, drinking and getting beat up on a regular basis. No one wanted to come around anymore except Mackenzie. So, while her siblings spent the summer at the Cooper Park Projects, Mackenzie stayed with Pat and Ray.

That's when she met Simon. His father was fixing up the building up the street from Pat's. By the time it was finished in early October, Mackenzie was so excited you would have thought she was moving in.

Sean hunted her down while she was playing with all the dirty kids on the block and brought her face to face with a light-skinned boy from down south who looked just like her. Light-skinned, with big ears, big teeth, and straight, light brown hair, it was obvious that he was bi-racial. Mackenzie liked him the moment she saw him.

Simon had two of every toy and shared everything with Mackenzie. They became close friends and inseparable on the weekends. They took turns playing in front of each other's houses, doing all sorts of crazy stuff, like playing with bugs, or skating up and down the streets making as much noise as they could and getting as dirty as they could.

Mackenzie only wanted to come to Pat's house because of Simon. There she had a friend, someone to play with. For the next three years, they continued to play on the weekends or during the summer, and when Simon went inside, they would talk through his window or she would sneak to the store for him and buy popcorn for them to share. And when his mother would come and yell at him for playing in the window, Mackenzie would sneak off his stoop and wander around the neighborhood until the sun came up, when Ray left to do whatever he did. Although she was terrified, to her it was better than being in that apartment with Ray, and watching him beat up on Pat.

Pat's drinking was far worse than ever before, and she started smoking marijuana with Ray on a regular basis. She didn't even know when Mackenzie wasn't in the house.

Food was scarce, and Ray wouldn't keep his hands off of Mackenzie whenever Pat was passed out. The sexual abuse she suffered would torment her for the rest of her life.

In between all of this, Pat had another baby girl, Samantha, but it didn't stop him from beating her up. It seemed like it was worse now. He did everything from hitting her over the head with a boot, or knocking her across the face with a steel pipe, to slapping her silly in the middle of the street because some man would look at her.

Whenever they went out of the house, Mackenzie would walk ahead with her baby sister Samantha so she didn't have to witness one of Ray's explosions, which could take place anywhere.

Some nights, when Mackenzie wondered the streets or slept in the hallways, she wondered what had happened to Pat and why Jun would allow this for someone he'd loved? Ever since Pat went away, she had never been the same. Some days, she would be so happy and hugged Mackenzie, and they would laugh at how Pat would change her voice and tell Mackenzie the story of Brer Rabbit. Other days, she would be on a warpath, making Mackenzie cry because she couldn't do anything right.

Deep down inside, Mackenzie knew that Pat needed her, and she just couldn't leave her here alone. The roaches, the drinking, the fighting - and yelling, and Ray's hands all over her- still wouldn't allow her to leave Pat.

By the end of the summer of 1982, Mackenzie had spent the entire summer at Pat's, and it was time to go back to Coney Island. Mackenzie took the train all the way back home after she snuck underneath the turnstile because Pat didn't have any money. When she arrived, everything was chaotic.

Jun had a three-year old son named Aaron that no one knew of. Vi had left him and was living across the street with her mother. Some white lady was living there, along with Aaron's mother, April, who was a mirror image of Pat, and her daughter Chelsea, who Mackenzie took a quick liking to.

There was no food, the furniture was gone, and the traffic was way out of control. Her old apartment was now a drug haven, infested with addicts, perverts, and whatever else walked through there.

"I will be starting the sixth grade in a few days and everything is a disaster!" Mackenzie told Erica, who was now testing the limits with her new boyfriend. Lauren was now withdrawn and didn't want to go out, while Eric was the complete opposite of what Mackenzie remembered. He was one of the most popular boys in the building, doing back-flips and having the prettiest girlfriends hang around him.

When school did start, Mackenzie was forced to realize that their economic situation had changed. They no longer wore Jordache, Sasson, or Gloria Vanderbilt, but old clothes that were sometimes dirty. They ate toast instead of pizza, and Kool-Aid and soda, was replaced by water.

At school, some of her friends even gave Mackenzie clothes to share with her sisters, and academically, she was no longer in the head of her class, she was far behind trying to deal with all the changes in her life.

Jun's attitude was really bad now; he was always mad about something and often left them for a few days with April. In between April's issues with Jun and their fighting, April spent countless hours in the bathroom or away from the kids trying to escape her pain.

Mackenzie, whenever she could, or whenever April wasn't busy, tagged along tying to keep her happy, sometimes wanting to tell her, "Leave Jun alone; he ain't no good!" But it was obvious that April was strung out on Jun as well as other things, which hurt Mackenzie because she knew April was special. She had a kind heart, and with all the mess going on, she did all that she could do for her kids, Mackenzie, and her siblings.

Now that money was no longer available, Erica would get money from somewhere and try to cook a hot meal for all of them and wash clothes in the sink so everybody had clean underwear for school.

And adding insult to injury, after another boring day at school, Mackenzie walked home, only to witness the cops taking Jun away in handcuffs. Erica was screaming and hollering, and all the adults that had been in the house, April included, were gone.

It turned out that Vi had betrayed him by going to the cops, telling them Jun sold drugs out of their home. The cops found pounds of marijuana and cocaine up in his room and arrested him on the spot.

Erica begged the cops not to take all of the kids. She called their Aunt Michelle, who spoke to the cops and said she would be there in less than thirty minutes to pick them up. Reluctantly, a police officer waited until their Aunt Michelle showed up, then told them they had to get as much as they could because they were boarding up the apartment.

Michelle, Jun's youngest sister, was athletic, fashionable, and smart. (She took trips to Africa for culture's sake.) She elegantly thanked the cop and reassured all the kids that everything would be okay.

Grabbing as much they could take in plastic bags, they, along with their aunt Michelle, took the train to the Cooper Park Projects.

This was yet another home for Mackenzie and her siblings.

Each morning, they would have to take the train back across town to Coney Island to go to school. Lauren and Mackenzie were both still at the same school and spent endless hours on the train talking and laughing before and after school. They became closer, and Lauren was beginning to talk more.

They were a year apart and mirror images of each other, only Lauren was caramel and Mackenzie was Vanilla. They stayed close while the rest of their family fell apart.

Mackenzie wasn't allowed to visit Pat anymore, so she and Lauren played at their grandmother's house during the weekends until one weekend, Mackenzie convinced Lauren to help her sneak over to Pat's.

They got their story together and ran errands the week before so Mackenzie would have money to get there and back and a couple of dollars for Pat.

Mackenzie made it there one early Saturday morning and found Pat seven months pregnant and looking like she was in the middle of a battle zone. Ray had been beating her up all day, and for the first time, Mackenzie ran and called the police.

By the time she made it back to the old burgundy building, the police were already there. Pat looked so worn out, and her bottom lip shook, trying to hold back her tears. The officers took Mackenzie, Pat, and her little sister Samantha to Grandma C's house. They stayed there overnight while Grandma C, once again, scolded Pat for not doing better for herself and her children.

Pat stayed there until she went into labor on the floor, telling Grandma C that this baby was going to kill her. She kicked, screamed, and moaned while pulling her hair saying that she was going to die.

After another son, David, was born early one Wednesday morning, Pat wasn't released from the hospital due to her blood pressure. Bureau of Child Welfare took both Samantha and David away. The doctor's said her blood pressure was just too high, and they needed to run tests. Upset and visibly angry, Grandma C finally convinced Pat that she had to stay so she could get better and be with her kids.

"Don't you want to get Samantha and David back? You can't do it if you're not feeling well. Stop arguing with these doctors and get yourself together, Pat. Now I mean it." With these words, Pat agreed to stay.

For two months, Pat stayed at the hospital, and one day Mackenzie over-heard Erica and Eric talking about Pat and being in a coma. Mackenzie didn't quite understand, but she knew it meant she was sleeping. She guessed Pat was tired of all of that beating and needed some rest.

Pat kept asking her to visit when they spoke over the phone, but Mackenzie always made some excuse. Now she really wanted to go but because Pat was in a coma, she wasn't allowed in the ICU.

Erica was old enough to visit, so she and Eric went, and when they came back Mackenzie knew there was something to worry about.

"She doesn't have any hair. Why they cut off all her hair and put those tubes down her mouth? Why they do that to her?" Erica screamed, asking Aunt Michelle questions she had no answer to.

With no explanation and only a hug, Erica cried on Aunt Michelle's shoulder while everyone else watched, tears rolling down their faces.

Mackenzie and Lauren were to graduate from the sixth grade on the next day, but somehow, that didn't seem too important right now. After Erica got herself together, she told Mackenzie and Lauren that Pat wouldn't have wanted them to miss it. "Go and have fun with your friends." So, with their big sister's blessing, they went. And although Mackenzie was a little nervous about her graduation, this news seemed to worry her more, although she didn't know how to express it.

Surprisingly, Jun showed up at their graduation, all smiles as usual, like nothing had ever happened. Even against her wishes, he hugged

Mackenzie and gave her twenty dollars and a kiss on the forehead before leaving to visit Pat in the hospital.

"Bye Daddy. Give Mommy a kiss for me," Mackenzie said, before running off to find her friends, who were in the gymnasium for a party for all those who had graduated from the sixth grade.

That following morning, Mackenzie woke up and snuck out of the house to meet her friends back in Coney Island. She hung out with them the entire day, until she left to go to Grandma C's for a graduation gift; it was there that she was supposed to meet Lauren.

Mackenzie beat Lauren there but was so excited she didn't worry about her lie and sneaking out because Aunt Cecile and her twin daughters were there. She was too excited. When she finally sat down after cooing with the twins and giving hugs to Aunt Cecile and Grandma C, their mood was pensive and sad. Grandma C came close by Mackenzie, touched her on the shoulder, and softly said, "Your mother passed this morning at six-thirty."

Mackenzie screamed out as loud as she could, and sobbed uncontrollably in her chair. The tiny apartment that Grandma C and her grandfather shared, seemed even smaller; everything felt like it was caving in on her. She even felt like she couldn't breathe.

Aunt Cecile and Grandma C held her and wiped her tears. She was eleven years old and had seen so much already. Drug parties, illicit sex, sexual abuse, emotional abuse, molestation, and physical abuse. But none of these things prepared her for losing her mother. She was lost, and for the next thirteen or fourteen years, she would have to find her way.

Chapter Three

Mackenzie and her sisters and brothers would endure all that one must endure when losing a parent. They would be separated.

The two kids that her mother had by Ray, Samantha and David stayed with BCW and were never seen again. Sean went back upstate with their grandfather, taking Eric with him. Erica went to stay with their Aunt Laura and their cousins now living in Crown Heights, and Lauren decided to stay with her best friend, Rochelle. Her mothers' only sister, Cecile, took Mackenzie in.

Aunt Cecile lived in the projects with her two daughters, who were quite a bit younger than Mackenzie. Mackenzie roller-skated over there and Aunt Cecile laughed because she'd only come with the clothes on her back and her roller skates. It was Mackenzie's task to baby-sit and make sure the house was in order. They lived in the heart of Brooklyn, in Bedstuy, in the Tompkins Projects, to be exact.

Grandma C lived right down the street with her grandfather in Marcy Projects. On Mackenzie's very first day there, Grandma C walked down to meet them, and they all went school clothes shopping.

Mackenzie couldn't remember ever feeling so special since Pat had passed away. Aunt Cecile made sure she had everything toothbrush, panties, socks, a book bag, clothes, and supplies, too.

Her seventh grade school year was beginning to look bright after all. She no longer had to wonder what was for dinner or if there would be tons of people in the house, passing around the mirrored tray and getting high.

After her first shopping spree, Aunt Cecile said that she was going to take all of them to church next Saturday so they could join the choir. Mackenzie froze with terror; she couldn't sing her way out of a free garage sale.

She was planning a way to get out of the ordeal, because she was going to make a fool out of herself.

All she could think was, *"What is Aunt Cecile trying to do to me? Doesn't she know I have been through an ordeal? I am suffering, and she wants me to go to church and sing in some choir with complete strangers."* Mackenzie was beginning to rethink her move over here when she was sidetracked by her first day of junior high school.

A bunch of kids met her outside to show her how to get to her new school. She thought to herself, *"This is the projects, right?"* Because at the Cooper Projects, there would be fighting at the bus stop, fighting on the way to the train station, just fighting wherever they could. They wouldn't try to help the new kid at all. Perhaps they would try to take her lunch money, but that was about it.

Her heart skipped a beat when she met the ringleader of good deeds, Sam. She forgot all about church and was taken aback when he said, "Hi. I'm Sam." Not only did she meet Sam, but also Tanya, Desire and Dominique, Rachel, Simone, and so many others on that day.

The strange thing about her first day of the seventh grade was that she was going to attend John Ericsson Jr. High School. It was considered one of the better schools, and it was located about fifteen minutes from the Cooper Projects.

Mackenzie was fortunate to know new kids like herself, and old friends that she'd grown up with, while spending several summers in the Cooper Projects at her Aunt Michelle's and her grandmother's house.

She was back on the upswing, forgetting about her obligation with the choir on Saturday and focusing on all of the new faces. There were cheerleaders, a band, and a choir at this school. Mackenzie smiled at the news because that's where a choir belonged to her, at a school and anywhere that didn't involve her joining.

Her mind was set on the new dance group the music teacher was starting up. They were called the Ericsson Rockers. Although she could never mimic Sister Sledge like her sisters, nowadays, she found dancing to be fun.

Mackenzie learned all the new dances instantly and was on the same craze as any other little tomboy, break-dancing and popping. She watched *Beat Street* repeatedly; She came up with her own routine and was just waiting for the chance to do it. She was going to get her chance at the Ericsson Rockers' tryouts.

After waiting around in the school's band room filled with groupie cheerleaders, tough b-boy, gangsta, graffiti writing break-dancers, and a few other spectators for about an hour, her time had arrived.

Each person would be given a sample of music to dance to for two minutes. "Show your best," they said, as Mackenzie sat and waited.

"Mackenzie," the small, static microphone called. "Mackenzie to the dance floor." Nervousness filled her body, and the whole room seemed to spin out of control.

Mackenzie walked up in her usual tomboy attire, which she had sneaked to school in her book-bag. It was jeans, sneakers, and a T-shirt that Sam had let her borrow for the tryouts. She positioned herself in the middle of the makeshift dance floor, which stood in front of a chalk-board that looked like a huge sheet of music paper. Then she shifted into dance mode. She began patting her feet, anticipating the start of the music. She shook her head momentarily and waited for the music to start.

The spectators sat, looked, and talked in small groups until the microphone said, "Are you ready?" Mackenzie gave a slight nod.

The DJ must have read her mind, because he played a sample of "Dance to the Drummer's Beat" blended in with some other funky beat that just caused her to lose her mind! She popped to the beats and manipulated the music as if it was her theme song. She moved her head to the beats in between popping like she was talking to her audience, and when she stopped, the crowd hollered.

Mackenzie was beat red in the face. She could feel the steam and sweat forming a trail down the center of her back as it always did when she over-exerted herself.

Mackenzie managed to dance to no end, letting out her frustrations, and hurt. She didn't allow fear to win today, and that caused a little smile to fall across her face as the on-lookers clapped continuously. Maybe she could join the choir, she thought, as she went back to her little area in the music room and watched the others try out.

When the tryouts were over, Mr. William, the music teacher, said they would find out on Monday who'd made the cut. There would only be ten, out of about fifty kids that tried out that day. A list would be ready and attached to the band room door by lunchtime. Mackenzie couldn't wait. And if the cheers from the crowd were any indication, she knew she'd made the cut.

She would have to wait an entire weekend, and probably would have to join the choir, and sing on Sunday, before she knew anything for sure. Mackenzie was going through a tizzy wondering. But way deep inside she knew she was in. Her confidence level was usually low, but today she felt different about herself.

"Damn!" she said, breathing a harsh sigh as she left the band room and headed to the bus stop.

Sam had waited for her at the bus stop and had tons of questions about the tryouts. Mackenzie did the best she could at trying to tell him how it went, pointing out to him all the people that were there. She told him she'd been scared to death. He laughed.

On their way home, she decided to tell him about her situation. After she let it out in pretty much one long, incomplete run-on sentence, Sam laughed hard at her, and she was pissed. It was still hard for Mackenzie to take a joke or constructive criticism; she felt as though they were picking on her or making fun of her. The toughest task she was facing these days was in not being so defensive. It was a hard task.

"Mackenzie, you should join the choir," he said, after about five minutes of nonstop laughter.

"Really?" she said, sarcastically, trying to avoid sounding defensive.

"Yeah! I sing in the choir at my church, and one day I want to have my own gospel choir."

Mackenzie couldn't believe what she was hearing. "You sing in the choir?" she asked, surprised.

"Un huh. I sing on the school's choir, too."

"For real? You're not lying, trying to make me feel better?"

Sam laughed some more, as the bus pulled up, "Why are you so scared to sing on the choir? It's for GOD, and Jesus; you know it's a good thing to do. It's far better than running the streets, getting pregnant, or doing drugs."

Sam made a lot of sense that day to Mackenzie, and considering her horrible background and the things she'd seen, church looked wonderful, and so did the choir. They continued their ride home on the bus, discussing church and the choir business and Sam's hopes to one day have his own choir. He talked about all the places they would perform, and the flashy clothes they would wear. Mackenzie listened attentively, and they enjoyed their bus ride home.

That Saturday, Aunt Cecile kept her promise and took the three of them to the church to join the choir. The organist told Mackenzie that she was a soprano and that Lena and Lannette were altos. Mackenzie was nervous, but she found her way to the soprano section and sat with the other young girls there. She was glad she wasn't alone.

They joined church on that Sunday during the service at which their choir sung. It was youth day. Mackenzie did her best, although she was terrified and sweaty, but she just kept thinking about what Sam had said, *"It's a good thing."*

When she made it back to school on Monday, she couldn't wait until lunchtime. But before she could make it over to the band room smiles, and pointed fingers and stares greeted her. "You made it," Sam said, coming up from behind and extending a high five to her.

He was acting like her friend, and she was wishing he would give her a hug and a kiss on the cheek.

That year, Mackenzie was selected as the only girl to be a part of the Ericcson Rockers and was given the name "Lady Pop." They did shows throughout the school year. She met some of the best break-dancers in Brooklyn, and every time she went somewhere, she was adored. The attention was great and did wonders for her ailing self-esteem.

During the eighth grade, most of the Rockers graduated, so she gave up performing, but her name never left her. She became closer with the kids in her neighborhood and frequented church more.

By this time at church, they had a new youth minister. She just couldn't believe he was so cute, stylish, and did everything for the Lord. When he preached on youth day, the church did back-flips. And when he sang, she couldn't do anything but cry. Wherever he went to preach, Mackenzie was there. In one particular revival where he preached, Pastor Grundy's church, Mackenzie just stood there, watching all the young people shouting, and praising God. The youth minister was calling young people up and telling them something, when suddenly, he looked at Mackenzie and called her up.

Mackenzie almost panicked; and began searching for her shoes underneath the pews. She quickly put them on and walked up to the altar. The handsome youth minister with pearly white teeth, naturally curly hair, and smooth, golden skin touched her shoulder and said, "God is going to use you, you just have to let go and let him use you."

Mackenzie didn't understand the words that fell perfectly from his mouth, but she accepted what he'd said and quietly walked back to the pews she was sharing with some friends. She held back the tears, that were forming in her eyes, and listened to the still voice inside her head that made her feel as though she wanted to scream out loud or run around the church at high speed. She knew the words that the youth minister had spoken had power, and to her it was as if he had hit the nail right on the head.

But instead of screaming at the top of her lungs or running in a sprint, Mackenzie sat quietly with her new church friends Red, Mishcah, and Willie. Out-side of school, she and her church friends did everything together.

Mishcah was the oldest, and Mackenzie gravitated to her because she was so strong. She always talked to her about relationship dos, and don'ts, faith, and having patience. Mishcah came from a big family, so Mackenzie was sure she knew exactly what she was talking about.

Red was the comedian and always had them stretched out, dying laughing, while Willie was the bearer of news, good or bad. They had their own little clique that kept them off the streets. They usually hung out at each other's house, mostly Mishcah's because she was older, had her own room, and the funniest older brother one could ever meet. Sometimes they just wanted to go over there so he could make them laugh. He called them the craziest things and made the funniest faces when he said them. He should have been an actor, Mackenzie often thought, because he could entertain them easily.

By the time ninth grade rolled around, Mackenzie was hanging out even more with her church friends and less with the neighborhood friends, and sadly enough, she lost good friends in the process, like Desire and Domonique. For some strange reason, she picked a fight with them, which was not a characteristic of someone going to church all the time, and she knew this. She picked a fight and they never forgave her, which hurt because she knew she was wrong.

Afterwards, Mackenzie quickly started practicing what she was preaching. Church became more than a hang out place. It became a place where she began to learn about Christian love, and the Lord and His requirements.

Willie and Mackenzie both joined the junior missionaries and frequently talked with their pastor, Pastor Batts, about living right and doing God's will. They all became close and life now seemed bearable.

Mackenzie was always referred to as the girl whose mother died but also the girl that truly believed and had something good to say.

She knew what she had done to Desire and Domonique was wrong, but turning over a new leaf made it easier to deal with. So, her ninth grade year was filled with church and getting to know the Lord as best as she could.

Now that Mackenzie was living in the projects, she realized that it took a lot of faith to get by, and she had to exercise that faith on a daily basis. Mackenzie could remember countless times that they were put on alert because some rapist was stalking the buildings, or times when rival projects would come and shoot up the park with guns for the hell of it. Or even worse, seeing friends succumb to the pressures of drugs and sex, seeing how in a year's time, the project's beauty queen could become the project's dope fiend.

Her past life of living on the streets while at Pat's seemed like a piece of cake compared to now. Seemed like then, things weren't as rough, and walking the streets late at night or sleeping on the stoops of Pat's old apartment had been a safe haven.

Mackenzie graduated from John Ericcson Jr. High School and received an award for perfect attendance that year, and that was the first day she looked in the mirror and saw who she was. It was at Michcah's when they all went to hang out after her graduation that she looked in the mirror and saw herself.

She was light-skinned, with long, dark brown hair, small eyes, and a small nose. Her smile was big, and so were her teeth, but she liked what she saw, even her jherri curl. She was happy that day, and a little okay that Pat was not there to share this moment with her. She only cried about five times that day compared to crying all day on her birthday, Pat's death anniversary, and Christmas.

She was even happy, considering she hadn't talked to Jun in God knows how long. It seemed like he'd died, too. The last she'd heard at their annual Easter dinner at Grandma C's house, Lauren and Erica said, he was living with some lady back at the Cooper Projects. *"Good for him,"* Mackenzie thought. *"Good for him."*

Mackenzie would be attending Edward R. Murrow High School in the fall, which was a school where there were no sports, just electives like broadcasting, journalism, and drama. Her personality was beginning to develop more, and she was still feeling confident after having been selected as one of the top dancers at her former middle school.

During that summer, while she waited for school to start, Sam became one of their clique's newest members. His pastor had died at his church, so he joined Mackenzie's church since it was so close, right down the street from their projects to be exact. He had broken up with his girlfriend, which made Mackenzie ecstatic. The time they spent together now made Mackenzie feel hopeful that one day they would be more than just friends.

They all got along fine. Sam and Red would come to get her and Mishcah, after they got their haircuts, and they would go back to Sam's house to crack up laughing, while drinking Pepsi or orange juice.

Sam lived with his maternal grandparents and older sister. They were such clean and nice people, and Mackenzie admired their sense of family closeness. Sam always fussed at the many chores he had to do, but Mackenzie was used to cleaning and helped him when she could. After Vi's tortuous Saturday morning cleanings, Mackenzie knew she could clean or do any chore. And Sam was happy that she could, cleaning and him just didn't get along.

The sad thing was that also that summer, Red's mother passed away. They all did their best to be there for Red, but that was the first time Mackenzie and the rest of her friends didn't see a smile or hear jokes from Red. He was sad and distraught because his mother had died right in the house with him, his sisters, and his nieces.

And in their projects, ten girls were raped that summer, and a new drug, crack, had hit the streets like wildfire. All too common were the faces of fallen neighbors, old friends, church members, and family members, who were literally being eaten alive by this new drug. Mackenzie worried about her father and hoped that his fate did not lie in that direction.

She stayed focused in spite of the outside turmoil and kept to herself when school started, since they all went to different high schools and Mishcah had already finished high school. Silently she rode the train, unlike her newer schoolmates, who caused havoc on the trains.

These schoolmates gave the adult passengers hell! They took their seats, poked fun at them, and often pushed them when they were trying to catch their train. On the subway system in New York's inner city, neighborhood kids were hell on the commuters.

Edward R. Murrow was in Flatbush in a white neighborhood. It was close to the NBC studios, so during lunchtime or off periods, Mackenzie would walk over there in hopes of seeing a cast member from the then popular "Cosby Show." She saw a few of the stars like Tempest Bledsoe, and Malcom-Jamal Warner.

During the tenth grade, she was branded a nerd because she did not socialize at all. Her grades, however, did not reflect nerd status. Mackenzie was still, in her own way, trying to cope, so her attention span was not that great. In most of her classes, she was quiet because she was daydreaming, hoping for a brighter future.

Chapter Four

Because of her constant daydreaming, Mackenzie passed the tenth grade with barely enough credits and became a junior. Her school was weird to her; most of the students were white, punk rockers, or wealthy and stuck up. The black students were pretty much the same, "Oreos" as they called them back then, pretentious, or wanna-be hoodlums. Mackenzie felt she didn't fall into any of those categories.

And finally, that school year, Sam and a schoolmate started their own Gospel choir. Sam convinced all of them to join, and they sang at numerous events in Brooklyn trying to make a name for the new choir. Mackenzie met many people through this affiliation and learned something new about church folk. They were a trip to her.

They were no different from any other group of people; jealousy, envy, lying, and backbiting were a way of life for many of them. You had to be this or that to be somebody, or dress like this, or wear this hat, and those shoes. This nature of going to church disturbed Mackenzie; she didn't like it.

Mackenzie was poor. She received a check of $49.00 every month from Pat's social security. Aunt Cecile wasn't poor, but she had two girls that attended private school, so basically Mackenzie had to use what she had of her own, which wasn't much.

This made things a little tough and made her frustrated with members of the church. Mackenzie just wanted to be as close as she could be to God. If it were up to her, she would wear a paper bag to worship and praise him. That's what she always told Sam, who constantly had her in and out of stores trying to find a dress to fit in her budget every month. This was something she didn't like about Sam.

Sam, along with the rest of the choir, didn't agree. They felt as though God wanted his children to have the best and wear the best, even if it meant not paying a bill to do it. Mackenzie couldn't and didn't understand their way of thinking.

So, she sang with the new choir wearing what she could, each engagement becoming harder and harder to bear financially. Not only were you to wear nice, fashionable, costly clothes, but you had to pay dues, give offerings, and pay to ride a van to get to an engagement. Her forty-nine dollars just wasn't getting it done. And Mackenzie was ready to quit Sam's new choir.

Halfway into her junior year of high school, Aunt Cecile said she was thinking about moving to Texas, as her job, the corporate office in which she worked, was relocating immediately. The news excited Mackenzie. She was ready for a change.

The projects were a complete war zone now. The occupants, were against the drug users and the drug dealers. It was nothing to see young, black, Uzi-toting, hoodlums running through the projects, seeing crack vials and addicts throughout the hallways, looking for the next high or house to break into.

Mackenzie was scared, and her errands to the local Key Food became harder each day as she tried to avoid drug addicts and their suppliers filling the halls. Moving to Texas didn't sound bad at all, even though it would be fifteen hundred miles away from anything she had ever known, distant family included. She was ready for a change.

Aunt Cecile shared her thoughts as well and decided that they needed to move. It was 1988 when they decided to get the hell out of there. Mackenzie knew she would miss her friends and church, but she was pretty much burned out with the new choir anyway.

Mackenzie, along with her friends, promised they would keep in touch and after the entire church prayed for them, Mackenzie, Aunt Cecile, and the twins all got on a plane and headed to Dallas, Texas.

During the plane ride, Mackenzie remembered all of the goodbyes and the many things about New York she would miss, like pizza from the corner pizzeria, and the faces that she knew there. So, while the twins played tic-tac-toe, Mackenzie turned her head to the aircraft window and cried herself to sleep.

They arrived in Dallas, shortly thereafter, and the huge airport seemed motionless compared to LaGuardia's airport. The patrons all seemed so quiet and peaceful, with no worries, unlike the fast-paced New Yorkers that rushed throughout the city daily.

They settled into the Marriott off of LBJ freeway almost thirty minutes away from the airport and ate cold cut sandwiches that Aunt Cecile had packed.

Early that following morning, Aunt Cecile enrolled them into school and Mackenzie was in for the shock of her life. The students seemed so much older. They had cars, jobs, and just a different attitude.

Mackenzie was introduced to her counselor and asked if she wanted to play a sport. She was ecstatic. "Basketball," she blurted out. So, she was enrolled into athletics, which met early in the morning each day. Mackenzie had played basketball every now in then in the projects with her friend, Buffy, and some of the guys her age when she didn't have church activities to attend to. For her, it was better than what her peers in the projects were doing. She picked up the game naturally and enjoyed the intensity of playing defense and getting rebounds and blocking shots.

That's how she met China. Ms. Athletics, China played volleyball, basketball, and ran track. She was also quite smart and played the viola. She was definitely different from Mackenzie's friends in New York.

China was tough, too. She would say, "Yeah, you from New York, so what? You in Texas now!" Mackenzie thought the approach was funny but real. They both had a strong belief in God and would have endless conversations about God and also about boys.

China had no problems getting the guys; she was shapely, with almond-colored skin and the biggest smile across her small, round lips. She made dark lovely. Her eyes were like buttons that fit perfectly onto her rounded face.

She also had an attitude that told the boys she knew she had what they wanted, and they could only get it if they treated her right. She was very mature and knew exactly what she wanted out of life. Mackenzie admired her more than anything.

By this time, Mackenzie was sixteen and was the epitome of plain. It didn't matter to her friends though, because she was accepted anyway. But Mackenzie was bothered by her plainness and not being a magnet to the boys. It made her feel like her stepmother Vi had been right, and all people saw her as Vi had like she was strange and unattractive.

For the remainder of the year, Mackenzie would go watch China and the other girls compete at track meets or hang out at China's house and talk and laugh or walk her dog, Macy. Sometimes they would go to the local recreational center and shoot around, which frustrated Mackenzie because, to her, China was a bully on the court. Her words seemed to penetrate Mackenzie in ways that made her re-think playing basketball. She didn't like to be picked at or made to feel uncomfortable because she played differently.

That summer, Mackenzie experienced heat like never before. It was so hot that she could have sworn she was on the other side of hell.

She prayed for winter to come early, but China said there wasn't a winter in Dallas, Texas. *"So get use to it,"* she told her. They laughed momentarily but Mackenzie's feelings were hurt because this heat was going to be too much for her.

"Mackenzie, do you have a boyfriend in New York?" China asked after their laughing spell. Mackenzie thought, it was odd they always talked about guys, what they liked, the silly things they did at school, or how fat or ugly one was, but they never talked about a specific one.

"No, just someone I'm in love with." Mackenzie said, not making much of it.

"Really? Who is he? What's his name?"

Mackenzie smiled and laughed a little at China's excitement.

"His name is Sam."

"Sam? Sam what? Like Samuel, Sammy, please tell me not just Sam."

"You are so crazy. His name is Sam Brian. I guess something southern. We all just call him Sam though."

"Are you two in a relationship, or you just like him?"

"I love him, and no we are not in a relationship"

"So does he know?"

"I don't know; I've never told him. We just hung out together all the time and went to church together."

"Have you ever had a boyfriend before?"

"Yeah," Mackenzie said with a hint of sarcasm. "Of course I have. I just like Sam now." She didn't want to tell China that she'd had plenty of boyfriends growing up, that she had been unattended outside playing with all the boys in the neighborhoods because that would mean she would have to talk about some of the bad stuff they did to her.

"Well, you should get over Sam. He's too far away. I have a friend from Sherman Texas you should meet."

Mackenzie nodded, trying not to think about the past.

"No, really, I think you will like him. His name is Demarcus."

"Corny," Mackenzie thought to herself. *"Why couldn't his name be Michael or something sexy like Xavier?"*

"Okay, I'll meet him. Just give me a warning so I can be prepared."

They laughed some more and then finished watching Spike Lee's *"School Daze."*

The two of them spent the remainder of summer just waiting around for school to start. Often times, Mackenzie would walk up to China's part-time job at Taco Bueno and get free food before closing time, then they would walk home, just talking.

If it was a Saturday night, they would hurry home so they could get ready for church that following morning. China belonged to a real small church in South Dallas off Martin Luther King Boulevard. It was nothing like her church, but it definitely had a sweet spirit.

China's entire family went there, everybody from cousins, uncles, aunts, to grandparents. You name them, they were there. After church, they always went to her grandparent's house in Oak Cliff and had the best Sunday dinner prepared by them.

When school started, the girls were finally seniors and were happy as ever. Mackenzie got her first job at the local movie theater so she could pay for her senior items for graduation.

China and Mackenzie were pretty close by now, and to Mackenzie, she was her best-friend even though China was so hard on her.

Two weeks before that year's Thanksgiving, China's friend Di invited her to a party in Richardson, Texas. She begged Aunt Cecile to let Mackenzie go and promised she would have her in at a decent hour.

Still a little concerned, Aunt Cecile only agreed after China's mom assured her that they would be okay and that Mackenzie could spend the night there when they made it back from the party.

China and Mackenzie were going to meet Di at the 7-Eleven down the street that Saturday. Di had a car so they would at least have a ride there and back. (Walking in Texas was absolutely unheard of.)

As they walked down the street to meet Di, China and Mackenzie were talking about boys, as usual, when they heard a horn and Di call out, "Hey, ya'll get in."

They sat in the back seat because some light-skinned boy was sitting in the front. Mackenzie thought to herself that he was probably Di's boyfriend. Then China nudged her and started smiling.

"Hey, Demarcus, you can't speak?"

Mackenzie's stomach sank, and nervousness took control.

"Hey, girl." He said, in a slightly mature voice. Then Di introduced the two. Demarcus was nonchalant, so Mackenzie acted the same towards him. Once they made it to the party, Demarcus and Mackenzie made eye contact a few times, but nothing major happened until she went outside to get the lip gloss that she'd left in the car.

As she was on her way back into the so-called party, which consisted of a bunch of teenagers standing around and booty music blasting in the background, Demarcus called out to her. "Hey Mackenzie, where you going?"

"Oh, just back inside with China and Di," she said, returning his nonchalant tone.

When he finally caught up to her he asked, "You having fun?"

She shrugged. "It's okay."

"I bet the parties in New York were way better, huh?"

"Actually, I really wouldn't know; I went to church all the time."

"Really? Wow. If I lived in New York, I would be out all the time."

Mackenzie laughed, thinking to herself that he obviously didn't know New York too well, a country boy like him, would get his ass eaten alive in New York.

"Well, New York is really not all that. You have to watch your back quite a bit, and it kind of takes the fun out of everything."

"Yeah, I guess if you put it that way." They both became quiet for a minute, and Mackenzie thought about how cute he was. She loved light-skinned men, with the exception of Sam, who, was a smooth, caramel brown. Light-skinned men didn't remind her of Ray and his big black hands all over her. Plus, they seemed to her to be a little soft, and she liked that.

Demarcus was every bit of that, soft spoken and polite. He had light brown chinky eyes and a little nose, all nestled above his full, pink lips. He had that kind of hair that made you think he was mixed. He was just a cute boy everything Mackenzie liked in a boy. It wasn't that his skin was light, but it was golden, like he should be in magazines.

"So what part of New York are you from anyway?"

"Brooklyn."

"Yeah? Have you ever seen any stars?" That was always the question from the people in Texas. They naturally assumed that because you were from New York, you knew stars. The only one who had never asked her anything silly like that was China, who could care less where she was from and who she knew.

"I don't know any stars personally, but yes, I have seen quite a few living in New York."

"I like your accent," he said, smiling at her. When she smiled back, he asked if she had a boyfriend.

"No, I'm single I guess."

"You guess? What do you mean? Do you have a boyfriend in New York?"

"Oh no, I was referring to the correct term to use, that's all; I have no boyfriend." He smiled again.

"Come on, let's go back inside," he said. He began walking with a confident stride and Mackenzie followed. They didn't dance together, but they stood together and watched everyone else. Occasionally, the two would share a laugh at China and Di, who were sitting at a table playing dominoes. They must have been winning because every time Mackenzie looked over there, they would be slapping high fives and laughing at their competitors.

After that night out, Demarcus and Mackenzie exchanged numbers and started going out right away. Demarcus called her every day, sometimes three or four times a day. When it had almost been a month, she realized that they still hadn't kissed.

All they did was talk on the phone. Although she was a senior in high school, truthfully, she was inexperienced. And since unwanted molestation and sexual abuse did not count, Mackenzie considered herself a virgin. She wanted to kiss Demarcus, and she knew he wanted to kiss her also, but whenever they came close on a few occasions, her nerves just got the best of her, and she avoided him.

A couple of days before her seventeenth birthday, when Demarcus took her to see Eddie Murphy's *RAW*, Mackenzie made sure she wore something cute. Her fitted black pants with the boots that Aunt Cecile had bought her for her Texas-style seventeenth birthday, and a red sweater, which was Lauren's favorite, was the perfect outfit. Demarcus had on blue jeans with a blue jean shirt and snakeskin cowboy boots. Mackenzie never thought she would ever think someone dressed in an outfit like that would appeal to her, but it did.

They walked hand in hand to his car and once they got in they listened to Bobby Brown's new tape. Demarcus thought he was a singer, so he would grab her hand and sing to her. All Mackenzie could do was laugh because he couldn't even sing, well at least not as good as he thought.

Watching *RAW*, they both laughed hysterically, sharing popcorn and Hot Tamales. After the movie, they drove back to Aunt Ceciles' and stood outside the house for hours, just talking. That was the good thing about being with Demarcus; they always had good conversation.

When their conversation died out, Demarcus cornered her and placed his smooth lips onto hers. Mackenzie was delirious. Everything was so soft and calm. She could have stood there, forever with Demarcus.

This was her first real kiss, and it was so soft and slow, like he cared. They kissed for a while in front her apartment. It seemed as though time stopped for them on that day, and after their first kiss, she knew they were truly a couple.

Chapter Five

Now that Demarcus and Mackenzie were kissing on a regular basis, she could feel him wanting to do more. And it was officially clear on Valentines Day because Demarcus did want to go all the way and Mackenzie didn't. After heavy petting, and kissing, she said no. Demarcus was visibly upset for the rest of the day. He began to respond to Mackenzie's concern with smart remarks and even went so far as to remind her that she was immature for her age.

Part of his behavior bothered Mackenzie, and for the most part, she began to question herself and whether she was ready to go all the way. But then she was reminded about the past that she had endured with Ray and the neighborhood boys, and she was obviously torn.

After Valentines Day, things went downhill. Actually, the weekend following Valentine's Day, Demarcus called and told Mackenzie he was going back to Sherman Texas for the weekend and that he would call her when he returned on Sunday.

Okay, she thought and made no mention of it. Actually, after hearing all of the girls at track practice talk about going all the way, sexing, Mackenzie decided she could go all the way with Demarcus.

So when he returned, that would be the perfect opportunity. So she thought.

Saturday evening, Mackenzie decided to call Demarcus and leave a message on his answering machine about meeting up as soon as he got back. To her surprise, Demarcus picked up the phone.

"Hey," she said, with a bit of worry in her voice.

"Hey, what's up?" His voice sounded as cold and flat as two-day old pancakes.

"I thought you were in Sherman for the weekend?"

"I was, but I had to come back early."

"Really, why didn't you call me?"

"Hold on a sec, my phone is beeping." Without waiting for a response, he clicked over.

Mackenzie probably waited on hold for about seven minutes; when she realized Demarcus wasn't coming back to the phone, she felt like her world was crashing in on her. Lying on her bed, staring up at the ceiling and feeling hurt, Mackenzie began to think.

What kind of games was he trying to play? She wondered. Mackenzie called China and managed to get everything out in one sentence, as she usually did when she was upset. They decided to meet at China's house and do some investigating.

Neither of them had a car, but China could drive, so as her mother slept, they slipped her keys off of her dresser and headed to Park Lane to find, in Mackenzie's words, "That no good bastard Demarcus." Mackenzie was angry, hurt, and anxious to find out the truth.

"We have to be back by at least by nine-thirty, 'cause my momma wakes up at ten to get ready for work. At least the car will have cooled down by then." China said, bringing Mackenzie out of her daydream.

"Yeah, that'll work. Let's just get there so I can see what's going on."

"Do you think he's with someone, Mackenzie?"

"I don't know. I just know he wanted to go all the way and I said no. Ever since then, he's been acting stank."

"Do you think you're ready to go all the way? I mean that is a big step. Just make sure that it's what you want and you're not doing it to please him or keep him."

"China, I do like him. I guess sex is the next step."

"Yeah, but you're a virgin. You're supposed to take this seriously and slowly. Be sure you have the right guy to be your first."

Mackenzie nodded her head in agreement with mixed emotions because no matter what, China always had to make Mackenzie feel like she was dumb, and she resented that.

"Demarcus is cool, and I know I introduced you to him, but to feel like you have to be with him because of me and where I am in my life is not a good idea."

China made a lot of sense. Mackenzie was definitely not where she or most of the other girls at school were. She was still a tomboy and would much rather play basketball than try and decide if she wanted to have sex with Demarcus, or any guy for that matter.

They finally made it to Demarcus's apartment on Park Lane, which was one of the busiest areas in Dallas. Many young people had their own apartments in this area, so it was nothing to see so much traffic. As a result of the high traffic, China and Mackenzie made it into his controlled-access apartment with no problem.

His apartment complex was pretty big, but Mackenzie remembered where his apartment was because it overlooked the pool and had weights on his patio. Demarcus had brought her over there once before to show it to her, and she never forgot anything about it. She often imagined living there with Demarcus or spending nights with him watching TV and talking all-night. But she figured now, if he was here with another girl, it was never going to happen.

China parked the car after Mackenzie gave her non-verbal directions through the parking lot, and they just sat there for a minute. "You sure you want to do this, Mackenzie?"

Hesitantly, she nodded and said, "Yeah."

They got out of the car and Mackenzie jumped when a Siamese cat ran his tail across her leg. Even with jeans on, the strong rub from that cat felt as though she were barelegged. For a moment, Mackenzie began to re-think her decision to come over here but that lasted for half a second because she continued on and ignored the possible sign that she should go home.

Demarcus lived on the second floor, so as she led, China followed. They reached the top of the step and she turned right. She was stepping forward to knock on Demarcus's door when it swung open.

Mackenzie was standing face-to-face with the prettiest girl she had ever seen. She was about five-five, had long hair pulled back into a ponytail, honey brown eyes, smooth caramel skin, and a heart-shaped smile. They looked at each other for probably five seconds until Mackenzie shook her head and saw Demarcus in the background in boxer shorts and nothing else.

"You ain't shit." China said from behind. She must have read Mackenzie's mind, because Mackenzie was speechless. All she could was look at Demarcus and shake her head. His eyes looked so pitiful, like he wanted to say something but just wasn't man enough to do so.

Ms. Pretty looked at Mackenzie, and then looked at Demarcus and said, "What's going on, D?"

D, I guess she's the main one because she's calling him by his nickname, Mackenzie said to herself.

"Nothin. Ummm, this is Mackenzie, a friend of mine from New York. I told you about her, remember? She from Brooklyn, where Big Daddy Kane stay."

Mackenzie couldn't believe him and the fact that he couldn't even acknowledge their relationship.

"Oh. Well, what do they want?" Ms. Pretty asked with a bit of an attitude. Mackenzie was feeling a little jealous and nervous as she began fidgeting with the seams of her pants.

"We don't want shit, trick. Who the fuck are you?" China said, with more assertiveness than any man would care to deal with.

"Let's just go, China," Mackenzie said, turning around, only to be caught in the middle of China's heavy hands getting a one and a two on "D" and Ms. Pretty.

China moved Mackenzie out the way and said, "Go head, do something, 'cause you know I know you ain't nothing but a punk, DEMARCUS."

By this time, Demarcus pushed Ms. Pretty inside and was standing face-to-face with China now. They were like two bulldogs, sniffing each other out when Demarcus stepped back and closed the door.

"Come on, China, let's go. He ain't worth it."

China kicked his door like it was a soccer ball, and they walked back to the car quietly. Mackenzie, with her feelings hurt, stared down at the pavement.

China kept quiet the entire ride back until they made it back to her apartment. "You know I can get some of my cousins from Oak Cliff to whip his ass. Just say the word."

Mackenzie was tempted. "I wish I could get that sorry ass punk beat down. Had we been back in Brooklyn, that nigga's nutts would be chopped off and sold on Graham Ave. as earrings," she said, rolling her eyes hard.

"But that's okay. I'm all right. I just no longer have a boyfriend, and I'm still a virgin. Could be worst; I could have slept with him, and surely I would feel worse than I do now."

"You are too nice." China said, looking at Mackenzie like she was the biggest fool.

"I'm just not into seeking revenge, just doesn't seem worth it. It would be wasted energy if you asked me. Besides, I've overreacted before, and it cost me two good friends."

China made an irritated sound and shook her head in pity.

"Well, are you going home, or are you staying at my house tonight?" They forgot all about the fact that they had to get back to China's house and bring back her mother's car.

"I just wanna go home, take a bath, and go to sleep."

"Mackenzie, DO NOT GO HOME AND GET ALL DEPRESSED OVER THAT NIGGA!" China blurted out. For some reason, China just felt like Mackenzie didn't know any better.

"I guess being a virgin gives me this stamp of stupidity when dealing with the opposite sex, huh?" Mackenzie said, snapping at China. She really wanted to go home and just go to sleep. Maybe that was depression, or perhaps she was just tired.

"China, I'm just tired," she added. "I'm tired of playing eye spy all damn night. Shit. Besides, it's February, we graduate in three months, and I have no idea what I'm gonna do after we graduate. You, you're already set, going off to play volleyball on a full scholarship. I don't have anything. Fuck Demarcus. I'm worried about other things. Give me some credit."

China looked at her and then gave her one of those nods like, "It's about damn time you saying something to stand up for yourself." They parted ways after China dropped her off and sped like crazy to get back to her apartment.

Mackenzie went into the house, said hey to Aunt Cecile and the twins, who were glued to the TV playing Nintendo's Donkey Kong. She went into her room and shut the door.

Mackenzie just sat there and thanked God for the small things, like having her own room finally, and also being able to shower in a clean bathroom and eat before she went to bed, unlike in the past when Pat was still alive.

She pulled off her clothes and left them right there on the floor, grabbed the robe that Aunt Cecilie had bought her last Christmas, and went to take her shower. The hot water covering her body seemed to sting, like it was trying to tell her something that she was obviously missing.

The water was poking at her shoulder, and she began to cry, wondering where she was going or what she was going to be doing once she graduated.

Mackenzie honestly had no clue. Her teachers here in Texas always spoke to her as if she were dumb. She guessed it was because she didn't say much in class, and they figured she was dumb. So many times she'd wanted to explain certain things to them or share with them the different ways of interpreting such stories as Mark Twain's *Huckleberry Finn.*

They were still portraying Nigga Jim as the fool, the dummy; if only they knew. Shit, Jim was the smartest person in that damn book! Mackenzie learned that, courtesy of her high school back in Brooklyn, which ironically had several Jewish teachers, that didn't mind telling her the truth. They shared knowledge in spite of what society wanted humans to believe, that blacks and Jews were sworn enemies. Mackenzie knew that wasn't true, and if you asked her, she believed the two had more in common than any other races.

Guess those teachers felt there was no reason to lie about such things as that. It would be a shame for someone with such credentials as a teacher, to lie about history, Mackenzie thought.

As a result, the counselors weren't sending for her during class periods to talk about college or future plans. She never said anything; she just sat and watched most of the kids that didn't wind up getting pregnant or being hauled off to "Juvy," getting ready for college.

Her tears fell like a waterfall because she was fucked. She'd always wanted to be a lawyer because it was like you were E. F. Hutton, when you spoke, people listened. But Mackenzie didn't know the first steps of getting there. She often dreamed of one day having her own practice and kicking ass in the courtroom. She would be well versed, intellectual, and always dressed to kill, knocking them dead just by being in the room.

If only she knew how to make that dream a reality. She wouldn't be standing in the shower butt naked, crying like a baby with the now colder water freezing her nipples.

That was the sad part of not having parents around to guide you, to make sure you chose the right path, or to hold you when you were hurt. Mackenzie felt her anger stirring and wanted to punch someone. She missed Pat, and Jun, too. She missed her brother's and sisters. She felt disconnected and, once again, lost. She cut the water off, barely dried off, and went to bed naked. She finally dosed off with her hands in between her legs and shivering because she was still wet.

Chapter Six

The month of May arrived quicker than she cared to think about. China and Mackenzie graduated, and China went off to college in South Carolina. She had to leave early to start workouts and all the other things you do when you get ready for a college-level education. That was the last time Mackenzie ever saw China.

Mackenzie was alone, until she met up with Nick. She had met Nick about seven summers ago, when, before Pat died, her paternal grandfather let all of his grandchildren come upstate for a month. That was the last time her, her brothers, and sisters, and all her cousins on her father's side had been together. It was probably one of the best summers of her life. They played baseball with a stick and an aluminum paper ball, and walked six miles to the store after they all stole change from their grandfather's jukebox. They also had a pet goat, until their grandfather cooked it and gave them its scrotums to play with because he had been drinking with his buddies and let his joke go to far. They went fishing at a nearby creek for dinner at least twice a week. And of course, they had their talent shows, during which Mackenzie sat with the boys, cracking up laughing at her silly sisters and cousins trying to sing or at her brothers dancing to *Flash Light* and *Ring my Bell*.

Nick hung around her oldest brother from time to time and was the boyfriend of one of their neighbors. Nick was mulatto; actually, he was Italian and Trinidadian. He was tall with curly hair, had light skin, dark brown eyes, and full lips. He was cute but as silly as ever.

He'd moved to Dallas because he'd finally broken up with his old girlfriend from upstate and wanted a new start. His brother lived here and said he should give it a try.

They ran into each other as she was walking past the check-cashing place and he was getting into his white pick-up, Mackenzie took a double look and said to herself, *"Damn he's cute,"* when he turned around, he said, "Mackenzie, is that you?"

She looked and realized that it was Nick. He was a man now, well, not technically he was only one year older than she was, so he was just eighteen. But something was different; he didn't have that goofy look to her. He seemed straight up, serious.

"Hi, Nick, what are you doing here?"

"I live here. What are you doing here?" he asked.

"I live here, silly, right around the corner."

"No shit? I live across the street behind the Chinese restaurant."

They stood there talking for a minute and exchanged numbers. They were both looking for jobs, so they decided to hook up later that night and see what they could come up with.

Nick was living with his brother and doing the bachelor thing. They had no furniture, just beds, a dining table, and a refrigerator filled with beer.

Luckily, the two of them found a job at a sorry telemarketing company and deemed each other brother and sister. Each weekend they hung out at the West End in downtown Dallas and tried to hook each other up with prospects that were out and about. Mackenzie always got to Nick because she would tell him that some pretty girl was staring him down, and when he would turn around, she would be butt ugly!

Cracking up laughing, Nick wanted to knock her out, until one day she couldn't get his goat anymore because he found the girl of his dreams when they were window shopping through J.C. Penney.

She was beautiful and wouldn't take her eyes off of Nick.

"Come on, Mackenzie; hook me up," he begged, until Mackenzie finally gave in.

"Okay, let me figure out what to say." But before Mackenzie could go to find her and hook Nick up, she was coming her way. Nick disappeared.

"Hi. I'm Tiphane. I was wondering if you and your friend wanted to come to my parents' Caribbean restaurant/bar this weekend?"

"Sure. Actually he's my brother though, but I'll tell him, Nick loves to get out."

"Oh, okay. Well, let me get you my number and y'all can call me Saturday afternoon."

"Okay, I'll pass it on to Nick."

Tiphane passed Mackenzie her number on a J.C. Penney card and she fled, trying to find Nick throughout the Prestonwood Mall. Nick was sitting at the Burger King in the food court, anxiously waiting on her.

"Did you talk to her?"

"Yeah, and you won't believe this. She invited us out this weekend to her parents' Caribbean restaurant/bar."

"You lying right?"

"No, I'm for real this time; she really did. Here's her number. I told her I would pass it on to you."

"Oh shit, damn. This must be my lucky day. I just talked with the guy at J.C. Penney and they said they were hiring a loss prevention officer, so I applied. He said more than likely I would get it."

"Wow, that's good, Nick. Guess you can kiss that tele-junk goodbye, huh?" They hated their job, which consisted of calling people and trying to sell them insurance. Each day that they drove there together, Nick and Mackenzie dreaded the stench of old the coffee and liquor-flavored breath of most of the employees.

"Well, I' think I'm going to join the army, Nick. I just have to do something with myself 'cause I'm bored."

"Are you nutts, girl? The army? You got to go basic, and do all sorts of crazy stuff for like two or three months. And then, you only get paid like four hundred a month."

Mackenzie knew all of that; she had already spoken to a recruiter. But since Nick was probably switching jobs and she had no car, she knew she had to do something.

"Nick, since when are you so negative and rude?" Mackenzie said, disappointed. "You know I have to decide for me. I don't have anything to back me up. At least if I go to the army, I can get money to go to college in the future. Damn."

"Sorry, Mackenzie. You right. At least you can go to school when you get out. How long will you sign up for?"

"Probably two years just so I can get something out of the deal. I think the recruiter said if I sign up for two years I can get a two thousand dollar bonus and ten thousand for college when I get out, or I can take classes while I'm in."

"You should do it. If I didn't mind having someone yelling at me and telling me when I could do something, I would join with you."

Damn, she thought. She'd forgotten about that aspect, but people yelling at her, wasn't something she hadn't experienced before, so she didn't let it bother her too much.

"Well, we'd better get home and figure out what you gonna wear on Saturday. 'Cause you can't wear those damn boots and a T-shirt, Nick." That was Nick's thing; he always wore boots, baggy jeans, a baseball cap, and a T-shirt.

Looking through Nick's closet was a difficult task. All of Nick's clothes were the same. With their puny paycheck from that sorry job, buying an outfit was out of the question. So, they went to Nick's brother's closet and sifted through his flashy shirts and nice slacks. The only problem was, Nick's brother was about 5'8, and Nick was 6'1 easily.

So the best they could do was decide to iron a pair of his better jeans and a T-shirt and clean off his boots. They only had two days before Saturday would arrive. So, Mackenzie helped Nick with his outfit, let him model it a few times, and made sure he wore the perfect jeans.

When Saturday finally came, Nick looked pretty good. He shaved and trimmed his mustache and cut down his hair some. *Lucky mulatto,* she thought. His hair just fell into place. Nick smiled, tilting his head like he knew he had it goin' on.

Nick called Tiphane and got directions. She said they should get there around seven or eight. Nick's face was glowing and Mackenzie was cracking up laughing.

Tiphane's parents' place was down in Deep Ellum on Elm St. It was a nice, small Caribbean Bar and Grill, with bistro tables, two bar areas, and a patio out back with more tables. There was just enough greenery and two palm trees out back to give it that Caribbean atmosphere.

The placed smelled of rich, authentic Caribbean spices, coconut, and pineapples. When they walked in, a short, light-skinned lady greeted them and showed them to their table. Nick informed her that they were meeting Tiphane and the lady smiled at Nick, then, looking at Mackenzie, she said, with her West Indian accent, "Just a sec. I'll git her for you."

Nick and Mackenzie looked at each other. "I wonder who that was?" Nick said.

"Probably your future mother-in-law." Mackenzie smiled at Nick.

"So you guys made it," Tiphane said, coming up from behind Mackenzie. The short lady who'd seated them accompanied her. "This is my mom, Marty. My dad, Franklin, is in the kitchen; he'll be out shortly."

Nick extended his hand to shake Marty's. Mackenzie followed and did the same. She left them and Tiphane sat down to talk, encouraging them to have something to eat or drink. Nick was ready to eat and ordered oxtails with rice; Mackenzie ordered a pineapple soda, declining any food, because she was quite picky.

"Mackenzie, we can make you some fries or something if you don't eat Caribbean food." Tiphane said. She must have read her mind and heard her stomach because Mackenzie was starving.

"You can do that, really?"

"Un huh. You want them seasoned or not?"

"Girl, I love French fries; I can eat them all day, no seasoning though."

"Be right back," Tiphane said and excused herself to the kitchen.

"I can marry her. She could be my wife." Nick said. His eyes were serious, so instead of poking fun at him, Mackenzie just listened as he sat there, staring after Tiphane, commenting on everything about her.

After they ate, Mackenzie, took a walk around to the patio and let Nick and Tiphane talk. She sat outside and decided she was going to the recruiter on Monday. Out of the blue, a tall guy approached her. He was wearing baggy blue jeans, boot's, a tan T-shirt, and an apron. "Hey, I'm Ken. Tiphane's cousin."

He was attractive with brown skin, and black, wavy hair that was cut down low. His eyes were dark brown and big, as were his lips, which had a mole on the left side.

"Would you like something else to drink?"

"Oh no, I'm fine."

Ken sat down beside her and asked, "So what's your name, and why are you out here alone?"

"Well, I'm not alone, my friends are inside, but I guess you know that. I'm Mackenzie."

"Nice, Mackenzie." He said, smiling. "I guess your friends need some time to talk huh?"

"Yeah, I guess."

He smiled again, "Tiphane pointed you out earlier, wanted me to meet you."

"Really." Mackenzie replied.

"I fixed your fries for you. Were they good?"

"They were great. Thanks."

Ken looked at her and she looked at him.

"Do you want to dance once they pull the tables back?"

Mackenzie continued looking at Ken as he continued speaking. "Yeah, at about 11 or so they pull the tables back and play the best reggae music, that's when this place is jumping. We bump and grind until about two in the morning." It was about a quarter to ten as Mackenzie looked at her watch, then smiled.

"Well, I can't dance reggae."

"Don't worry, I'll guide you."

They both smiled. Ken and Mackenzie sat there for the next hour or so talking about religion, and goals.

Surprisingly, Ken wanted to be a lawyer as well. In fact, he'd just finished up undergraduate school at SMU. He worked at the Caribbean grill with Tiphane's family for extra cash.

He and Tiphane were first cousins, their mothers were sisters, and Ken's family was still in Antigua, where they ran a small resort. He was an only child and very close to his cousin Tiphane.

Ken had planned on attending one of the best law schools in Texas down in Austin this fall. Obviously, money was not an issue for him. When she told Ken about her idea of going into the army and possibly going to law school after she finished undergrad, Ken nodded and said she should go for it. In fact, he listened attentively to everything that she said. This was something Mackenzie was not used to.

"I could see you as a lawyer. There's something about you that is so cutting edge, like you're not to be messed with, intimidating."

Mackenzie had never thought that. "Really?" she said.

"Yep. Come on, they should be pulling the tables back now. I wanna dance with you."

Ken grabbed her hand and they went back inside. Tiphane and Nick were already on the dance floor, dancing closer than close, like it was their own private party. Mackenzie couldn't help but smile. Nick seemed so happy.

Then Ken grabbed her close and they danced reggae all night, sweating and carrying on in between laughs. The place was packed in no time, and the music just wouldn't let you sit down. The music and smells of a Caribbean atmosphere made Mackenzie forget her life and its uncertainties.

When the Dee-Jay flashed the lights, everyone knew the cue and started clearing the dance floor. Ken walked her outside where they met up with Nick and Tiphane. "We gonna go get something to eat," Nick said. Mackenzie wasn't hungry just tired, and her feet were killing her.

"Well, I can give Mackenzie a ride home."

Okay, she thought. *"I'm gonna kick Nick's ass, for pushing me off on Ken."*

"Cool." Nick said, whisking Tiphane away.

Ken looked at her and asked, "You ready?"

Mackenzie, filled with flattery, responded, "Sure."

Ken drove a little black CRX, which was odd because he was around Nick's height. But with his seats pushed way back, he fit in just fine. "Where to?"

"Oh, I live off of Spring Valley and Coit. You know where that is?"

"Yep, no problem."

They drove home listening to Bird "Party A" on the radio and laughing at Nick and Tiphane being glued to each other on the dance floor.

When they arrived at her apartment complex, Ken jumped out, and opened her door for her. He walked her to her apartment, as they dodged the sprinkler system and then stood at the bottom of the steps.

"Well, I should get going," Ken said lightly, clearing his voice.

"Yeah, I'm going to church tomorrow, I have to get up early."

Ken extended his arms for a hug, and Mackenzie moved in to hug him. But he didn't move his head; he just kept straight, towards her face, and kissed her. Mackenzie was caught off guard, but he just paced himself and waited for her, as she kissed him back.

They kissed for a while, and he wasn't too bad a kisser, but sad to say, Mackenzie couldn't get her mind off of Demarcus. So, she ended the kiss and told Ken, "Good luck with your law school studies." Then she went upstairs and let herself in without ever looking back.

Mackenzie laid out her clothes for church, showered, and went to sleep. Later, Aunt Cecile came to wake her up to tell her Nick was on the phone.

"Mackenzie, wake up. It's Nick."

Clearing her throat she told him, "I know, nigga. What you want?"

"Mackenzie, she gon' be my girl. We going out tomorrow to her parents' crib for dinner. She said you can come; Ken's gonna be there. You gon' go?"

"Nick, I'm hanging up. Call me tomorrow, I can't believe Aunt Cecile woke me up for this call. Bye."

That Monday, Mackenzie didn't go to work and decided to join the army. The recruiter said she could leave by the beginning of September, which was about three weeks away.

He told her she could enlist for two years, then, she took some test that stated she'd qualified for several jobs. She chose occupational therapy. She would do basic training at Fort Jackson in South Carolina, then come back to Texas to train for occupational therapy at Fort Sam Houston in San Antonio.

Over the next three weeks, she ran two miles everyday back at her old high school and practiced push ups, and sit ups, practically dying. Nick was so wrapped up in Tiphane, that they didn't hang out much, just driving to work together for two out of the three weeks she had left. Every other sentence was about Tiphane.

Mackenzie was happy that Nick had found his girl, because when they'd first met up, he had been broken down over his old girlfriend from upstate.

The day before she left, Nick, Tiphane, and herself, went to have dinner back at her family's Caribbean Grill. They laughed, drank pineapple sodas, and Mackenzie said her goodbyes. Aunt Cecile picked her up and Mackenzie was on her way to army life.

Chapter Seven

"*What have I done to myself?*" was all Mackenzie could think of. For the next four months, she would be living in a huge room filled with women of all types. There were absolutely no men, except two air-headed drill sergeants, who were nuts. They seemed to get pleasure out of yelling and scaring the hell out of her.

One the biggest and meanest of the two was from some small town in Georgia. The other was some small-time, wanting to be big-time, ex-drug addict that couldn't keep his eyes off of some of the younger girls.

Drill Sergeant Jack and Jack-off made her life a living hell. She was constantly in the pushup position. And she knew it wasn't because of her behind, because she didn't have one. Her name was "dick head" and "pea brain" for the next two months.

Luckily, Mackenzie felt like she got over Demarcus during basic training and made lots of friends. Besides, they were always so tired and trying to keep each other motivated, they didn't have time to talk about loser ex-boyfriends.

Halfway through, they learned how to shoot the M-16 rifle and learned about various other weapons the U.S. military used for war.

When some of the women couldn't quite learn how to shoot, they all had prayer service in the barracks in hopes that they would pass. Failing meant you would be set back and couldn't graduate with your class. By the Grace of God, they all passed.

When she graduated from basic training, she and some of the other women went off base and rented their own rooms to relax. In a sense, they were going to let their hair down.

After getting settled into their rooms, it was more than obvious that many of the women were planning to meet up with some of the guys that were also in basic across the way. There was some guy she would always see during chow time who would wink at her. Quite naturally, that man was at the hotel waiting for her after they all got their rooms. Most of the guys who were just finishing basic thought many of them would be horny as hell. Not at all, as far as she was concerned, but Mackenzie didn't mind having male company just to talk to.

This man was gorgeous, with a nice brown complexion, full lips, and neatly trimmed, wavy hair. That always seemed to be Mackenzie's type of guy, guy's with good hair. They hung out all day and night laughing and talking about basic training and how tough it was and glad that it was finally over.

Then they kissed until the sun came up because she wasn't about to give it up to someone she'd just met. He kept asking her to let him eat her out, and she just kept saying NO.

After their long night of kissing, Mackenzie went straight to her job training at Fort Sam. She never saw or heard from him again, but she did get a real good lesson in kissing that night. Always follow the leader and never be too aggressive. Kissing is an art; one should try and master it.

Now AIT, this place was supposed to be more relaxed than basic. There were guys everywhere. And it was official: Mackenzie was finally over Demarcus.

On the weekends, they partied hard at the Enlistee club for trainees, dancing with guys, close to sexing on the dance floor, which was tiny. In fatigues and brown T-shirts, they partied hard. And it was nothing for her homegirls to leave with one of the guys and not come home until the next day. Of course, they were far more advanced than she was; most of them had kids, husbands, or boyfriends at home.

Mackenzie wasn't even trying to go there. She was waiting for her ideal man to be her first. She didn't meet anyone there but did manage to get some stares and occasional winks from guys after she danced with them. But none of them had that spark she was looking for.

Mackenzie took it all in stride and during quiet time, kept to herself, especially during shower time, when this one woman in particular, who looked liked a ripped boxer, and was probably toothless would always catch her taking off her robe. Mackenzie would usually wait until everyone was out of the dorm when she took her showers on the weekend. She wouldn't even see the woman around, but as soon as she made it to her bunk and began to disrobe and get dressed, she would come from nowhere. Mackenzie would be standing there, butt ass naked, answering stupid questions about the weather while this "woman" surveyed her body with her eyes.

Ugh. Just the thought upset her. The woman never propositioned her; she just liked looking at her something that made Mackenzie furious.

"At least say something so I can say HELL NO!" Was Mackenzie's position on it.

When Mackenzie finally turned eighteen that December, Nick and Tiphane sent her cookies and Aunt Cecile and the twins sent her a Mickey Mouse watch. It was not exactly how she'd planned to spend her eighteenth birthday, but it beat being in the streets somewhere hungry.

When Christmas came around, they were all allowed to go home for two weeks. Mackenzie was headed back to Dallas, walking straight up like a real nerd and happy to be able to eat home cooked food again.

Nick and Tiphane were exclusive now and welcomed her back with a little get together at their new apartment in far North Dallas. It was nicely decorated with all light gray furniture, matching gray carpet, an oak entertainment center, matching tables, and a bedroom that was filled with a full-sized bed with tons of pillows across it.

There were new faces around, but Mackenzie didn't see Ken. She was actually a little sad, as she'd wanted to see him. She guessed law school was keeping him pretty busy or some woman was.

"Oh well" she thought, *"I hope he's happy."*

After the little get together, they all went down to the Caribbean spot and sat around and talked, waiting for the servers to push the tables back.

This only made Mackenzie want to see Ken more. But as soon as the tables were pushed back, a short guy asked her to dance. It felt like he came up to her kneecaps until he got real close, and she felt his touch on her thigh. Suddenly, the word *short* and *small* just didn't seem appropriate. Mackenzie forgot all about Ken.

They danced the entire night, with him being silly like it was his own party and Mackenzie laughing because he would make her laugh with his outrageous dance moves until the Dee-jay started flashing the lights.

They followed everyone else out and stood waiting for Nick and Tiphane.

"My name is Silas…and yours?"

"Mackenzie. Nice to meet you finally, after you've gotten me all sweaty."

They laughed at the obvious. Mackenzie's bun was sweaty and falling down.

"So, you like to dance reggae huh, Ms. MACKENZIE," Silas said, with authority. She was actually feeling something.

"You wanna go get something to eat?"

"Well, let me find my friends first; they may want to do something."

"All right, I'll wait right here." Silas said, as Mackenzie went in search of Nick and Tiphane. Mackenzie went searching up the street to Nick's usual parking spot and found him and Tiphane exchanging kisses and touches that belonged in private.

"Hey. You guys going home or out to get something to eat?"

Wiping his mouth, Nick replied, "What you go'n do?"

"That guy Silas wanted to go get something to eat. You guys want to come." They looked at each other, and Mackenzie knew what that meant.

"Do you need us to go?"

"Nah, he's harmless, too short to pose a threat." They all laughed for a second, and Mackenzie left them standing there hugging and kissing again and went to find Silas. He was standing there waiting on her.

They joked about each other's dance moves and walked to Silas's truck.   Little Silas drove a big pick up, and it seemed as though he needed a booster seat. It was nice though, a spoiler kit, rims, and leather seats. Silas blasted MC Breed and Mackenzie enjoyed his company. There was something about Silas that she was attracted to; he was sexy to her.

She sat and thought about how his lips moved when he talked, and how his hands moved when he was trying to be cool, obviously overcompensating for his height.

Silas drove fast and with control to IHOP on Skillman, and they sat and talked. Silas was from California and attending college in Texas at UTA on a track scholarship, which explained his muscular tone and physique. He was currently studying criminal justice and had future plans to work in parole.

Not only did Silas have his "stuff" together, but he was funny. All through the night, he would change his voice and imitate Eddie Murphy.

Silas thought Mackenzie was crazy to be in the army and too pretty for that. Mackenzie laughed because she thought that it was funny. They ordered chicken tenders and French fries after Silas finally stopped making their waitress laugh so much. When it came time to eat, that little guy ate quite quickly. Mackenzie cracked up laughing at him. She told him he looked like he was in the military because of the way he ate, non-stop without looking up!

"So, you wanna come back to my place and hang out for a little bit?"

Mackenzie was a little hesitant, but in a way, she was anxious to be alone with Silas. He just had that effect.

"Yeah, sure, why not, I've been bored out of my mind ever since I joined the army."

"Cool. I live in Grand Prairie, not too far from Six Flags."

"You will give me a ride back? I stay in Dallas on Spring Valley."

"No, I was thinking you could walk back. It's about 40 miles, you know, give or take a few."

Mackenzie squinted, her eyes and looked at Silas, who started crackin' up laughing before she could say anything.

"You're so crazy. Come on, let's go," she said, as they got up and walked out to Silas's truck, which was being admired by a group of young teens.

"Okay back up, move away from the truck," Silas said, talking through his hands like he was using a bullhorn. The teens scattered, and the two of them got in, blasting MC Breed, and driving down Central Expressway to I-30.

Silas had a nice efficiency apartment that was barely decorated. You could tell he was a student because there were books everywhere and only a desk and a bed.

"I don't drink, but I have some cherry Kool-Aid with lemon if you want?"

Yep, he's a brother, thought Mackenzie. *The red Kool-Aid was a dead giveaway.* Mackenzie laughed to herself and then said, "sure, that would be fine."

Mackenzie put down her little jacket and sat Indian style on Silas's floor. Silas bought her Kool-Aid, and then threw down some pillows to join her.

Silas was short, but he was attractive, too. He was caramel-colored with a cute smile, semi-big eyes, and fresh, white teeth. He was also bald, clean, and neat. Even his sagging pants and oversized shirt looked neat, and he spoke well when he wasn't joking around and being silly. Mackenzie was definitely attracted to him.

"You have a boyfriend, Mackenzie?"

"Nope. Single."

"Why, you like guys don't you?"

"Ha ha, very funny. I may be in the army, but *I like boys.* Smart Ass."

Silas laughed and asked if she wanted to arm wrestle for a dollar.

"How about five, cheapskate?" she said, as Silas sat up and started talking mess while rolling up his sleeve.

Mackenzie rolled up hers and they locked hands. It was tough trying to be serious because Silas started his Eddie Murphy routine, but Mackenzie finally got the best of him when she took her free hand and tickled his neck; he squirmed.

"Yuk, you do like girls don't you? Because you just did a girl move, squirming and stuff."

Silas fell out laughing and then busted out and said, "I can show you how much."

Oh damn, she thought, *me and my big mouth.* Silas started looking her in the eyes and came close to kiss her.

He moved in close enough to touch her lips, then called out, "Psyche!"

Mackenzie couldn't help but laugh, and in the same spirit, she pulled him close, and kissed him on the mouth.

"What you scared now?" she whispered.

He smiled and said, "Are you scared?"

"Nope." She replied, then she kissed him again until he started feeling on her in ways she couldn't describe. Silas had what her army buddies called dick appeal. Something about him wanted her to allow him to be her first because she knew she would like it.

Mackenzie remembered hearing some of the girls in the army saying how much they hated their first time and how badly it hurt. That alone made her dread having sex.

But Silas was different; the way he was kissing and feeling all over her, made her just want to lose it. And she did. Silas was slow and a professional at this sex "stuff." He did everything to a rhythm, from undressing her to walking over to get a condom, and when he pulled her on top of him, the size of his penis didn't even matter; he made hurting feel good.

By the time they finished, she was shaking like a leaf and dying for more. That night, morning, and afternoon, Silas showed her a reality she never thought existed. In fact, he was so sweet, he made it feel like what she was doing couldn't be wrong. And turning eighteen didn't seem so bad anymore.

They took a shower together and Silas washed her, and then cracked up laughing about her ugly feet. And as she washed him, she told him he needed vanishing cream for his black ass, which didn't match his face. Mackenzie was feeling all grown up being with Silas; she never imagined that her first time would be like this. She broke all of her rules about sex. And, strangely enough, she was okay with that.

Mackenzie couldn't wear any of his clothes home because she knew she would be busted. It was bad enough that she was going to have to lie to Aunt Cecile about where she'd stayed last night.

So she called Tiphane and asked her to promise her she wouldn't tell Nick what she'd done last night, but if Aunt Cecile ever asked, she said, "Tell her I stayed with ya'll last night." Tiphane agreed, and the two exchanged a few laughs and then hung up.

For the next two weeks, Silas and Mackenzie hung out whenever his schedule permitted and "did their thing" whenever they could. She never told Silas that he was her first and just basically enjoyed him until it was time for her to leave.

Mackenzie was so wrapped up in Silas she didn't even see China, who was home for the holidays, which was how she preferred it.

And Christmas was a crying shame. Silas didn't go home, so she spent most of her time with him. Their gifts were each other all over his tiny apartment. New Year's was pretty much the same after she left church with Aunt Cecile and the twins. She lied, telling them she was going to Nick and Tiphane's for a party.

Mackenzie dodged Nick so much during her trip that he called and told her he was pissed at her and was about to disown her, then hung up in her face. Silas had that attraction though; she just couldn't help it. Some day she would tell Nick, and he would understand. At least she hoped so.

All the way to the airport, Aunt Cecile complained about her not being around at all. Mackenzie told her she was sorry and if she came home for Easter, it would be different.

Before she left, Silas and Mackenzie exchanged addresses and promised they would do their best to keep in touch.

Chapter Eight

When Mackenzie made it back to the base, she was happy as ever. Most of the girls came back with their stories and issues; some were broken hearted because they had been dumped over the holidays; others were ecstatic because they'd finally gotten the man of their dreams. But Mackenzie wasn't saying anything. She just kept her smile on her face and reminisced about Silas, "his big penis", and how they'd had sex four or five times a day whenever they saw each other.

Countdown to getting out of the service felt better and she was charged up. Mackenzie only had another year and seven months before she could get out.

She was scheduled to graduate from Occupational Therapy school two weeks after she returned from Christmas break. When she received her orders, she was happy to find out that she would be stationed at Fort Gordon in Georgia and not overseas. Mackenzie was even told by some of the prior service soldiers, that more than likely, since she'd only enlisted for two years Fort Gordon would be her only duty station.

Graduation from her job training was literally a fiasco. A couple of the girls got into fights with some civilians over some of the male soldiers, the barracks were filthy due to soldiers leaving and not cleaning up, and the drill sergeants seemed to have disappeared. She was just anxious to start her tour so she could hurry up and be done.

Fort Gordon, as she was told soon after she arrived, was considered the party place to be. They said working there would be a "piece of cake." In other words, for the most part, you would work only half a day. In addition, guard duty meant bringing a book or a pillow your choice.

The clinic she worked at was very low key, with one other tech, and an officer to oversee them. The officer, Captain Lockley, was a lot older than they were, probably thirty-five. He wasn't married and just as nerdy as he wanted to be.

However, he didn't mind talking to her, even though she was only an E-2 and an enlisted. The two were not to be dealing with one another as far as the military was concerned. In fact, when she told him why she'd joined the army and her plans of someday going to law school, Captain Lockley told her that she should go and even suggested that she go to a highly recognized school right in Dallas, Southern Methodist University. He even told her that he knew several of the law professors there and would put in a good word for her. Mackenzie said she would love to take him up on his offer, but she had to finish or go to college first. He agreed but gave her his information anyway.

For the next eleven months, Captain Lockley taught her so much more about the OT field than she'd learned at Fort Sam. He gave her good books to read and challenged her mind every chance he got. He kept her sharp and on her toes for the most part, and for that fact, she would always be grateful.

On evenings whenever he could, Captain Lockley would meet her outside of the base and teach her how to drive. He thought it was funny that she didn't know how. That captain broke many rules to help her. That was one thing Mackenzie had never experienced. Aside from her Jewish teachers, back in Brooklyn, Mackenzie didn't think that white people cared. Captain Lockley was truly an asset to Mackenzie and a true friend.

At the end of that year, 1990, Capt Lockley was given orders to go overseas to Germany. This hurt Mackenzie, because for a white man in his thirties, he was unique. Not having a wife and kids and a picket fence meant nothing to him; he loved the army and was well versed, in literature, history, and technology.

Before he left, Captain Lockley gave her the best advice anyone had ever given her. "PFC Kennedy, when your tour is up, get out and go to school. Most of all, remember that you have to be one step ahead."

Captain Lockley was actually going overseas for the rumored war that was about to take place in Kuwait.

When Christmas arrived that year, Mackenzie met Aunt Cecile and the twins in New York and stayed at Grandma C's house. She had forgotten how much of a good cook her grandma was.

Mackenzie saw most of her brothers and sisters and looked at recent pictures of her father, which Lauren bought over on Christmas day. They were pictures of his third wedding. He had finally left that "mean-ass Vi" for good. *How nice for him,* she thought. However, it was too little too late. He'd even had the nerve to send a message to tell her happy belated birthday. Again, Mackenzie said, "Too little, too damn late!"

Looking at the pictures, she felt tears filling her eyes. She missed her blood and how Jun smelled. "That mean mutherfucka always smelled good." Mackenzie could tell from the pictures that he had given up his habit because he had put on some weight. *Maybe there is hope,* she said to herself, wiping away the tears that did manage to fall.

After Christmas dinner, Mackenzie said goodbye to her brothers and sisters and promised she would do better to keep in touch. They hugged as if it were the last time they would ever see each other.

Mackenzie called Sam as soon as they left and begged Aunt Cecile to let her walk up to Tompkins to see him. After Sam said he would meet her at the train station of Myrtle and Marcy avenues, Aunt Cecile agreed.

It was like old times because everybody was there at his house Red, Willie, Mishcah, and some of the members from their old choir.

Sam was still looking good and a magnet to all the other girls that were there. Mackenzie was even surprised to find out that he now had his own choir, and that's who most of the other people were.

They played "truth or dare" that night, drank Pepsi, and then went their separate ways until church that Sunday. Mishcah sang that Sunday and of course had the church doing back-flips. Mackenzie saw her youth minister who was all smiles. He asked about army life and *Texxxxaaass,* as he jokingly put it.

It was nice being back in New York, but it was also sad to see how dismal things looked in Brooklyn. Mackenzie knew she could never live there again. It was like a ghost town, and the only people that roamed the streets were those in search of another high.

Sam and Mackenzie managed to get one day of hanging out when he skipped out on class and they went to lower Manhattan to window shop. They talked for hours, walking up and down the city. Finally, they stopped and ate at Ray's Pizza in the village.

When Mackenzie told Sam about Silas, he was attentive. He said he'd always thought she would wait until she was married. Mackenzie told him she'd always thought so, too. But Silas had that *Dick Appeal,* and Sam just fell out laughing when she told him about it.

Sam told her about his newest girlfriend and how he was thinking about getting married once he finished college. She sang with his group and was originally from New Jersey. He wanted Mackenzie to meet her, but their plans just didn't meet up. Besides, Mackenzie wanted to avoid the woman that had finally won Sam's heart.

When she left New York, they vowed that they would be friends forever, and whoever got married first owed the other a bottle of cologne or perfume. The price had to be over a hundred dollars, of course; Sam had expensive taste.

When she made it back to Fort Gordon, things were crazy. The talk of war was becoming more of a reality. A lot of the soldiers were leaving and security was tight.

Mackenzie panicked. The clinic was shut down because there wasn't another OT officer there to run it; most of them were being pulled over to Germany to await injured soldiers. That was the good thing about occupational therapy: you would be called to the rear of the war, not directly into the front lines.

OT technicians, were responsible for setting up a clinic that helped soldiers work with injuries or disabilities caused by the war or injuries they'd received doing other tasks for the military.

Mackenzie only had until the end of July and she would be through. She was counting on that notion to get her out of being pulled overseas or extended.

She was blessed to find out that she would do the remainder of her time at Fort Hood in Kileen, Texas, about an hour away from Dallas.

And while many of the U.S. soldiers were fighting by the time she made it to Kileen in early February, she was put on guard duty at the gates, mess hall, or wherever they could put her until she left.

Mackenzie often wondered how it happened, and so did many of the other soldiers who were shipping in, and out on a daily basis, coming or going overseas. She decided that it had to have been Captain Lockley's doing; His father was a Brigadier General in Virginia. Mackenzie figured he was making sure she took care of her business when she got out of the army.

When July finally arrived, she was happy. Mackenzie called Nick, Aunt Cecile, and Silas to tell them she would be home in less than thirty days.

Nick was still a little mad but after she told him the truth about Silas, he called her a dirty dog and said, "Next time, make his ass take you somewhere nice!"

Aunt Cecile was delighted that Mackenzie was finally coming home, because the twins were "growing up far too fast." Mackenzie couldn't catch up with Silas and was a little bothered.

They hadn't communicated too much after their two-week excursion. In fact, Mackenzie had probably talked to him a total of three times, and they'd probably written each other double that. He would always be remembered as the guy that had *dick appeal!* Mackenzie quickly rearranged her thoughts and realized that Silas was long gone. So, she was leaving behind two things at one time, her feelings for Silas and the army.

Mackenzie had to turn in all of her stuff, and go through so much paperwork, medical exams, and clearance that she regretted ever having gone into the military. But had she not, she wouldn't have met Captain Lockley or cracked up laughing several nights while enjoying talking with the other soldiers there.

Part II:
Living to Survive

Chapter Nine

Back in Dallas again Nick, Tiphane, and Mackenzie started hanging out. They often hung out at the Caribbean spot, talking and drinking their pineapple sodas. Nick would often order Guinness Stout or a Heineken behind Tiphane's mother's back, which probably wouldn't have been a problem because Marty loved Nick to death. He wouldn't dare disappoint her.

After two weeks of being back, Nick said they should try some of the other clubs in Deep Ellum or just walk around and look at all the "freaks." Deep Ellum was notorious for attracting different people.

So they walked around just looking, saying amongst themselves, "Damn, we've been missing out!" It was such a true reminder of New York, with people everywhere, walking, talking, and drinking. It was a trip for her. Mackenzie and her friends had been so consumed with the Caribbean place that they'd never looked any further or paid attention to anything else.

After walking past one club in particular, *The Aqua Lounge,* they all decided to go in because it had the longest line and a drag queen at the front door, choosing whom he wanted to let in.

Nick was cheap, so he basically swindled the three of them in for free, telling the drag queen that they were all visiting from New York and wanted a cool place to check out. The drag queen was so taken by Nick's lie, that he didn't bother to check identification. He went on and on about trying to save enough money to get to New York for a modeling career.

"Yeah, you could make it. They dig stuff like this in New York."

"I know. They're going to love me in New York."

They all laughed at his dramatic display and filed into the club. The place was wild. The music was loud and people were everywhere, sitting in lounge chairs, dancing on speakers, and dancing all over the place. The club had a unique smell that floated through the air, which was hypnotic to Mackenzie. Nick looked at Tiphane; neither of them were impressed. But Mackenzie was sucked in the moment that drag queen had let them through the door.

They finally left when the club closed at four in the morning. Nick and Tiphane swore they were never coming back because they said the people were too weird. Nick said they all looked like they were on something. Mackenzie was just so taken by the party atmosphere, that she hadn't seen anything unusual.

From that day on, she was hooked. Now the club scene was all her. It was 1991, she was about to be twenty, and it was a time to be unique.

Mackenzie applied for a job at Lady Foot Locker, got it, and was making good money to support her party habit. Every weekend she had to have something new on. Most of the girls always gave compliments and asked where she shopped. Mackenzie never told because she liked the status of being unique. Still, the following weekend, someone would try to wear something similar.

Once she got the hang of the techno and house music, Mackenzie couldn't sit down. She walked in the club dancing and left dancing, all the while, keeping to herself. When someone finally asked where she was from and she told them "Brooklyn, New York", her popularity soared.

Mackenzie was put on the infamous *guest list* and was considered one of the regulars. *Isn't it funny how we all need to be associated with something, and if we're not careful, we'll associate with anything?* She thought to herself.

Right about now, Mackenzie was hooked, as if it were crack. She had to be there every weekend. She opened the club every Friday and closed it every Saturday night. Each time she walked to her car, a Geo metro she'd bought with her army bonus money, high on 7-Up, she would think about how she had been banging it down on the dance floor. Mackenzie felt like she was on the rise.

Mackenzie was enjoying the attention and pretty much forgot all about Silas, Ken, and Demarcus and anything that reminded her of being a woman. It was nothing to dance on top of the speakers at the club with other girls, or to leave the club or some after party and head straight to work.

On one of her weekend shopping sprees, she went to the mall with the twins. Minding her own business, dressed in a T-shirt and sweats, she saw a handsome guy coming in her direction.

He was light-skinned, with chinky eyes, and was well dressed Demarcus!

"That no good bastard!" she thought. He had the nerve to be grinning at her.

"Hey Mackenzie," he said.

"Hey Demarcus."

"Oh, I don't get no hug?"

Mackenzie wanted to tell him, "Hell no, you don't get no hug, but I do have a size nine to put up yo' ass!" In the middle of Valley View's food court, Mackenzie was fuming and wanted to hug Demarcus all at the same time.

Ignoring her disposition, Demarcus came close and gave her a hug anyway. Demarcus appeared even older now. His smell was still the same fresh. Mackenzie wondered what he would think when she told him about Silas. She wanted to rub it in his face that she and Silas would fuck until the sun came up, and he'd shown her things with such sensitivity, it was a damn shame. But she declined, hoping to get him at a later time when it might *really* hurt.

Letting go of his embrace, Demarcus said, "Say, Mackenzie, won't you let me get yo' phone number? I've been trying to find you."

"Really, where have you been looking? Cause Aunt Cecile never said anything about you trying to find me. And besides, I went off to the army after high school."

"So when you gon' come see me?" he said, causing her to fume. Mackenzie couldn't believe him; it was as if nothing had ever happened. She wanted to walk off and leave him standing there. He made no mention of Ms. Pretty, or that night, nothing.

But the truth be told, Mackenzie was weakened by Demarcus still. After seeing him again after so long, she was awakened and needed to be close to him again. Mackenzie was back at his same old apartment that night.

Demarcus's apartment had been redone. He had all leather black furniture. Demarcus was still the want-to-be singer and played BBD's single, *I Do, Need You* and sung along with his little mic.

"Always the entertainer, never a true romantic. If I wasn't so hot and bothered, I would have told him to be original, nigga!" Mackenzie said to herself.

After his so-called serenade, it was like a dream come true for Mackenzie. Demarcus and naive Mackenzie kissed like old times, only this time, she wasn't thinking of ways to end it before they went all the way. Instead, she was anticipating the sex and how he would feel inside of her.

Taking off her fitted red top first, Demarcus tasted her. When he unbuttoned her black Levis, she kissed his lips, hoping that he understood how badly she wanted him.

Fully undressed, Demarcus spread open her legs and let his tongue do crazy stuff that Silas had never done. She squirmed and trembled as she arched her back in ecstasy. When he finished, Demarcus asked if she wanted to "do" him. Mackenzie told him she didn't know how, because she didn't, and last she'd heard from her old army friends, "That was for nasty girls to do."

Demarcus covered up his penis just like Silas had always done and grabbed her from behind. It was a position that Mackenzie favored. She backed into Demarcus as he pushed deep inside and quickly had another orgasm. Sex was still a very good thing, she decided. From behind again, on top, and then against the wall, Mackenzie came like Niagara Falls.

They were asleep on the floor for a couple of hours when Demarcus's phone woke them up. After he briefly talked on the phone, he asked if she would shower with him. She ignored the phone conversation and obliged.

Of course, before any showering could take place, Demarcus wanted to fuck again. This time, Demarcus was so damn hard, his dick was a brick sword. Straight up, Demarcus sat up against the shower wall and pulled her on top of him, with no condom. He moved her up and down and she arched her back in the act of ecstasy, then she grabbed his head and held on while he fucked her good, she was dizzy by the time they climaxed together, with him still inside of her. Her mind was spinning out of control.

Shaking and taken by this wonderful, new experience, Mackenzie was all smiles. They washed each other off and went back to his bedroom where they were at it again. This time, he pulled her on top of him as he lay on the bed, holding her hips so she could move in rhythm with him. Hugging his muscle with hers, he exploded as he pulled out, jerking and making sounds as his cum covered her stomach.

He rolled her over after he stopped jerking and carrying on, and went down on her, sucking and licking until she came as well. And like two people after a good meal, they fell fast asleep.

Mackenzie dreamt of the two of them together again, and in a much more adult situation, and it was all bliss. She had awakened a few times in the night to make sure that her eyes weren't deceiving her. It was finally a dream come true.

That following morning, Mackenzie felt as though she was in the twilight zone. Demarcus was already awake, dressed, and buzzing around his apartment. There was no "good morning" or "how did you sleep?" He was cold as ice when he finally asked her, "Are you gon' take a shower here or when you get home?"

"I guess now," she said, confused.

"Well hurry up, 'cause I got to go." And that was all he said to her except for mumbling, "I'll talk to you later" when they walked to their cars. Although she wouldn't dare show it, she was hurt.

Mackenzie continued to club and started going from Wednesday through Sunday. That was her way of not letting the episode with Demarcus bring her down. She gave up the idea of going to school that January; she just wasn't ready. She waited for Demarcus to call again in hopes that things would be different.

In the midst of all the madness, the club scene was changing. Many of the girls who usually had some guy tagging along, were all of a sudden drawn to each other. Maybe it had been like this all along and she had simply been too wrapped up in herself and her image to see it. Her mind was stuck on Demarcus and the night they'd spent together. She didn't want to accept the fact that Demarcus could care less about her and the night they'd spent together. She even made an excuse about the phone call in the middle of the night that he'd received.

Mackenzie kept her distance from the clinging, because she didn't feel it was necessary. In fact, besides China or Tiphane, or her distant sisters, Mackenzie never liked females around her. They always had some drama or issues or were mad because they didn't have what she had.

Then she met a girl named Erasmus. Everything she believed about women was about to change the boundaries, her insecurities, her trust issues, and the issues of love.

Chapter Ten

Erasmus and Mackenzie were both connected on the basis of their fashion sense. Erasmus was crisp from head to toe. There was no doubt after talking in the bathroom, and exchanging fashion tips that they would be friends for life. For a white girl, Erasmus had her fashion together and was beautiful, Mackenzie thought. Her long, curly, red hair, tangle-free, defined cheekbones, and pretty teeth provided a replica of Andi McDowell.

There was one slight problem though: Erasmus was extremely moody. On Fridays she would be cool, and then on some Saturdays, she was as rude as she wanted to be. Mackenzie figured she was probably schizophrenic or, one of those drug addicts that hid their problem well.

They would meet at the club and depending on which day it was, they would laugh the entire night. Then Mackenzie would dance, while Erasmus drank and took many trips to the bathroom with groups of people. On some nights, Mackenzie would see Erasmus just watching as she danced. She would have a little smile that made Mackenzie feel confident, kind of like her home girl's got her back. When they weren't at the club, they spent countless hours on the phone, hanging out at

Mackenzie's, going out to eat, or just sitting and talking while looking deeply into each other's eyes.

Often after Erasmus would leave, Mackenzie remained caught up in each experience, wondering why it felt so good to sit and talk, looking deeply into each other's eyes. She had never felt this close to a woman before.

Mackenzie truly believed that she was her only friend there, and for the most part, she had proof. There was one other girl who'd always tried to be Mackenzie's friend. She would always ask her if she wanted another 7-Up or she would just come up to Mackenzie and speak or compliment her outfit, which made Mackenzie feel awkward.

One Friday, Mackenzie and Candie were in the restroom and she asked if Mackenzie had ever done any drugs.

"No! Not at all."

"Well, that's good, but if you ever want to get some X."

"Some what?"

"You know, ecstasy, the stuff that makes you feel bad ass. It's like you love everybody. You will dance your best on that shit."

"Really?" Now that's deep."

"If you want, we can do some tomorrow night. Just let me know."

Skeptical, Mackenzie told her that she would let her know. Candie, the short, blonde, petite woman then handed her a piece of paper with her phone number on it.Mackenzie thought long and hard about their conversation in the bathroom. "*Why was she asking me to do drugs?*" she thought.

That night, while finally getting to sleep, Mackenzie dreamt about crazy stuff and saw crazy things; it was as if there was chaos everywhere. For some odd reason though, she was still intrigued about this X drug and decided she would try it. Besides, dealing with Demarcus and his rude ass just made her feel compelled to go and hide. She didn't want to face that first Silas was gone and now Demarcus. She couldn't deal with what she might be doing wrong; taking X was an escape.

Mackenzie decided not to tell Erasmus about her decision because the one thing she did not want with her new friend was a friendship based on getting high. She still had images of Jun and his many friends and how they sat around for hours just getting high. Mackenzie just wanted to try some X this one time, and besides, at times, Erasmus could be very judgmental and downright ignorant!

When Mackenzie went to the Candie's house, she saw some people she knew from the club. Once she came in though, they all left, and the two of them were alone. She explained to Mackenzie that X was a pill, and it would take about thirty minutes before she felt anything. Once it hit her system, it would feel like she was floating on air.

Mackenzie checked the pills to make sure they were both taking the same pill, and then they took their pills with some Sprite. Candie told Mackenzie not to take any alcohol because she wouldn't need it. Mackenzie said, "That's no problem because I don't drink," sounding proud of herself, not realizing that she was making one of the biggest mistakes of her life. And, of course, she was lying, because Erasmus would sneak her a drink every now and then because she said Mackenzie needed it so she wouldn't be so "anal," as she so rudely put it.

They drove to the club in Candie's car because she said not everyone can drive under the influence. They made it to the club and Mackenzie still didn't feel anything, but thirty minutes hadn't passed either. For some odd reason, she wanted to feel the effects of the drug. She wanted to see how she would dance and what others would say. She wanted to feel good and forget for a moment.

She sat down on some of the lounge chairs with Candie because she said it would be best if they were sitting down when the drug hit them.

They sat down for about five minutes when Mackenzie felt her body lean over to the side by itself. Candie smiled at Mackenzie and said, "Do you feel it?"

All Mackenzie could do was smile. She couldn't even get up, so she just sat there until she saw Erasmus. When she saw her, she tried to get up and walk over to her but fell flat on her behind. The dark, smoke-filled club, now spinning, made Mackenzie close her eyes, and try and catch her breath.

Erasmus rushed over. "What the hell is wrong with you, Mackenzie?" Erasmus looked at her with a deep stare, as if she knew she was going to tell her something she didn't want to hear.

"Girl, I took some X." Mackenzie started laughing as soon as the words fell out of her mouth.

Erasmus grabbed her chin and made her look her in the eyes. "What do you mean you took some X?" Where did you get it? Who gave it you?"

Mackenzie pushed Erasmus away and simply said, "I said I took some X."

With disappointment in her eyes, Erasmus asked her again, "Who did you get it from?"

When Mackenzie told her who, Erasmus walked off mumbling, "I should have known that bitch would be after you."

Erasmus came back over once she'd calmed down, and Mackenzie told her not to worry. "I know I'm wrong for taking this drug, Erasmus, but just watch over me. Candie is trying to set me up. She said I would be able to dance; I can't even stand up." Although Mackenzie was experiencing her first high that felt good, she knew she was wrong. What would her mother say? What would her father say? Would he want his baby girl to be where he was? All those questions danced around Mackenzie's head while she floated to a place she knew she should be far away from now.

That entire night, Mackenzie just sat on the lounge chair staring into space. She didn't even hear any music that night or dance.

When the club was closing down, Erasmus helped her up and asked where she'd parked. When Mackenzie couldn't manage to get out any words, Erasmus walked through the crowd, grabbing the dealer by her shoulder, and screamed and hollered at her, while Mackenzie tried to hold herself up with the wall.

When Mackenzie came to, she felt like a stampede of wild elephants had trampled over her body the night before. She was stiff and could barely move in Erasmus's twin bed the two were sharing.

"Well, well, well,...Sleeping Beauty has awakened."

Rolling over and bumping into Erasmus, she asked her where she was and what time was it.

"My house, and it's about eight thirty, **PM.**"

"Did I drive here last night? Where's my car?"

"No, I did, and my brother went with me to pick up your car while you slept." All Mackenzie could remember was making it out of the club, and everything seemed different.

Interrupting her thoughts, Erasmus blurted out, "What the fuck were you thinking? Don't you know, X has heroine in it?" Mackenzie was frozen when those words fell out of her mouth.

"Heroine, as in dope and nodding?" she asked, in complete shock.

"The very same. Mackenzie, I don't understand you. You barely drink and then BAM, out of the blue, you decide to take heroine."

"Erasmus, quit it with the theatrics. Had I known it was heroine, I wouldn't have taken it."

"You know what, that's beside the point. What are you doing hanging out with that bitch anyway?"

"I don't even know, I guess I had a lot on my mind."

"Yeah, that's what most junkies say when asked how they get hooked!"

"Hold up, I'm not a junkie. I just made one bad decision that's all. It's not like I'm craving the shit now."

"Well, I hope not."

"Fuck you, Erasmus. Where the hell are my keys? I need to get home." Mackenzie, fully dressed, stumbled out of Erasmus's bed, searching for her keys. When she found them, she left, trying not to disturb her family.

She was so damn mad at Erasmus on the way home; she'd made her feel so low and trashy. "She is definitely the pot calling the kettle black. Guess she thought I didn't know about her coke problem because she damn sure has one. Mood swings, erratic behavior, and trips to the mutherfuckin' bathroom please! With mutherfuckers with sunken in faces. She had a lot of nerve putting me down. I know all too well the signs of a coke addiction, courtesy of that wicked bitch Vi and none other than Jun." Mackenzie said, with authority in her voice, driving down Interstate 20 back to Dallas.

After that encounter, Mackenzie suddenly felt the need to correct her mistake. She was saving up a little money for classes in the fall of

'92 but decided to use the money to move out. She had only been out of the army for two full months and one of those months had been used to party nearly everyday on top of work.

There was one available apartment at an apartment complex on Walnut and Audelia. It was cheap, small, and for the most part clean. Mackenzie moved in right away, against Aunt Cecile's wishes. Aunt Cecile said she should stay home and at least wait until she started going to school.

Instead, Mackenzie packed all of her belongings, stuffed them into her Geo Metro, and never looked back. Nick and Tiphane sold her their bed, because they said they needed a new one. She took it and made the best of her situation, having her own apartment with no furniture and only a bed.

Mackenzie got a phone in her own name, electricity, and some groceries her first day at the apartment. When she called Aunt Cecile to tell her the new number, Aunt Cecile told her that Demarcus had called, and wanted her to call him as soon as she got his message.

When Mackenzie returned his phone call, he asked if she wanted to come over that night. He said his car was in the shop, and he really needed a ride to and from work if she could help. Eager to hear from him, Mackenzie quickly replied yes and made arrangements to pick him up that night in East Dallas, where he worked as a security officer. And all she could think was, *He needs me.*

Mackenzie arrived at his job about thirty-minutes early and just sat there thinking. She hadn't experienced a set back or flashback from taking the X, so she felt she was clear. However, she was disappointed in herself for being so weak and vulnerable. How could she have fallen for the biggest trick in the book? She asked herself. Then she realized that her life was in jeopardy. All the things her youth pastor had told her, about Satan wanting to kill and destroy God's children became clear as day.

Mackenzie was going to have to devise a plan if she wanted to survive, and the first step she would take, was to end her friendship with Erasmus and Candie, and to stop partying. A month was enough!

Chapter Eleven

"Hey you," Demarcus called out, as she sat there in deep, tear-filled meditation.

"Hey, yourself," she said, happy to see his face and smiling.

Demarcus sat inside her car and gave her a soft kiss on the cheek. Mackenzie blushed a little and began their drive to his apartment.

On the way home, they talked about the latest music, New York culture, of course, and his new waterbed, which some ex-girlfriend had bought him. Also, the fact that he had moved to another apartment since the last time she'd seen him.

Demarcus went on and on about his new waterbed and swore it had been bought by his ex but that he was single again. Naive still, Mackenzie believed him and believed there was still hope for them as a couple. Her mind began making preparations to be a part of his life. Once again.

When they made it to Demarcus's new apartment, she saw that it was definitely nicely decorated, to say the least. They watched Def Comedy Jam and old tapes of the Martin show, cracking up laughing for at least two hours.

Since both shows were filled with strong sexual content, Demarcus was up in her face in no time. They took separate showers and then met up in the middle of his waterbed, ripping off what little clothes they had on.

Mackenzie was so preoccupied with the movement of his new waterbed that she couldn't really concentrate on the sex. The bed was completely uncomfortable, although, very nice. It was all black with leather trim.

Mackenzie felt like she was having sex in the middle of the ocean, and she kept feeling like she was drowning, with him pushing into her, making her head swirl around. She felt sick to her stomach. Their rhythm was definitely off that night. Their rendezvous, which ended as quickly as it started, left Mackenzie wide-awake while he fell fast asleep in no time, and again she was hurt.

As she was off the next day and had planned to be recuperating from a long night of steamy sex, Mackenzie had extra energy. She cleaned up his entire house from room to room, walked to a nearby grocery store because she had let him take her car to work, and bought some groceries.

Upon her return, she fixed some pepper steak that she had learned how to cook thanks to Captain Lockley, along with rice and broccoli.

When Mackenzie finished her domestic duties, she watched some TV and realized that she was bored out of her mind. She figured she would call Erasmus and tell her she was leaving the whole scene.

When she reached her, Erasmus had so much to tell her that she couldn't get a word in. "Mackenzie, there's this new club in the gay area that has straight night on Thursday's. You wanna go?"

"Oh no, I'm not going to some straight one night, gay the next, type of club. Sorry."

"Well, what are you going to do tonight? Do you want to go catch a movie?" Mackenzie began twirling the back of her hair, trying to get up enough courage to tell Erasmus that she was through with the club scene. "Erasmus, I'm staying in with Demarcus tonight, doing the domestic thing."

"Really. Humph. You two like a couple now?"

"Well sort of. We are definitely leaning towards that again, I'm sure." Erasmus wasn't too happy that Mackenzie wasn't going out and the mention of Demarcus seemed to make her cringe. She sighed and cleared her throat when Mackenzie told her about staying in that night.

When Mackenzie finally told her she was through with the whole scene, Erasmus lost it. "What the fuck do you mean you're not hanging out with us anymore? Is it because we're white and you're black? That's racist, Mackenzie."

"No, it's not because you all are white. It's the fact that you people don't seem to try and understand the struggles, the differences, the hurt, and pain associated with drugs and how they have torn up many of our homes, as far as blacks are concerned. And you guys with your money, and beautiful homes, just get high for the hell of it, go to rehab, and just start right back over again. I learned that in the one month I've been hanging with ya'll and it makes me pissed off! All you guys do is party while Mom and Dad foot the bill. Hell, I have to work and take care of me. And going to those damn clubs, is not taking care of me!"

After Mackenzie let out her campaign speech about drugs and their effects on blacks, Erasmus hung up in her face. Mackenzie looked at the receiver and hung up, glad that she didn't have to argue with Erasmus anymore.

Mackenzie was expecting Demarcus any minute, so she didn't even bother to call Erasmus back. As far as she was concerned, their friendship was over.

Just then, Demarcus began to fidget with the door as his keys dangled. Mackenzie ran and sat down on the couch, adjusting her breathing, and waited until he opened the door. "It smells good in here. What did you cook?"

"Oh, just some pepper steak, with gravy, rice, and broccoli."

Still smiling, he walked over, sat down beside her on the couch, and kissed her softly on the cheek. He whispered slowly in her ear, "Thanks for dinner."

Blushing, Mackenzie turned towards him and they kissed. Slowly, he began to take off her clothes, exposing her bare body. "I want to make love to you." Demarcus said, looking into her eyes. She smiled as he stood and removed his clothes, and he was at full attention close enough to her lips that had she been that type of girl, it would have been like a baby and its pacifier.

He pulled her up to him and picked her up to straddle him as he slid inside. "Uhm," she muttered. He felt so good inside that any doubts she'd had about him were erased. Up against his living room wall, they passionately made love. After his wall, they move to the couch, again with her straddling him, moving up and down, scratching his back, panting, and losing control.

Neither of them wanted to climax because they slowed down enough for him to pull out and turn her around. He pulled her in hard and with control, and they moved together with such intensity that he had them both hollering, then screaming in ecstasy as they came together with him still inside of her.

Mackenzie wanted to explode, but she managed to hold it together until he did pull out. She made her way to the bathroom as Demarcus pretty much passed out on the couch, and she took a bath slowly, trying to figure out what had just happened. Mackenzie felt different. Even as good as Silas was, she had never felt like that.

When she finished her bath, she made her way to his bedroom and left him still sleeping on the couch. Demarcus never came to bed that night, and Mackenzie didn't sleep too well because his phone kept ringing every time she dosed off! Message after message contained some love struck female begging him to pick up the phone.

With barely any conversation that morning, they rushed out really early because she had to drop him off to get his car and then rush off to work herself. To be honest, she really didn't want any conversation from Demarcus. She was quite content leaving him at the service center and just saying "Bye." That morning, she wasn't feeling him or the fact that the food she'd prepared had gone untouched last night.

Once she made it to her job, she grabbed her extra uniform from the back of her car and went into work. Today, she wasn't about to let her day be ruined by the insensitive, rude coworkers that pissed her off every chance they got.

Usually she made a big deal about being the only black sales person there at Lady Foot Locker. She was miserable there. Every time something came up missing, she was the one to be "suspect" or questioned simply because she was black. She was questioning her employment there and why she didn't just quit. Mackenzie knew she could use her GI Bill money for school and try to get a loan, but for some reason, she just didn't do it.

So many times she wanted to tell them, "Those who accuse are usually the ones who are guilty!" *"Hell"* she thought. *"I'm too scared to steal, and furthermore, I'm used to not having and know how to do without."*

They watched her like a hawk, but today, she wasn't going to let their ignorance bother her. She worked her eight hours and went straight home.

Mackenzie was feeling pretty low, like she was coming down with the flu. She showered and still felt horrible. So she decided to go out and get trashy drunk in hopes that she would feel better tomorrow. The pressure was too much, and her good girl image wasn't enough to get her through. For a brief moment, she saw Pat, drunk and passed out on their old, broken down sofa. She wanted to be there, too, and forget her worries. She could no longer resist the temptations of alcohol or anything that wasn't good for her. The sermons of her youth pastor, the visions of her broken home with drugs and alcohol, all went out the window.

Mackenzie went down to Deep Ellum against her decision to stop hanging out and decided to go to the club ONE and drink herself crazy. On Fridays, they had seventy-five cent drinks. The woman at the door had let her and Erasmus in a few times, knowing they were underage, so she figured she would again if she asked.

After a few words and a little conversation, the woman let Mackenzie in. club ONE was like a whole other world in Deep Ellum. It was a male gay club that was very dark and filled with smoke and white men. There were some women there, but they were groupies or club heads that had graduated from the Aqua Lounge. For the most part, it was ninety percent white men.

The bathroom was co-ed, because there were so many drag queens. Most of the time, you wouldn't know who was what. The strobe lights, smoke, and huge blocks on the dance floor gave it the party image that most people were after.

After her first drink, Mackenzie spotted Erasmus with her entourage of white male friends going towards the bathroom. She started to leave when they walked right beside one another, giving no acknowledgement of each other's presence. Mackenzie felt Erasmus accepted them not being friends, so she decided to stay.

She wasn't going to let her make her leave so she went to the bar to get another drink. Once she finished the drink in two gulps, she left and walked down the street to the Aqua Lounge so she could dance. After all, ever since her Ecstasy trip, she hadn't been back.

For a Friday, the club was dead. She walked around to see who was there. There was no one except the usual crowd and damn Erasmus, whom she could have sworn, was following her.

Without giving her eye contact, Mackenzie left and went back to club ONE to have some more drinks. On drink number three, which was her limit, she began to dance. Just feeling the music, Mackenzie felt someone dancing close behind her and smelled a familiar scent. It was way too close for comfort. Mackenzie turned around, and she was face to face with Erasmus. Expecting the worst, Mackenzie looked at her and gave her one of those "don't fuck with me" looks when she pushed Mackenzie into the wall. *"Ah damn"* thought Mackenzie; she was ready to whip ass when Erasmus grabbed her chin and looked at her, penetrating her soul and causing Mackenzie to feel uneasy.

She was speechless and couldn't move. There was something in Erasmus's eyes that Mackenzie had never seen before. Even in the darkened club, her eyes lit up the place. It was like time just stood still.

Mackenzie didn't bother to fight her off because she had a grip that made her

re-think whipping ass. People looked at them standing there with Erasmus holding her chin like she was some six-year-old being scolded for doing something she had no business doing.

It was as if Erasmus wanted to say something but just wouldn't. Mackenzie knew she wanted to say something but just couldn't find any words. After several seconds passed, Erasmus grabbed her chin harder and angrily said to her, "I need to talk to you." She proceeded to push her up against the wall harder. "You made me do it."

What the hell is this crazy girl talking about? Mackenzie asked herself, confused.

"What are you talking about, Erasmus, and let go of my fuckin' chin." She was deeply frustrated at "this idiot" who had her pinned up against the wall making accusations about things she did not understand.

"It's your fault, you weren't there for me. And I…"she paused for a moment "…and I got with Michelle."

"What the fuck are you talking about?" Mackenzie asked, with her chin gripped in Erasmus's hand.

"Michelle, Michelle. I got with Michelle last night." Erasmus blurted out, staring her dead in the eyes. Michelle was another girl at the club who occasionally danced on the speakers with other girls. At times, she was their third wheel partying or standing around the club as if they owned the place.

Mackenzie felt like she'd been hit with a ton of bricks and tried to ease herself away from Erasmus, but Erasmus grabbed her arm and pulled her towards the bathroom,cutting through everyone in line. They grabbed the next available stall.

Chapter Twelve

The inside of the bathroom stall was quiet and still. The nasty floors covered with wet toilet tissue, cigarette butts, and tiny plastic baggies, seemed to comfort Mackenzie, who looked down, avoiding Erasmus. Her mouth still open, she felt the germs tickling her throat. She couldn't close her mouth, due to her disbelief. In her mind, all she could think of was the last conversation Erasmus and she had had about all of the girls at the club changing, and wanting to be with each other instead of men, and how they said they never would change.

"Why Erasmus?" Mackenzie asked, with her head still down. "I thought you were stronger than that. How could you do that?" Mackenzie picked up the spare roll of toilet tissue, threw it at Erasmus, and turned to walk out of the too small, nasty bathroom stall. Before she could get herself through that door, Erasmus pulled her back and turned her towards her. She gripped her forearm and made her look at her.

Out of fear, tears filled her eyes. Erasmus pulled her in to her and kissed her on the side of her mouth.

"Please don't do this. Stop please," she asked Erasmus. Her mind was rambling and the bathroom was becoming hot. Mackenzie felt like she couldn't breathe.

Erasmus, being bold, moved in even closer and put her lips on Mackenzie's. Standing there in complete awe, Mackenzie's legs felt like lead. Erasmus did it again, this time, with more intensity. Mackenzie couldn't have fought her off if she wanted to because something was definitely going on there.

After several of her kisses, Erasmus opened her mouth and her tongue touched Mackenzie's lips, and as she dared to utter another plea for her to stop, their tongues touched, and they kissed with passion, questions, desire, and for Mackenzie, confusion.

For a minute or so, she forgot where the she was and what was going on. When she realized it was Erasmus and herself, standing there kissing like two young adolescents exchanging their first kiss, Mackenzie backed up and bolted out of the bathroom stall. She pushed her way through the drag queens, club groupies, and straight men that were out on the prowl.

She pushed the many people coming in and walked out of the entrance with tears rolling down her eyes. She left the club in what looked like, Flo Jo at her Olympic extravaganza!

By the time she made it to her car, her face was soaked with tears. None of her feelings made sense, because what she had just experienced felt good. Never had she kissed anyone with such intensity and a passion that brewed and made her insides liven up.

Inside her car, she sat for a moment, grabbing the steering wheel in hopes that her little Geo Metro would take her as far away from there as possible. As she started to put the key in, there was a tap on the driver's side window. It was Erasmus. Mackenzie looked up at her nemesis and turned the key in the ignition, driving off erratically through the streets of Deep Ellum, dodging in and out of the Friday traffic.

She drove around Dallas for what seemed to be eternity until she finally wandered to this guy's house, Rod, who was having the after party at his house that night. Her intentions were not to party. Mackenzie was angry and looking for Erasmus. She had to know what had just happened between them.

After parking her car on the little street down the block from his apartment, she walked up Gilbert Street mad as hell. She wasn't getting away with what she'd pulled, Mackenzie thought. She had better have a good excuse for shoving her tongue down her throat, getting her head all messed up. Mackenzie wanted to blame Erasmus, although she'd enjoyed the kiss. She wanted to know why though. Why did it happen?

There were tons of people standing outside the apartment talking and drinking, and some sitting outside of his doorway, which overlooked the pool. Erasmus was nowhere to be found outside, so Mackenzie proceeded to go into the barely lit apartment that smelled of weed and patchouli.

It was dark inside, and filled with people standing around and sitting on several of the sofas that filled his living room. It was as if his apartment had been made for hanging out, like a miniature club. Still, there was no Erasmus, which was strange. Mackenzie couldn't recall Erasmus having ever missed an after party, especially if the club was boring that night. Mackenzie guessed for Erasmus there was a lot of excitement at the club that night.

Mackenzie said her hey's and her hello's and went upstairs, where the smell of weed was intoxicating. She hated weed more than anything, since it reminded her of the glass mirror and pipe her father passed around with his friends. He always had to be smoking a joint like it was a normal cigarette. Even when they didn't have any food, he had his joint.

There were two rooms upstairs and a bathroom, and all of the doors were closed. Mackenzie knew what that meant; they were getting high. She wasn't about to break up their private parties, so she turned around to go back downstairs when she heard Erasmus's voice.

All of a sudden, her bad attitude was gone, and she was scared to death. She walked down the stairs slowly, like she was in a horror flick, cast as the cool ass, only black, person in the movie. Her heart was beating heavily, echoing in the background with each step she took.

At the bottom of the steps, Erasmus was standing there looking like she was waiting for her. "I've been looking all over for you." Those words seemed to echo because it felt like everyone in the room stopped when their conversation began and started looking at them.

"We need to talk."

Mackenzie didn't say anything; she just walked in front of Erasmus and let her

follow. She still wasn't able to speak to her; the words just could not find their way out of her mouth. *What was she going to do once they were alone?* She thought.

They walked outside towards Mackenzie's car. She was still in front of Erasmus because she was too afraid to be next to her, walking her little walk, swinging her arms, when in mid-stride, Erasmus grabbed one of her arms. She stopped her, and pulled her over, and they kissed again, this time, with no hesitation.

It was better than the first time. Erasmus pulled her face into hers, over and over again, and she was taken. Under the darkness of night, Erasmus and Mackenzie kissed until they moved over and leaned on someone's car and started kissing again. Her mind, her body, and her soul were awake. Each touch from Erasmus's tongue was a reminder of this.

After kissing for quite some time, Erasmus asked if she'd ever done this before, and if she was okay. Wiping her mouth, Mackenzie replied, "Never done this before, and I guess I'm fine. How about you?"

Holding her in her arms, Erasmus replied back, "I'm doing fine now."

Mackenzie leaned on Erasmus's shoulder, quiet for a moment, then spoke.

"Look, it's late, and I better get going. I got to be to work at eleven." All of a sudden, she realized the need to end what was going on.

"You want some company?" Erasmus asked, before she could leave.

"Damn," she thought, trying to find an excuse. "Well, I'm really tired. We can hook up tomorrow after I get off of work."

Erasmus seemed a little disappointed. She rubbed the side of Mackenzie's face, sending chills down her spine. Mackenzie knew she couldn't come home with her. There was just no possible way that was going to happen. Mackenzie felt she just couldn't. She kept trying to convince herself as Erasmus rubbed her face again.

The two couldn't get in to her apartment fast enough before they were kissing and undressing each other. Erasmus smelled so fresh, new, and her hands all over Mackenzie sent her into an erotic trance.

In the middle of her empty living room, both undressed, Erasmus lay on her and kissed her. Mackenzie's fingers played in her long, red, curly hair while Erasmus outlined her eyebrows, eyes, nose, and lips.

Then Erasmus tasted her in ways that she'd never experienced before. Slowly and passionately, she used her tongue as a navigator on the road to Mackenzie's paradise. Unable to fight the passion and pleasure, she came. They laughed, and then they did it again.

The sun woke Mackenzie up, with Erasmus's red hair across her face and her arm covering her breasts. "Erasmus, you up?" There was no response, so she slipped from underneath her muscular, swimmer arms and went to take a shower and brush her teeth.

Mackenzie felt like she had a hangover times ten, with added queasiness in her stomach that had caused her to throw up twice before she made it into the shower. *"Damn,"* she thought. *"I must have the flu."*

Out of the shower, she dried off and slipped on her robe. She had to call in sick, but she didn't want Erasmus to know. She just wanted and needed to be alone today and assess last night's escapade.

Erasmus was up and searching for her clothes and trying to pull her hair together all at the same time when Mackenzie opened the bathroom door. "Hey."

"Hey, how are you feeling?"

Mackenzie was going to have to lie. "I'm fine. Did you sleep okay?"

"Yeah, I did. Very well actually."

"Well, I set out some towels and an extra toothbrush for you. The bathroom is all yours." Erasmus smiled and said thanks, then walked naked past her and went into the bathroom holding her clothes.

Mackenzie went in the bedroom and lay in bed until she heard the water stop, then she pretended to get dressed so Erasmus could leave.

She was glad Erasmus had decided to follow her in her car instead of riding with her last night. She couldn't face being alone with Erasmus any longer. Erasmus walked out of the bathroom with her hair wet and pulled it back into a bun. She was all smiles and half dressed in her bra and jeans. Mackenzie ignored her wanting eyes and asked if she knew how to get back to Arlington from Dallas.

She replied yeah and continued to get dressed. "Are you leaving out with me?"

"No, it's still fairly early so I'm going to make some phone calls I need to take care of."

"Okay, well, call me later. Maybe we can hang out later or go get something to eat."

Mackenzie nodded, trying her best to hold down the contents now dancing around in her stomach. They said their goodbyes, and then Mackenzie immediately went to the kitchen sink, puking her insides out. After she was done, she finally decided to call Lady Foot Locker and let them know she wasn't coming in. Her manager wasn't too happy, but when Mackenzie started gagging in mid-sentence, she understood that Mackenzie wasn't lying.

She lay in bed the entire day and ignored her phone, which seemed to ring off the hook. In between sleeping and throwing up all day, she was angry with Erasmus. She wanted to blame her for last night because she felt like she'd taken advantage of her. Although she didn't fight it, she knew she couldn't blame herself. It had to be Erasmus's fault.

She decided she couldn't see Erasmus anymore and that their friendship was over. She was going to have to figure that out, because she wasn't giving her a call. She had to fight those feelings that were stirring inside.

Mackenzie stayed home for the next three days, lying around like she was going to die. Surely the flu shouldn't last this long, she thought to herself.

By Tuesday, she felt better good enough to go back to work. She was greeted by her co-workers, with insincere, "Are you feeling better?" and "What was wrong?" questions. She barely gave up any information and remained grouchy and rude the entire day.

She made it through that day and Wednesday also. When it felt like her sickness was letting up, she decided to go out to the Aqua Lounge and again, get drunk. She was going to get rid of this flu if it was the last thing she did.

Mackenzie drank so much and danced so hard, she was not aware of Erasmus until she cornered her on the dance floor, asking why she hadn't returned any of her calls. "I didn't know you called, Erasmus. I don't have an answering machine, remember? How am I supposed to know you called?"

With her piercing, almond-brown eyes, Erasmus looked at her and said, "Bullshit. What's up with you? Why are you acting funny all of a sudden? I thought you..."

"See Erasmus, that's the problem you thinking for me." In the middle of the dance floor, like war was about to break out, Mackenzie decided to put her foot down. "Look Erasmus, sometimes when a person drinks, they make mistakes. What happened between us was definitely a mistake. I'm sorry, but I can't do this." Mackenzie looked at Erasmus, daring her to respond against her wishes. Erasmus walked off, then called her a black bitch.

Later on in the restroom, Mackenzie was talking to one of the drag queens about her nausea and throwing up, when Erasmus walked out of one of the stalls and snapped, "Your dumb ass is probably pregnant."

"Fuck you, Erasmus. How would you know?" Mackenzie gave her one of those looks like, "You know, I know better."

"You're a cold bitch, Mackenzie. A cold bitch!" Erasmus said, harsh and angry. Mackenzie and her drag queen friend walked out and left Erasmus standing there.

Chapter Thirteen

That following Sunday, Mackenzie went out again, this time trying to overcome the dizzy spells and nauseating feelings that had kept her up most of the night. It was a boring night at the Switz Lounge this particular Sunday, and for fear that she would throw up on the dance floor, she passed on drinking, which had now become a normal habit.

Out of desperation and loneliness, she decided to call Demarcus and tell him that she had been feeling really sick lately. As soon as she picked up the phone, Erasmus grabbed her arm and said, "Who are you calling, Demarcus?"

Damn this bitch is bold, Mackenzie thought to herself. "Why?" she asked, pulling her arm away.

"No reason, just be careful. It's not like you can trust him. Or can you?"

"Whatever Erasmus."

"Hello."

"Hey Demarcus. It's Mackenzie. I need to talk to you."

"Right now?"

"Yeah, right now. This can't wait."

"Hurry up," he said, and hung up in her face. Mackenzie had known all along that the flu shouldn't last this long; it was time to think that she might be pregnant. She was just dreading his response.

When she made it to Demarcus's house, he opened the door in blue, checkered silk boxers. "I think I'm pregnant, Demarcus."

"Come here." He pulled her close and closed the door. Right there on the floor, he fucked her like she was some whore or something. It hurt worse than she'd ever imagined sex could; it was like he was trying to pull out whatever was inside her.

When he finished with her, he got up and went to the bathroom, then washed his dick off in the sink. She never heard the shower, just the faucet. Then he went into his bedroom and slammed the door.

Mackenzie gathered her clothes and went into the bathroom to take a shower. There were ladies things everywhere a pink razor, hair cosmetics, and an extra toothbrush. She should have left then, and she knew it. But she was way too tired, so after her shower, she put her clothes back on and went and slept on the couch.

Mackenzie woke up maybe an hour later, fighting for her life. It was dark for the most part. There was just the reflection from the light that was on, from the patio. Thick hands were wrapped around her neck. She couldn't scream because nothing would come out. She tried, but it was only a slight whisper.

Demarcus looked into her eyes as he tried to squeeze the life from her. As she felt her life slipping away, she cried out to God to have mercy on her. The more she prayed for God to help her, the more it seemed that Demarcus was choking her.

When he realized there was a will stronger than his, exasperated, he let go. "Bitch, if you tell anyone, I swear I will kill you for real the next time." She could barely move and was too afraid to breathe.

"Get the fuck out my house. Don't ever come over here, talking 'bout you might be pregnant. You too stupid to have a child."

She couldn't believe her ears. But in spite of what she wanted to hear, if she wanted her life, she had to get out of there.

Demarcus glared at her and said, "I said, get the fuck out, NOW BITCH." She got up off the couch, stumbling, trying to look for her keys. He threw them at her face and she could feel the blood. She didn't react, she just tried to catch them before they hit the carpet and went for the door."Let me get that for you." He yanked the door back on her and shoved her out, all in one motion.

Mackenzie was too ashamed to cry; she held her head down and walked to her car. She decided not to call the police because she just couldn't replay that scene over in her head again. She couldn't call her family in Brooklyn because they would make her come home, and telling Aunt Cecile would just crush her because she thought the world of Demarcus. She remembered Pat, too, and all the embarrassing remarks, people made after Ray beat her up. Mackenzie didn't want to go through that. She just knew she was done with Demarcus for good now.

Passing by incoming cars, Mackenzie looked down as she walked to her car. She made it home and washed off her face and neck. She knew she couldn't go to work with these bruises, which would definitely have shown up by the time she made it to work at twelve.

She decided she would call in sick. Then she sat on the side of the tub and began to turn on the bath water, asking God for a sign? Was there something she was missing?

After a much-needed bath, she fell asleep on the floor in the living room for the entire day and part of the night. She woke up to the sound of someone banging on her door, like they were insane.

"Shit," she thought. *"How did Demarcus find me? He's never even been here. I was always at his apartment."*

"Open this fuckin' door, I want my speakers."

"Speakers?" she whispered, getting up to go to the door. "They must have the wrong apartment."

She tiptoed over to the door and proceeded to look through the peephole, when she saw the African guy that had let her check out some of his old car speakers to see if she wanted to buy them after they'd flirted over a brief conversation. She'd forgotten all about the damn speakers that had barely played in her Geo Metro.

Standing there for a minute, she was about to back away when her entire front door came crashing in on her. There was bright red blood everywhere. Mackenzie screamed so loud that her neighbor ran out and all she could think was, *"This bastard has kicked in my door on me. What the fuck!"* She was hysterical for the most part.

When she came to, she was at Parkland Hospital in the emergency room. "Mackenzie, what happened to you?" Hell, she wanted to ask Chris, her neighbor, the same thing.

"Why am I here?" She tried to sit up but her head felt the worst, like wild elephants again. Then she remembered someone banging on her door, asking for some damn speakers.

She didn't tell her neighbor Chris about the African guy or the doctors that she was probably pregnant. Parkland was so busy they were glad she was awake and alert so they could discharge her to use the bed.

They brought her clothes and some discharge papers, and she was on her way.

Chris informed her that it was about three thirty A.M., and all she could think was, *"In the last twenty-four hours, I've been raped, strangled, and hit by a door. These ass whippings have to stop."*

Chris drove her home and she asked if she could come to his apartment and use his phone, afraid to go in her apartment alone. He said no problem. He even offered her his couch. But she declined.

She was so shaken she couldn't remember Erasmus's phone number, so she had to call information, but she promised her neighbor she would pay for the charges when he got the bill.

"Erasmus, this is Mackenzie."

"Yeah, what's up? Ms. Mackenzie? It's pretty late to be calling don't you think?"

Mackenzie sucked her teeth. "Why did I even bother to call you? You don't care anyway. Bye."

"Wait a minute, Mackenzie. What's going on?" Erasmus heard her fighting back her tears.

"It's nothing, I'll be fine."

"Well, you don't sound fine. Where are you?"

"I'm at a friends."

"Who, Demarcus?"

"No, Erasmus. Why would I be at his house and calling you?"

"Forget I even asked that. Just tell me what's going on?"

"I don't even know where to start." Mackenzie said, as tears rolled down her face.

"Lets just say that in the last twenty-four hours, I feel like I've been through hell and back." Mackenzie heard talking in the background. "I'm sorry, are you not alone?" Then she heard some female in the background asking Erasmus, "who are you talking to?"

Angry and feeling rejected for the second time in less than twenty-four hours, Mackenzie hung up in her face. She thanked her neighbor for his help and assured him she would be okay, then went back to her apartment with the broken front door. It just hung from the hinges.

She was exhausted. Tomorrow was Halloween and she had to be at work by one and then by seven in the evening, she would have to pass out candy to all of the kids that came to the mall to trick or treat as opposed to doing it the old school way. "Scary asses!" Mackenzie muttered to herself.

She lay on her bed staring up at the ceiling, thinking about how quickly everything had just crumbled for her. She should be in school right now, not worrying about what the hell she was gonna do now that she might be pregnant? Not to mention that the father was a complete asshole!

Sigh after sigh, she began to feel more afraid. What was she doing in this apartment with the door hanging off the hinges? What if the guy came back? Then she heard soft knocking at her door. *"Shit, not again."* she thought. She grabbed her aluminum baseball bat and headed to the door.

"Who is it?"

"Mackenzie, open up. It's me, Erasmus."

"Go away, Erasmus. I don't need your help. I don't need anything from you."

"Mackenzie, you door is hanging off the hinges, let me come in."

"Thought you were busy with one of your girlfriends. What happened, you two run out of things to do?" Mackenzie snapped, sounding jealous.

"You're not being fair, Mackenzie, now open the door."

"NO, now go home to your little girlfriend."

Erasmus fidgeted with the door for a moment, and then walked in. Mackenzie walked into her bedroom as Erasmus followed.

"Oh my God, what happened to you, Mackenzie?" she asked.

"I don't feel like talking about it. I thought I told you to go home." Erasmus walked over to her and touched the bandage on her head, then her eyes looked down to her neck.

"Who did this to you. Was it Demarcus? I told you to be careful, but you just won't ever listen." Erasmus said, as she shook her head.

"Erasmus, before you start trying to be eye spy, you need to listen. *Go home. I don't need you here. Get out.*"

"Mackenzie don't, I'm sorry. She's not my girlfriend. She was just a friend, hanging out, that's all."

Mackenzie rolled her eyes at her weak excuse.

"At three thirty in the morning, at your parents' house. Please, Erasmus. I've heard enough. Now either you leave or I'll call the police, and considering that they've been here once tonight, you won't stand a chance."

Erasmus looked away, feeling helpless. "All right, I'm leaving. You know where to find me."

"Yeah, yeah, yeah. Just get the fuck out."

"She has some nerve coming over here with the scent of some other girl's pussy on her breath, Mackenzie thought. *No thanks, I'm tired of being second."* Mackenzie washed her face and prepared for bed. She made a mental note to find a Planned Parenthood that would be open on a Saturday, and then fell into a heavy sleep.

She rushed through the morning after waking up late and went to Planned Parenthood just before work, fighting back her tears and the need to be with Erasmus.

Just as quick as she went in, she came out, and the news was just as Mackenzie thought, pregnant. Four to six weeks, to be exact, as the doctor told her in an uncaring, and nonchalant manner.

She went to Lady Foot Locker, mad as usual, and didn't say much until her manager told her she needed to speak to her. Basically, she was tired of her attitude, her calling in, and her complaining about the schedule. The manager gave her a choice to either get it together or find another job.

Unbothered by her manger's ultimatum, Mackenzie took out her store keys to hand them to her manager with the same attitude that had landed her in this position in the first place and waited for a response.

"Wait a minute, Mackenzie. You are a good employee; I'm sure we can work this out."

"Yeah, this bitch just doesn't want to have to work the rest of the day; if I leave, she wouldn't have no one else to work," Mackenzie thought to herself.

"Look, I'm tired of the bullshit around here. I don't have time for the games. I come to work to work. Not to be friends with ya'll. I can find another job with less bullshit to put up with." Mackenzie said to her red-faced manager, who seemed helpless against Mackenzie and her bad attitude.

"I don't want you to quit."

"Well, don't give me the option and I won't."

"Look Mackenzie, your attitude."

"You know what take your keys." Just as she started to hand them to her again, she felt a real sharp pain, like cramps from hell.

"You okay, Mackenzie?"

"Yeah, I just need to go to the restroom."

Chapter Fourteen

The small bathroom in the back of the store seemed to smother Mackenzie, as she lay on the floor with the worst cramps she'd ever had. She was hot, sweaty, and panting for dear life when her manager knocked on the door.

"Mackenzie, are you okay? Should I call the ambulance?"

Answering her seemed like the hardest thing to do, and when she finally did, there was no response.

She had taken off her uniform because her body temperature felt as though it had reached a hundred and ninety-nine. She lay there in a fetal position, holding her stomach. Her cramps were more intense than ever, and she swore she was going to die. Silently, she began to pray.

"Mackenzie, the ambulance is here."

"Ma'am, are you okay? We need to come in." Mackenzie just stayed there until they opened the door. "Mackenzie, oh my God, what happened?" By this time, Mackenzie was speechless and allowed her naked body, lying in a pool of blood, to speak for itself.

She was rushed to the hospital while the pain of her cramps escalated heavily. The paramedics asked if she was pregnant and she told them yes. They began to speak in code and then quickly gave her an IV.

At the hospital, the doctors put her in a room and came to speak to her shortly thereafter. Mackenzie was told that she might miscarry and to remain calm. There was nothing they could do. It was just a matter of time before she would either pass through the tissue, or the cramps would let up.

They explained to her that if she passed all of the tissue, they would have to do a D & C to clean out her insides. If her cramps did let up, they would modify her care plan and keep her overnight for observation. In the meantime, the nurses took all of her insurance information, and she just waited in between cramps for all of this to be over.

"Ms. Kennedy?" The petite nurse in pastel, flowery scrubs said, as she walked in.

"Yes."

"Sorry to bother you, but you have a visitor." Mackenzie nodded and the nurse quickly exited.

"My manager is so nosy," Mackenzie thought. *"I knew she would come, asking twenty questions."* Mackenzie then heard a slight knock and turned over to avoid contact with her manager.

"Mackenzie, I'm so sorry." She rolled back over to see if her ears were deceiving her when she saw Erasmus, red-eyed, and with tears rolling down her face.

"This is not going to keep me calm!" Mackenzie thought to herself, as she rolled her eyes at Erasmus.

Erasmus walked over to the hospital bed and grabbed her hand. Tears rolled down her face, too, as Erasmus pulled up a chair and sat beside her holding her hand.

"We'll get through this."

"I can't believe this is happening to me." Mackenzie said.

"Listen, don't think about that right now. You need to relax and get some sleep. We'll talk when you get up. There are a lot of decisions we have to make."

They sat there quietly for the next couple of minutes until Mackenzie fell asleep thinking about her comments and the word "we" that Erasmus kept reiterating.

Erasmus was sleeping in the chair when she woke-up a few hours later. Mackenzie stared down at her perfect face. She seemed to be at peace, quite different from how she had been at the club scene and the bathroom scene, Mackenzie thought to herself.

She also thought about that night they'd spent together, and about how soft her body was. She was as gentle and soft as a cool summer breeze. It was just enough.

She dosed off for a couple of hours and woke up again when she felt someone stroking her hair.

"How are you feeling?"

"Hey, I'm okay, just a little tired."

"Well, the nurses said we could go home as soon as you woke up. I can drive you if you want. You and the baby are going to be fine."

"Uh sure, that's fine. I kind of don't want to tell my aunt. She'll just want me to move back home."

Erasmus just smiled. "Well, I called your apartment management and asked them to fix your door. It should be fixed when we get home."

Erasmus kept saying "WE," and that began to bother Mackenzie, but she didn't bother to question her. She didn't want to argue with anyone right now. The nurse bought in her discharge papers and told her what she could do to feel better. Rest was basically all that she could do. She then proceeded to sign herself out.

Erasmus took her home and made sure she had all that she needed. Erasmus said she needed to run some errands and would be back shortly.

So, Mackenzie went to sleep, letting Erasmus find her way out. She woke up about eleven that night sad, and a little worried. It was Halloween, 1991, and Mackenzie was about to be twenty and expecting a child. So much had taken place since she'd left the army only three months ago.

A knock at the door and keys rattling interrupted her thoughts. Mackenzie jumped up and quickly walked to the door. "Who is it?"

"It's me. Erasmus. I forgot I had the keys; they're a little stuck." Mackenzie unlocked the door and let Erasmus in.

Erasmus brought in some groceries and an overnight bag. "I thought you could use some company. I bought you some soup, mac and cheese, and ginger ale. My mom always says, ginger ale is a cure all." They both laughed and then put up the groceries.

Erasmus ran Mackenzie a bath and fixed her some macaroni and cheese with a glass of ginger ale. She sat in the bathroom, watching Mackenzie eat, and playing in her hair. Then she washed her back, her face, and the rest of her body, paying close attention to her stomach.

They slept comfortably that night, with Erasmus holding her and Mackenzie falling asleep to the sound of Erasmus breathing on the back of her neck. She was comfortable because she liked her being there, although she didn't want to admit it. But at that moment in her life, it was peaceful, and she felt she needed Erasmus there.

For the next few weeks, Erasmus stayed with her in between going to her parents' house in Arlington. She would go home to wash their clothes, sometimes with Mackenzie with her, and sit around with Erasmus's younger brother, who was quite the comedian at the tender age of seven. Her folks were very friendly, hard working individuals that never questioned their acquaintance, at least not to Mackenzie.

After being absent from the club scene, Erasmus and Mackenzie decided to go out to a private party for some old friend of Erasmus at the Aqua Lounge. Mackenzie actually wasn't going to go until Erasmus convinced her to go and unwind. "You need to start going out again, at least until you start to show," she pleaded with Mackenzie. And after hearing several reasons why she needed to go out, Mackenzie finally agreed.

Mackenzie saw many of the same old faces and wasn't too impressed. Erasmus was buzzing around, so she pretty much stayed to herself. In fact, Erasmus disappeared for a while, and when Mackenzie found her, to tell her she was ready to leave, she was in the bathroom stall with the birthday girl.

"Don't let me interrupt you, but I'm ready to leave." Erasmus looked at her like she was busted, and Mackenzie looked at her like she was, too, then she walked off. Grabbing her from behind, wide-eyed, Erasmus asked, "What's wrong?"

"Nothing. Just enjoy yourself." She loosened herself from Erasmus's hold and went outside.

Mackenzie sat on the curb and talked to some guy for a minute, trying to ignore her fatigue, her changing body, and the need to eat anything in sight, then found her way back into the club. Unexpectedly, she was offered some acid from the guy outside who had tracked her down once back inside, and without thinking too much about her condition, she accepted it. "Erasmus won't be the only one having fun tonight," Mackenzie said to herself, then she went to the bathroom to take her acid tablet.

When it quickly hit her, she felt much better. She danced and ignored the fact that Erasmus was up under the birthday girl the entire night. Mackenzie danced on the bar with other women and laughed with others at the club high on acid and ignoring Erasmus's presence. The intensity of the LSD-laced tablet was an escape from her worries. The tracers on the club walls, the tingling in her throat, and the heat that filled her body was all she needed to forget any and everything until Erasmus grabbed her arm to told her she was ready to leave.

"Fuck off and get your friend to go home with."

"What are you talking about, Mackenzie?"

"Oh okay, like you weren't all up under that girl."

"So? She's a friend, and it's her birthday. Stop being selfish, Mackenzie. Now let's go."

"I'm not going anywhere with you. As you can see, I'm having fun now, and I'm not going to let you fuck it up."

Mackenzie walked off and started dancing with some girl, touching and dancing for a few moments, which must have sent Erasmus over the edge. She yanked the giggling Mackenzie off the dance floor and pulled her into the bathroom. "What the hell is wrong with you?"

Seeing tracers up against the bathroom wall, Mackenzie couldn't concentrate on Erasmus's words and started laughing.

"Mackenzie, are you on something? Did somebody give you something?" Mackenzie kept laughing until Erasmus grabbed her by the chin and looked into her eyes.

"Shit." Erasmus grunted. "Come on, we need to get home."

"Why do you keep saying we? You're not my girlfriend, and I'm not yours."

Erasmus just grabbed Mackenzie by the hand and they walked out of the club, with Erasmus leading the way to her parents' car. Mackenzie sat in the car and had to close her eyes. The acid was causing the streetlights to look much brighter and move towards her. She was breathing fast and started feeling paranoid.

"Mackenzie, what did you take tonight?"

"Acid, and why do you care, Ms. Socialite?" Erasmus was quiet for a moment. While Mackenzie began looking in the passenger side mirror; she jumped back, frantic, as she believed that her face was melting.

"Mackenzie, we can't be together if you're gonna start taking drugs. What about the baby are you crazy?"

"Be together? Be together when? At your convenience? When you're at my house away from your friends and family? When? When you're not afraid to accept that I'm black, from the projects, and was raised in a broken home. When Erasmus? When?

"And this is not your baby. You don't have to worry about me, or this baby."

"We can talk about this later."

"Yeah, that's what I thought." Mackenzie said, trying to agitate Erasmus. Mackenzie began to play with the mirror and laughed at her hands, hallucinating to no end. When they pulled up to her apartment and got out, Mackenzie asked,

"Where are my keys?" She stumbled over to the driver's side of the car.

"I have them right here. I just want to make sure you get up okay."

"Just give me the damn keys, Erasmus. I don't need you to see if I get up okay."

"Well, what do you need?"

"You couldn't handle what I need, Erasmus. Just give me the keys." She stumbled once again over to Erasmus trying to get her keys out of her hand, but she wouldn't let them go.

"Give me the damn keys!"

"No," Erasmus said, as the onlookers passed through the parking lot paused to look at the two of them.

Mackenzie pulled back her hand, as if in slow motion, and slapped Erasmus across the face. Erasmus stood there for a moment, then walked upstairs to Mackenzie's apartment. Mackenzie stomped up the stairs behind Erasmus, cursing, and pushed her into the apartment, trying to get her to fight her. She pushed her several times around the apartment, but Erasmus just looked down, avoiding eye contact. She looked at the faded gray carpet, then at the bare white walls, trying to avoid an obvious explosion that Mackenzie wanted to start.

"What's wrong? You always grabbing on someone, pulling on my damn chin, like I'm a child. You scared?" She pushed Erasmus harder up against the wall and grabbed her shirt collar. "Doesn't feel too good, huh?" Mackenzie looked in Erasmus's eyes, and took her small hand, gripping on her black, fitted top.

Erasmus was twice as strong as Mackenzie, but out of rage or a reaction to the acid, Mackenzie continued to pull at Erasmus's collar as if she were an easy target. She held her there for a few seconds, then in one sudden motion Erasmus flipped her around and pinned her up against the wall.

Erasmus kissed her passionately. Mackenzie was suddenly aroused and wanted Erasmus more than anything. They moved into her bedroom and fell onto the bed, groping and feeling all over each other. They undressed each other and took turns giving the other pleasure. The acid made Mackenzie experience intensity in sex that she had never felt before, she was hooked.

Erasmus finally fell asleep when the sun was coming up. The acid had Mackenzie wide-awake staring at tracers on the wall and occasionally playing in Erasmus's hair thinking the strands were like tiny spiders crawling.

"Thank God I'm off today," she said to herself, and then continued to stare at the wall, not able to make much sense of the many colors she saw or why her hand kept looking like it was turning into smoke.

When Erasmus finally woke up, she wanted to talk.

"Mackenzie, I was crazy about you the moment we met in the bathroom stall. Michelle was my first because I was mad that you were with Demarcus."

"Well, I've never been in a relationship with a woman before and actually never wanted to be. I don't know if I can." She told Erasmus she'd always believed that she was heterosexual, and never thought about being with her, but she did like what they shared. And after much silence and thought, Mackenzie asked, "Would you hurt me like he did? Can you say you would be willing to be there for me no matter what? And what about this baby? Can you handle all of that?" Erasmus pulled her close, held her hand, and promised Mackenzie that she would be the best girlfriend she'd ever had. They smiled and shared a kiss before making love again.

Intertwined, Mackenzie looked into Erasmus's eyes and promised Erasmus that she wouldn't take drugs again. Then they had sex again, more intense and promising than any time before. Later that night, they went to Erasmus's house to get most of her clothes.

Chapter Fifteen

For the next three years, Erasmus and Mackenzie would be together as girlfriends. After her lease was up, they moved to the gay area of Dallas, in Oaklawn, right off of Douglas Street.

Erasmus's parents gave her their Mazda and Mackenzie still had her Geo. They turned their little, one bedroom apartment into a cozy spot filled with candles, a black futon, and the full size bed that Nick and Tiphane had given her. Mackenzie ignored her life as a heterosexual and eliminated her friends that were not gay. The idea of the two of them being so young, gay, and Mackenzie having a child, was very welcomed in the gay community. They were the ideal couple in the eyes of the gay community.

In the matter of family, Mackenzie was welcomed at Erasmus's house, but she couldn't dare take Erasmus to Aunt Cecile's house as her girlfriend. Instead, they went over there on occasions but as friends, until Mackenzie was too far along to hide her pregnancy. The twins thought Erasmus was weird because she was white. She always told them Erasmus was her best friend and her being white didn't mean anything.

"Dang, you act like she's somebody special. Shoot, she's white and nothing special," Lanette snapped, as Mackenzie returned from showing Erasmus to the restroom on one evening, something she did every time Erasmus accompanied her to Aunt Cecile's. It was their secret time to kiss, flirt, and listen for the sounds of the baby.

"Well, she's my friend, and to me, that's special." Mackenzie blurted out before she could think about it. Her emotions were out of control, and she couldn't hide the love she felt for Erasmus.

Whenever they left and went home, they sat up talking underneath the smell of vanilla scented candles. Mackenzie played in Erasmus's hair and she rubbed her feet.

"Do you think we could take a trip somewhere, Erasmus? Maybe go to the Riverwalk in San Antonio." Mackenzie asked, as she twirled Erasmus's hair around her small finger.

"Yeah, that would be cool, our first mini-vacation. As soon as the baby is born, we can go." Erasmus stood up and pulled Mackenzie to the bathroom and undressed her.

"Have you thought about a name yet?"

"No. It's all been so surreal, I haven't been able to think, to tell you the truth. I don't know what I would do if you weren't here."

"Oh sweetie, you're tough; you could handle it."

"No I couldn't. Promise me you won't leave me to do this all alone.

Promise me, Erasmus." Mackenzie pleaded with Erasmus as they stood in the middle of the bathroom, undressed, the sounds of the running bath water echoed in the background.

"Mackenzie, I promise I will be here. Are you all right? I mean, where is this coming from?"

"I don't know. I'm getting fat, you're so beautiful, in shape. You could be with anyone if you wanted to."

"Wait, you're are just as beautiful, and beside all that, this is where I want to be. I love you."

"Do you mean it?"

"Yes. Now come here and kiss me with those pretty full lips of yours." She pulled Mackenzie close and they exchanged a soft and meaningful kiss."

The entire year of 1992 was ideal for them as a couple. The birth of Jasmine in early July was a moment of peace for them. She was tiny, with reddish brown curly hair, and white as snow. She arrived quietly and on her first day home, amongst many of their friends, she slept quietly as they all buzzed around her.

It wasn't until the second year that their relationship began to suffer. Erasmus stayed at home to watch Jasmine, who she'd nicknamed Jay-Jay, and made new friends while Mackenzie continued to work long hours at Lady Locker, which led to both of them starting their habits again.

Mackenzie, feeling neglected, started to use acid on a weekly basis. She barely made time for Jay-Jay, who was still quiet and clung to Erasmus. Not only was substance abuse a problem, but cheating and fighting as well.

Although still a couple, on any given night out at the clubs, while Jay-Jay stayed with Erasmus's folks, girls would throw themselves at Mackenzie and perform sexual favors in the bathroom stalls. Erasmus was so high most of the time, she didn't even notice. Mackenzie became a sexual magnet and cheated with no problem. Every weekend at several gay clubs like JUGS, Club Mesha, or TRAXX, there was someone new. Black, white, Hispanic, it didn't matter.

They did acid together and laughed until Erasmus would find her after her high wore off and was ready to leave. They stopped talking like they used to and fought endlessly because of their substance abuse. The combination of Mackenzie's LSD habit and Erasmus's problem kept them at each other's throats as Jay-Jay sat quietly, witnessing everything.

Mackenzie hid her drug problems from her family and employers, but it became a complete problem for her. The guilt was an enormous weight every time she looked at Jay-Jay's pretty brown eyes. Sometimes she would hold her and smile when she grabbed her index finger and used it to teethe or hold back tears as Jay-Jay would fall asleep in Erasmus's arms as she tried to sleep off her high.

Their apartment wasn't much of anything, and all of the things they'd promised they would do became just that, promises. With Erasmus's friends coming in and out at all times of the night, it was just like Jun's, but Mackenzie was so messed up on LSD she didn't even bother to question it or make the connection.

On her twenty-first birthday, Erasmus was so messed up they fought at the club and then went home and passed out when they couldn't fight each other any more. Bruises, scratches, and broken lamps were enough to end that night's fighting. It was just good that Jay-Jay was spending the weekend with Erasmus's family.

It was 1993, and Mackenzie was exhausted. The drugs were wearing her down, and Erasmus was out of control. Sometimes she came home and sometimes she didn't, causing Mackenzie to stay at home with Jay-Jay and missed work, which was causing a financial strain. Mackenzie paid most of the bills and used the money that her folks sent over for Jay-Jay's savings. Things became so bad, that she began getting money from some of the other girls she was messing with to pay their bills.

"Where have you been, E?" Mackenzie asked, after one of Erasmus's extended disappearing acts.

"I've been out. Why?"

"For three days?" Mackenzie asked, cleaning the month old dishes that were in the sink while Jay-Jay sat in her high seat playing with one of her toys.

"Look, I'm tired. I need to get some sleep."

Mackenzie was getting upset, "Tired from what? You're not working. I' mean, what has you so tired? If anyone in here should be tired, it's me. I have a job."

Erasmus glared at Mackenzie and started to walk over to her, then threw up her hands instead and walked into their bedroom.

Mackenzie cut off the water, dried off her hands, then picked up Jay-Jay, and followed her. "Erasmus, we need to talk. I can't keep paying these bills by myself. You need to get a job or,"

Erasmus was sitting on the bed when she looked up to cut off Mackenzie's words.

"Or what? You'll get one of your girlfriends on the side to move in here and help you take care of Jay-Jay? You think I don't know that you've been cheating on me? You think I'm stupid? Everybody knows what you do with your little friends in the bathroom, Mackenzie."

Mackenzie, feeling a little embarrassed as Erasmus turned the tables on her, placed her free hand on her hips and said, "If you would stay home and stop getting high every damn day, I wouldn't have to cheat!"

Erasmus threw down her shoe and stood up. "So you don't do drugs now? You don't trip on acid every weekend or throughout the week? People talk, Mackenzie. I know who you get it from, when you get it, and who you do it with. You're just able to hide it at your job, but what's gonna happen when you get caught? I don't have a job, and I don't have to worry about getting caught."

Mackenzie looked at Erasmus and laughed. "Erasmus, you sound stupid. You need to get a job because I'm not going to keep paying these bills by myself. Or you can leave. It's up to you."

"I have a job. She's in your arms, remember? I take better care of her than you ever have, and if it wasn't for my folks, Jay-Jay would probably be in CPS care. So don't tell me about a job. You're a fuckin' unfit mother."

Mackenzie turned to walkout of their bedroom and Erasmus slammed the door at her back.

Mackenzie was ready to give up. Erasmus was right; she was cheating with several women, and it was like the two of them were only together for the image, and more importantly, she *was* an unfit mother. Mackenzie finished up the dishes, put Jay-Jay to sleep, and left them both asleep in their bedroom.

It was Thursday, so she went to FISH DANCE, to score some acid. As usual, she needed to escape. While there, she met a girl named Josie. She was the same age as Erasmus but much more serious and in control of her life. She was about to finish college and held down a part-time job. They stayed in the bathroom stall and talked for what seemed like hours. That night, Mackenzie stayed sober.

Josie was a beautiful blond with a bob that hung behind her ears. Sleeping with Josie seemed to give her peace in her now turbulent life.

For two weeks, they hid their affair from Josie's significant other and Erasmus and became close in a short period of time. They talked on her lunch break and secretly saw each other when Erasmus was gone or when her significant other was at work. She encouraged Mackenzie to apply to college and stop wasting her time with the likes of Erasmus.

When Christmas Eve arrived, Erasmus sobered up and took Jay-Jay to see her parents. Josie came by and told Mackenzie they had to end their affair. Mackenzie was crushed because Josie seemed to be her only link to survival. *"We can't do this anymore."*

She softly said as Mackenzie pondered telling her that she wanted to be with her and was going to leave Erasmus.

But she knew at the time that Josie was out of her league. She had a home, was financially stable, and was about to hold a college degree with a future in a promising career. Mackenzie had Jay-Jay.

Josie gave her a Christmas gift: a full tuition at a junior college for the spring of 1994. Mackenzie gave her all that she had, one last night of sex. When she left, Mackenzie cried herself to sleep because life for her now was out of her control, and she didn't know how to stop it.

Erasmus woke her up in the middle of the night, ransacking their apartment. "What are you doing?" Mackenzie asked, in complete shock.

"We're leaving, I need to get our things."

"You're what? What do you mean, we? Who's leaving?" She couldn't believe her ears.

"What do you mean. Who's things?"

"Mackenzie, we can't do this anymore. I can't"

"E, what are you talking about? Come on, it's Christmas. Calm down. Did you and your folks have a fight again? Was Jay-Jay acting up?"

"Mackenzie, you need to listen. I said we're leaving. That's it. There's nothing to talk about."

Mackenzie ran her hands through her hair in disbelief. She needed Erasmus. Although they had their problems, she couldn't imagine being without her and little Jay-Jay. The reality of her motherhood finally sank in. She wasn't ready to face life alone.

"You can't take Jay-Jay. She's all I have. What am I supposed to do?"

"Mackenzie, what you said the other day made a lot of sense. I can't give you what you need anymore. So, be free and see who you want to see. Do what you want to do. But I'm taking Jay-Jay because you can't take care of her; you don't even know her, or her sleep patterns, her food tastes…"

"What the fuck are you talking about? She eats baby food, damn it!" Mackenzie slammed her hand against the wall.

"That's what I mean. She's eating table food now."

Mackenzie looked down at the floor as sweat formed at her temples. The faded gray carpet gave no sympathy, just the notion that she would be alone and Erasmus and Jay-Jay would be gone for good.

Someone knocked at the door as Erasmus moved things around in the bathroom and went in and out of their bedroom. Jay-Jay sat upon the bed and watched. Mackenzie was too ashamed to even pick her up. She walked out to answer the door.

"Who is it?" Mackenzie asked, wanting to get back to Erasmus to convince them to stay.

"I'm here for Erasmus."

Mackenzie opened the door and saw one of the mulatto girls from the club. She looked at her, confused, when she said again, "I'm here for Erasmus." Mackenzie looked back towards their bedroom.

Erasmus walked out of the bedroom with some of her things. Holding Jay-Jay, she went over to the girl. "I thought I told you to wait in the car?"

"I know, baby, but I thought you would need some help with your things and Jay-Jay."

"Excuse me. What the fuck is going on here?"

"Mackenzie, this is who I'm with now. She's my girlfriend, Nia."

Mackenzie began to lose it, pacing.

"Why," she asked. Erasmus ignored her and Mackenzie's empty questions fell on deaf ears. Erasmus placed things in bags and walked in and out of the apartment, taking things downstairs to Nia, who was now waiting by the car and holding Jay-Jay.

She paced in a crazed state of mind, and then watched the two of them load everything into her Mazda, including her daughter.

When the door shut one last time, it felt like Mackenzie's whole world closed in on her. She paced the floor the entire night. The acid flashbacks were causing her to panic. That Christmas morning, she climbed into bed and stayed there for the next couple of days until she couldn't feel anything except the need to end her life.

Her mind was just about gone, so Mackenzie swallowed as many pills as she could find and chased it down with some vodka they kept in the almost empty apartment. There was no more Jay-Jay and her half smiles, her diapers, toys, or tiny clothes. Mackenzie believed she couldn't live any longer. The silence that filled the apartment sent her over the edge.

She jumped into her car, attempting to drive as far away as possible. But she had nowhere to go. Nick and Tiphane had no idea how her life had changed, and Aunt Cecile would go crazy if she saw Mackenzie like this a skinny, sunken in paranoid person.

After driving around much of Dallas, weakened by the pills and alcohol, Mackenzie passed out at an intersection. When she came to, she was covered with charcoal and surrounded by doctors and police officers staring at her. They had pumped her stomach, trying to save her life from a near overdose.

When she finally answered thier many questions and convinced the doctors and psychiatrist that she was okay to go home, Mackenzie went home by the bus her car was impounded. Disappointed that she was still alive, she made plans to go out anyway. She showered, ignoring the headaches that tap danced on her head, then got dressed and went out to the VILLAGE STATION to dance with the gay guys she'd met a couple of months ago while out at Sue-Ellen's.

Mackenzie, dancing with her entourage and drunk to no ends, wasn't paying attention to the group of women that came in looking for her, until she was dragged off the dance floor by the four of them and led upstairs to the patio.

"You're Mackenzie, right?" one of them asked, scaring her. The stud woman glared at Mackenzie, pushing her up against the patio rails in the midst of gay men with drinks in their hands.

"Yeah, I'm Mackenzie. Why?"

The three others looked at Mackenzie as each spat at her face. "Yeah, we got something for you, bitch."

Mackenzie, realizing she was in for something she had not planned on, tried to get away but the four of them surrounded her, taunting her and calling her names. "Dirty bitch. Bet you won't mess with my girl again."

"What are you talking about?" Mackenzie asked, trying to get away from them.

"Oh you don't know now, huh?" The stud woman slapped Mackenzie across the face, which signaled the others, who began slapping, punching, and kicking at Mackenzie. She couldn't get a hit in to save her life. Then the stud woman grabbed her by the elbow and the four of them lifted her up and threw her over the patio.

The crowd of men underneath broke her fall, but they didn't do anything to help, just cursed her because they'd dropped their drinks *"thanks to her little ass flying through the air."* the Fabio look alike said, as he and his entourage made a fiasco over the ordeal.

"Shit. You skinny, bitch. You just made me drop my drink," one of them said, they walked off ranting and raving headed to the bar. Mackenzie stumbled to get up, limping, she moved through the crowded VILLAGE STATION as people stared. Some of them she knew, some of them she didn't, but none of them helped as she made her way out of the club.

"You can't come back here anymore," one of the owners scoffed at her. Then another told her, "You're banned; don't ever come back."

Outside, she walked past Elle's to catch a cab, as pointed fingers, stares, and laughter greeted her; the news had already hit the circuit. Mackenzie was at rock bottom.

"Damn, what was that about?" Mackenzie asked herself, as she opened the cab door. She sat inside and sighed momentarily when a

bottle shattered across the front end of the cab. Mackenzie snapped out of her daze as the cab driver sped off.

"Where to, ma'am?" the Indian man asked, as he looked through the rear mirror. That's when she realized that her cheating and disregard for others had gotten her beat up. The many women that she'd cheated with had certainly been attached; after all, she had been.

"Ummm…Skillman and Walnut. Please."

"That's a lot of money," he said, looking at Mackenzie. She knew she had spent all of her money on alcohol and was betting on getting a ride from her gay friends.

"I know," she replied, knowing she couldn't pay.

"Don't worry, looks like you had a rough night. It's on me." He looked up again, this time smiling.

"Thanks," Mackenzie replied, hoping that he wasn't expecting anything for his kind gesture.

The cab driver drove Mackenzie home with no problem, occasionally watching her through the rear view mirror smiling.

He dropped her off at her apartment and told her to be careful, watching to make sure she made it into her apartment as she waved goodbye. By the grace of God, she'd made it. The pain from Erasmus leaving still hurt deeply as well as her ego from getting beat up. Mackenzie knew she had to save face or just do something different 'cause this wasn't getting it. That following morning, she quit her job at Lady Foot Locker and told Aunt Cecile she was going back to New York to visit. Mackenzie was going to hide and devise a plan. She made up in her mind that she had to bounce back or be defeated for the rest of her life. More importantly, she was going to get Jay-Jay back.

Arriving in New York, they had planned to spend New Years with Sam and his gospel group at church, and for the first time, she would be filled with the Holy Spirit.

"I'm tired," she told Sam as she stepped off of the train, halfway incoherent, dizzy, and psychologically in need of more acid.

"Then give it to God," he simply replied. "Give it to Him, Mackenzie. He already knows; he's been waiting on you."

She looked at Sam and saw the sincerity in his eyes, the tears that were a true symbol of unconditional love and true friendship.

"Come on. I want to show you something," Sam said, grabbing her hand and taking her to his car.

"This is nice." Mackenzie remarked at Sam's new car.

"Oh it's just a rental, but I'm saving up for my own."

They sat quietly, holding hands as Sam zipped through the evening traffic. "When Grandma told me you were coming, it was perfect. You don't need to change; I want you to come just as you are."

"Where are we going?" she asked, trying to hold her eyes open.

"Church. Tonight my choir is singing at a program."

"But I look awful. I haven't changed since yesterday."

"Mackenzie, don't worry about that. The days of dressing to impress at church are far gone. It's about God, his word, and getting your breakthrough.

"It's not about what you have on. It's about your state of mind, your state of being. Are you living the way God wants you to live? Are you free? Or are you in bondage, caught up, a slave to Satan?"

"Aren't we going to be late?"

"Actually, we're right on time." Sam pulled up in front of the huge church and called out to someone, then the two went into the church as the person he'd called drove off in the rental car.

Sam held Mackenzie's hand as they walked down the aisle of the church to where his choir was sitting. He smiled and greeted people while Mackenzie took in the freshness in the air and the peace that was welling up inside.

As they took their seats, it was time for Sam's choir to sing.

"Are you okay?"

"I'm fine. Go ahead. I'm okay, I promise."

With a rendition of a song that Sam and one of his musicians wrote, *No Hiding Place,* the church was spiritually on fire.

Mackenzie thought about what Sam said about God waiting on her and instantly, she knew why she was there. "Thank you, Lord," she cried out. "Thank you, Jesus." She yelled at the top of her lungs, as she thought about what she would have been doing back in Dallas. "Hallelujah," she screamed, and then took off running and shouting across the altar. She broke loose and was finally free.

She ran around the huge sanctuary and at that very moment, she was delivered from drugs and the many sexual escapades that had filled her life. From that moment on, life for Mackenzie would be different.

Mackenzie decided not to visit her family because of what she now looked like. Her frail, 100-pound body with sagging eyes that seemed to carry more baggage than she wanted to talk about kept her away. She stayed with Sam at his grandparent's house for a week, trying to get her strength back as well as her weight.

"So, what are your plans when you make it back to Dallas?" Sam asked while they talked over breakfast.

"Yeah, it's not like I can just stay here forever."

"Well, whatever you were running from, you have to face it back in Dallas," Sam said, looking deep into Mackenzie's eyes.

"I know. There are some things I have to face. Some things I have to fix," Mackenzie replied, thinking of Jay-Jay and how much she missed her tiny little hands and the half smile that always seemed to be on her face.

"You okay?" Sam asked.

"I'm fine, just ready to move on and make things right."

"Sounds like you do have a plan."

"Yep, but it's going to take a lot of work to make it happen. I'm determined to turn everything around."

They talked some about old times and old friends, and then made preparations for Mackenzie to leave the following morning. She took the train back to Dallas anxiously and decided she would use Josie's gift and start school that spring. She had to make up for lost time. She had to make up for almost losing her soul; she had to stay free from drugs.

Mackenzie went to the community college and took the necessary tests to get enrolled, then enrolled in a total of five courses. She got her books from the library or made copies from most classmates until her GI Bill would be ready.

The toughest obstacle was making her way to classes daily and holding onto her apartment without a job. She could deal with living off of Ramen noodles; because of her poor eating habits and severe drug usage, her stomach couldn't take much anyway. And with the many flashbacks that she continued to face, she spent a lot of time praying instead of eating.

After three months of riding the bus and borrowing money from a classmate, Mackenzie finally got a job at a homeless shelter for teens. But she was so behind on her rent she was forced to give up her apartment, so she moved in with a classmate named Amos. Even her money from the GI Bill wasn't enough.

Mackenzie told Amos all about her problems and her issues with women. He never judged her or asked for any money while she stayed with him. She stayed with him from the beginning of spring until the end of the fall semester.

Once Mackenzie began feeling better, her face and her sagging eyes seemed to perk up. Amos encouraged her to find another apartment. "I don't mind you staying here, and I enjoy your company, but part of getting better means you have to step out on your own."

"I know; it's time to take that step." Mackenzie thanked Amos for his advice because she knew he was right.

"I'm here if you need anything, Mackenzie."

"Amos, you've done so much already. A place to stay, bus money, food, listening. Thank you so much."

"Anytime."

Since she was working again, what she saved up she could use to get back on her feet. He also encouraged her to find Nick and Tiphane, since she talked about them so much.

Mackenzie was a little nervous because she felt like Nick would be mad at her for disappearing. She had always been in Dallas and so were they, but with her lifestyle, she'd stayed away out of fear. What would they say if they knew she had been living with a woman? But it wasn't until one day while she was working at the homeless shelter for teens that she realized she needed to find her friends and get back their friendship.

There were no lesbians in her life anymore. She was through with them for good. Mackenzie went back to the Caribbean spot and looked for Nick and Tiphane. The club was the same, and had the same enticing smells of Caribbean spices. She spotted Nick across the room behind one of the bars.

When she walked up, Nick looked as if he was seeing a ghost. "What's up, Mackenzie? Thought you was dead."

Mackenzie smiled and leaned over and gave him a hug. "Not yet."

He was hurt because it showed in his eyes. She passed on the drink he offered and they talked for hours until Tiphane showed up. She looked great. After hugs and questions, the three continued to talk about old times. Nick and Tiphane now owned the Caribbean Bar and Grill. Her parents had moved back to the islands and left it to them.

They told her Ken was finishing up law school and engaged. She smiled. When they asked where she had been and what she had been doing, she lied and told them only about the last year of going to school.

They exchanged numbers and promised they would meet that Sunday to watch the Super Bowl at the bar.

Mackenzie was glad she'd met up with them. She felt a lot better. She even decided to take Amos up on another of his ideas, to buy another car.

Actually, Aunt Cecile was buying a new car and gave her the old Honda Accord. Mackenzie found an apartment in East Dallas. It was an old garage turned into an apartment on Concho Street. It was small, cozy, and efficient. The landlord would let her rent it only if she had a cosigner, so Amos agreed to co-sign for her. She moved in shortly after that.

Mackenzie was one semester short of transferring to the University, so she enrolled one last time at the community college. That spring semester of 1996, she breezed through the course work.

She was single and only had time for work and school. She would meet up with Amos at times for a movie or coffee. Other than that, she stayed buried in her books and still fighting the flashbacks through prayer.

When summer arrived, Mackenzie enrolled at the University and tried to get ahead with her studies. She took classes in both summer sessions in between working at the emergency shelter.

By the time the fall had arrived, she was ahead of her schedule by at least a semester. Mackenzie was fortunate that many of her needed courses were offered in both summer sessions. She took her upper level social work classes and began preparing for her senior year and an internship.

Her life was once again back on track. She didn't go out at all anymore and was finally over the hurt and pain caused by Demarcus, Erasmus, and losing Jay-Jay. She was experiencing life freely. Cooking dinner in her apartment and watching TV alone-brought peace because one day, Jay-Jay would be there with her.

Then, on a typical day after classes, Mackenzie was taken aback when two police officers came to her apartment and arrested her for writing hot checks. She called Nick and Tiphane after nearly fighting for the phone down at the Lew Sterret jail facility and asked them for their help. They told her not to worry. They would call Ken and get everything taken care of.

PART III:
TELLING THE TRUTH AND WINNING & LOSING ALL AT THE SAME TIME.

Chapter Sixteen

So here she was, sitting in Lew Sterret, in a crowded cell with all types of women who'd committed all types of crimes. She could hear them talking about how they'd lied to the cops that arrested them or how they were so damn high they didn't even care that they were being arrested, raped, robbed, or beaten. And while many of those women reminisced about their highs, she sat there quietly, thanking God for her deliverance from drugs.

Mackenzie had been there for twenty-four hours when one of the guards buzzed open the door and called for her and seven other women. That left about two dozen others still there.

The guard briefed them on how to sit in the hearing room and how to respond to the judge, then he began to put chains on their hands and feet. Mackenzie promised herself she wouldn't be afraid; she knew God had delivered her, and there was no way she was going to prison now.

At the hearing, the judge called her name and informed Mackenzie that her attorney would be picking her up. *"Attorney?"* she thought. *This must be serious.*

The judge looked at her sternly and then nodded. Makenzie sat in the too small, dark courtroom until the guards came to get her. They took her to the property clerk and let her get her keys and jacket.

Mackenzie was escorted to a room where a young man sat as though eager to meet with her. He stood up and extended his hand. "Hello, Ms. Kennedy, I'm your attorney, Julian Taylor. I will be representing you and your case."

"Hello sir. It's very nice to meet you. But I'm confused. I don't even know why I was arrested."

"Why don't you have a seat and we can discuss the contents of your case."

Mackenzie was beginning to get scared because Mr. Taylor seemed so serious. His presence was demanding and powerful. The crisp black suit wasn't helping either.

He was probably a few inches taller than she was, about a hundred and sixty pounds, clean, shaven, and bald. His skin was the color of cocoa butter, and he had greenish-gray eyes. When he did smile, she saw that his teeth were pearly white with a slight gap between his two front teeth.

"Now, Ms. Kennedy, the State of Texas claims that you are responsible for writing over twenty-thousand dollars in bad checks back in 1993. They have been after you for some time but lost track of you after you left Dallas."

"Okay wait, there's been some mix up. I don't even have a checking account, and I've never left Dallas. I've been staying with a friend and attending school. In fact, after I finish my internship and three other courses, I'll graduate."

"Ms. Kennedy, they have your signature."

"They don't have my signature because I don't have an account."

"I can't help you if you're not going to be honest."

"No, you can't help if you're not going to believe me and do some damn research. I have no reason to lie." Mackenzie was really getting pissed at this green-eyed punk! What good was he if he didn't believe in her?

"Well, you are free to go for now. Your friends made bail for you. I'll be getting in touch with you by tomorrow."

"Thanks, you have a good day." Mackenzie stood up and was escorted out by the guard. She signed some papers and was on her way.

In a daze, as she walked through corridor after corridor until a familiar voice said her name. It was Tiphane.

Mackenzie walked up to her and asked where Nick was. She informed her that he was outside with the car because he didn't want to pay to park. *"Still a cheapskate,"* Mackenzie thought to herself and shook her head.

"Tiphane, thanks for getting me out. I have no idea what this is about. I don't even have a checking account. I paid my bills with money orders or Erasmus handled it."

"Who's Erasmus?"

"Old roommate," Mackenzie replied, trying to avoid any further conversation about Erasmus.

"You don't think she had anything to do with the fraud. Do you?"

"I hope not. She's the last person I want to see right now," Mackenzie responded again, trying to avoid the subject.

"So what did Jay say?"

"Who's Jay?"

"The attorney Ken recommended."

"Oh, he said his name was Julian or something like that. I wasn't really listening to his name; I wanted to know why I was being arrested."

"So what did he say?"

"Well, he thinks I'm lying first of all, then he went on to tell me that the State has been looking for me and it doesn't look too good that I was on the run. Yadda, yadda, yadda."

"He said that?"

"Yep, and I told him he wouldn't be able to help me if he didn't believe me and that he needed to do some damn research because I don't even own a checking account."

"Wow, was he rude? Ken said he would be great."

"Stuck up, rude, it's all the same. He said he would call me tomorrow."

They made it outdoors, and Nick was standing out front up against their 5series, all black BWM. When they walked up, he just shook his head. "Nick, that's out of character for you. It's not nice to judge," Mackenzie said with a slight attitude.

"Why didn't you tell us you were having problems?"

"Because I wasn't. Those charges are very much erroneous."

They all got in the car in silence and drove to the restaurant. "We have to start getting ready for the night crowd. You in a rush to get home?" Tiphane asked.

"Well, I have classes to consider and a project due. But if you guys have something to take care of it's okay." Mackenzie's flashbacks were starting again, and she knew she needed to be home praying. Her throat was burning and her mind was beginning to ramble. It was becoming hard to focus.

"Tiph, why don't you take Mackenzie home and then come back. I'll get things started here."

"Okay, I'll be right back."

"Thanks Nick. I appreciate your help and as soon as I get some money, I'll pay you guys back."

"Don't worry about it. That's what friends are for," Nick said, giving her a wink before she and Tiphane left.

Tiphane drove her home and they talked about all of the different scenarios that could have taken place. Of all of them, the one she feared the most was that Erasmus would do this to her.

Mackenzie made it to her evening classes late but was able to turn in her project. She did, however, miss her two morning classes. She knew she was going to have to do some serious explaining to her instructors.

When she finally made it home, she soaked for hours in hot water, bleach, and rubbing alcohol. What was she going to tell her instructors about missing class this morning? Would her absence affect her grades? All these questions danced around in her head. Her finals were in less than a week.

She must have dosed off when her phone rang. Worried that it was Mr. Taylor, Mackenzie hurried out of the shower to answer it, splashing water on the linoleum floor.

"Hello?"

"Yes, this is Mr. Taylor, may I speak with Mackenzie Kennedy?"

"This is Mackenzie. Can I help you?"

"Ms. Kennedy, I realize that it is pretty late, but I really need to set an appointment with you as soon as possible. Can you meet me, let's say tomorrow at about nine A.M.?"

"Well, I have class tomorrow morning. I'll be through by noon though."

"Where do you take classes?"

"In Arlington. But I can drive to Dallas to meet you."

"Okay, let's meet at say one o'clock at the TGI Fridays in the West End. Will that work?"

"Sure. I can find that."

"Okay well, I will see you then."

Mackenzie barely slept that night, tossing and turning, worrying about what Mr. Taylor wanted to meet about. She actually woke up an hour early and was early for class.

She caught up with both of her instructors and explained why she'd missed her classes yesterday. Her grades were above average, so her instructors seemed to understand.

After reviewing for finals in both classes, she was released early. Mackenzie drove into Dallas, searching for the West End and the TGI Fridays that Mr. Taylor recommended. It was the same one that she and Nick had walked past on several occasions so many years ago.

After locating it in the center of the West End, she parked her car and went inside. She was fairly early, so she ordered some fries and lemonade trying to ease the constant hunger pains in her stomach.

Just as she finished her lunch, Mr. Taylor walked up beside the table. He was dressed in a navy, pen-stripped, single-breasted suit that made his eyes appear darker than they were the other day.

"Enjoying your lunch?"

"Yes, I uh… made it here early so I decided to eat something since I skipped breakfast this morning," Mackenzie replied, trying not to talk with her mouth full.

"Did you possibly order me something?"

She looked at Mr. Taylor with some concern.

"Just kidding."

She laughed a little and downplayed his request as he sat down. Mr. Taylor ordered lemonade and began to discuss Mackenzie's situation.

"Okay, here's the deal, the charges have been dropped. You were right. You do not own a checking account and did not own one in 1993. In fact, the signatures don't even match."

"How'd you match the signatures?"

Mr. Taylor smiled. "When you signed out yesterday and signed in the day before. Those signatures matched identically. The others were way off."

"So who *did* sign them?"

"Well that's for them to investigate. My job is done."

"Well, thank you. I really appreciate your assistance."

"Well, thank you for reminding me of my job responsibilities."

"What do you mean?"

"Your comment about doing research was a definite hit below the belt."

"I'm sorry, I was just worried. I couldn't understand how this could happen," Mackenzie said, trying not to sound too trite.

"Well, you're a free woman now, and all charges have been dropped. So you can finish up school and go on to save the world."

"I don't know about saving the world."

"You are a social work major, and isn't that what you guys do?" Mr. Taylor said, as he sipped his lemonade.

"How stereotypical of you, and how'd you know I was in social work?"

"Your friends told me, and sorry about the comment just a little humor."

"No problem. You just got me off the hook. I'm just happy for that."

"So what do you plan to do in social work, if I may ask?"

Mackenzie readjusted her small frame into the seat that was almost too small for her. "Actually I wanted to get my master's and open up a center for runaways or troubled youth. But now I'm beginning to think about my passion."

"Passion, huh? And what would that be?"

"Would you believe Civil law, to be exact."

"Really, have you applied yet? Or taken the test?"

"Well, I haven't told anyone, but I plan to take it in January. And possibly attend SMU."

"Well, you do have your plans set. When do you graduate?"

"In May."

"Wow, you're focused. That's really good. Exceptional."

"Thanks. I need to make up for lost time," Mackenzie replied, forcing a half smile.

"I understand. Well, Ms. Kennedy, all I need is one last signature, but my secretary is currently drawing up the papers. So, as soon as they are done, I'll give you a call and possibly swing by so you can sign and I'll give you a copy. Is that okay?"

"Yes. That will be fine."

"Well, are you ready? I can walk you to your car."

"Yeah, I'm through here." They both stood and prepared to leave the restaurant. Mackenzie stopped and paid for the tab, declining Mr. Taylor's attempt to pay.

Mr. Taylor was the perfect gentleman and walked her to her car to make sure she made it off okay.

Because he was a lawyer, Mackenzie was shocked to see that he was not married. She thought being in a traditional field like his would definitely mean he was married. *Maybe he was engaged like Ken was*, she thought.

Chapter Seventeen

ater that evening, Mackenzie went into her job and worked a double shift, using the time at the shelter to study for her finals and fill out her law school application.

Mackenzie went straight to class, fueled by water and a granola bar. She was wondering about Mr. Taylor for some odd reason and why he'd insisted on bringing over the papers. He was just being a true friend and rare gentleman, she figured, and didn't think about it again.

After finishing up classes, she went home and fell asleep. Mackenzie had slept for what seemed like an eternity when her phone rang.

"Hello?" She struggled with the phone. "Hello?"

"Hello Mackenzie. I mean Ms. Kennedy."

"Yes, this is Mackenzie."

"Hi this is Julian, Julian Taylor, your attorney."

"Oh yeah. Hi. How are you?"

"Pretty well, thank you. Listen, I have those papers. If you want, I can bring them over."

Mackenzie looked over at her little alarm clock, which read seven eighteen P.M. "Yeah, yeah that would be fine."

"Okay. Just give me the directions, and I'll be there shortly."

Mackenzie gave him the directions and headed straight to her bathroom to take a quick bath, realizing she should have done this after class. Her bathroom, which only came equipped with a tub and a hanging shower that could not stand upright on its own, was Mackenzie's haven. Oftentimes, she would spend a couple of hours there when she had time, but today she knew that wasn't possible.

She bathed, pulled her hair back into a ponytail, and brushed her teeth. She decided to throw on some old army fatigues and a fitted T-shirt. Just as she was searching for socks in one of her handy bins, there was a knock at the door.

Mackenzie quickly put on her socks and went to the door. Mr. Taylor was standing there in blue jeans and a light sweater with a pair of Stan Smith Adidas on.

"Hi Mr. Taylor. Come on in."

"Thanks. How are you?"

"Pretty good. Can't complain. And yourself?"

"Doing just fine. Well, your place is nice and cozy."

"Thanks, it's just a little something to get me through school."

"Well, it's nice."

"I just moved in not too long ago, so I haven't been able to furnish it. Except for

the bistro set in the kitchen. We can have a seat in there."

They sat down and went over the paperwork. She signed and he gave Mackenzie her copies.

"Would you like something to drink or perhaps a piece of fruit, Mr. Taylor? I hadn't cooked this evening, being a little lazy." She said with a smile.

"Please, I insist that you call me Julian. And actually, I was wondering if you wanted to grab a bite to eat at a little spot I know of not too far from here."

"Well, uh, I guess that would be fine. Let me just slip on something else."

"You're fine. Actually, I'm a little overdressed."

"Are you sure? It won't take but a minute."

"I'm sure. You look great. Very comfortable."

"Okay, let me grab my sneakers, keys, and a jacket, and we can head out."

"Okay."

Mackenzie went into her bedroom and searched for her keys. She discovered them underneath yesterday's clothes. Smiling, she re-pulled her hair back and put on some chapstick and her sneakers, and then went back into the kitchen. "You ready?"

"Yep."

Julian had a nice, champagne-colored, S-Class Mercedes Benz Sedan that was fully equipped. His leather seat hugged her behind and caused her to feel so relaxed she wanted to kick off her shoes.

Julian opened the sunroof and put on some jazz as they drove to the lower Greenville area. They talked briefly about the upcoming Cowboy season and the possibilities of another Super Bowl.

"Do you eat fish, Mackenzie?"

"Yes, whiting or flounder."

"No catfish? You must be from the East Coast."

"Yeah, I'm from New York, Brooklyn. And I do eat catfish. I didn't until I moved here, though."

"Yeah, I don't even think they serve catfish in New York," Julian said, laughing.

"You're not from the East Coast are you?"

"No, no I'm a country boy. Born and raised in Oklahoma."

"So what, you don't like the East Coast?"

"Yeah, I've been to New York several times. It's a great place to visit and shop, but I would never live there. Too fast for me, I'd rather live in Houston or L.A. They're big cities, yet there is something that prevents them from being like New York. I'd probably say the space that it offers. New York is very crowded."

"Interesting."

"Well, come on, let's get something to eat. I'm starved." Julian stepped out of the car and walked around to assist her.

"Thanks."

"You're welcome, Ms. Mackenzie." They smiled and exchanged looks, then proceeded to the restaurant.

They walked up the block and across the street to a place called Aw Shucks. It was a very small place that smelled of seafood. Julian placed their orders at the stand up counter, and then they seated themselves on an outdoor patio.

"Do you drink, Mackenzie?"

"Not anymore."

"Really? That's good. You are very focused."

"Yeah, I just want to finish school and move on to the next level. I'm tired of being poor."

"I know the feeling."

She looked at Julian, shocked because he wasn't doing too badly to her. His nice suits and a big fancy car hardly qualified for being poor.

Then Julian went on to tell her that he was an only child, raised by his single mother in a small town in Canyon, Oklahoma. He said things were pretty tight growing up, living on a teacher's assistant's salary. His father left before he was born, so it was just he and his mother.

Mackenzie told Julian about her many brothers and sisters and growing up poor, too. They laughed about eating fried bologna and Vienna sausages.

Things became personal when Julian asked why she wasn't married. When she told him that she hadn't found the right guy yet, he laughed because he said his mother was always asking, "when are you getting married," and his replies were always the same: "I haven't found the right woman yet."

They sat and ate catfish and fries and talked about everything under the sun, sometimes bursting into laughter. Julian was six years older than she was but didn't look a day over twenty-one. Mackenzie told him her birthday was actually coming up and he couldn't believe she was as old as she said. He asked what were her plans for her birthday were and when she told him "to recuperate from finals," he laughed.

They talked until the restaurant closed, and then walked back to Julian's car. The night was slightly chilly and Mackenzie was glad she had brought her jacket. The gentle wind was causing her nipples to harden.

"So you really want to go to law school?"

Mackenzie turned and nodded her head, signaling a yes.

"It's pretty tough. You think you don't have a personal life now. Just wait until law school. You're going to go full time right?"

"Yeah, if I can qualify for some type of assistance."

"Well, you know SMU does offer three spots to minorities in what you would call a stipend in which they get donators to pay about 75 percent of your tuition and book costs, but you have to work for a law firm that is pre-selected by them."

"Really?" You're kidding, right?"

"No, I know at least two guys that used the program and are quite successful today as lawyers. Right here in Dallas."

"So how do I apply? And why didn't you use the program?"

"I never heard of it until I moved here. It's like a secret type thing that SMU does; you know, trying to give back but not wanting the public to know that they help minorities get law jobs. Kind of like a double-edged sword."

"You would think they would want the public to know that they are sensitive to minorities and the financial difficulties that they face."

"But this is a Republican state. For them, it's never good to help minorities."

"Well, that is true."

"I'll find out all that I can and then let you know what you need to do. You're trying to go by next fall, right?"

"Yeah."

"Okay, I'll let you know right away."

"So what type of law did you study? Criminal?" They both laughed.

"Actually, I'm in the what you would call entertainment/sports sector of law. I represent high profile athletes and entertainers."

"Really?" So doing my case was definitely a favor, huh?"

"Not really. Ken and I went to school together and we always felt, as African American men in this field, that we should always try to help our people out."

"Well, I'm sure glad you guys helped me. You get federal time for crimes like that."

"Well, you know, they say the federal system is like being on a vacation."

"It's not one I want to go on," Mackenzie said.

"I hear you."

By this time, they were on their way back to her apartment, listening to jazz. His car warmed up quickly and sent her back to that euphoric state of wanting to kick her shoes off. Julian drove slowly and Mackenzie enjoyed the company of a man.

By the time they pulled up to her pale blue and brick red garage apartment, Mackenzie was in her own world filled with power suits, a nice car, and a beautiful home. She was a top-rated attorney with a bon-a-fide A-list of clientele.

"We're here."

Mackenzie snapped out of her daydream and looked out of the window at her garage apartment. She let out a soft sigh.

"You okay? You seemed to be in your own little world. I didn't want to disturb you," Julian said jokingly.

"I'm fine, just a little tired."

"Thanks for having dinner with me. I hate eating alone."

Red light, she thought to herself. *"He must go out every other night with a different woman. I should have known that a good-looking, single man like him was probably a magnet for women."*

"Well, I'll get that information for you."

Mackenzie had already forgotten about law school, so busy daydreaming that she was a lawyer already.

"Sure. That would be great."

Julian helped her step out of the car, and then they walked over to her door.

"Good night, Julian. I appreciate all that you've done. I had a really nice time."

"Maybe we can do it again sometime or another?"

Mackenzie paused, and then responded, "Maybe, but you know I have school and all."

"Right. I'm sorry. I shouldn't be so forward. Well, you have a good night, Mackenzie."

"You too."

Mackenzie opened her door and then waved to Julian as he started his car to leave. Once inside, she forgot all about her evening with Julian and resorted back to her current way of living. No love, no lust, school and work only. Succeed she must.

Chapter Eighteen

The clock read 2:01 A.M. Her body was sweating profusely, and she was shaking all over. This was probably the sixth or seventh time she had had this dream in the last two weeks.

The first time she' had the dream she thought for sure that she was crazy. *"Why would I be dreaming about sex with Julian?"* Not only was it good sex, but it was slow and intense. It was like he was right there with her in her bed. And each time in her dream, they climaxed together. Then she would wake up and no one would be there. She even felt as though she could smell his scent- whatever it was.

Mackenzie couldn't understand it. After Demarcus and then Erasmus, she thought she was through with the sex thing, on both sides of the fence. Besides, it had probably been a month or so since she'd had dinner with Julian.

Even on her birthday, she'd celebrated alone by sleeping off her finals and the two days of back-to-back, double shifts at the emergency shelter. She was just coasting, waiting for her last semester of classes. She'd even convinced the dean of social work to allow her to use her work experience at the shelter as internship work, so nothing would prevent her from graduating in May. So, why was she dreaming about him?

Mackenzie used the remainder of the break to study for the LSAT and spent countless hours at the library's computer lounge going over the test questions.

When classes started, she was fortunate to find that her GI Bill would be on time this semester. And she would be receiving a little more than last semester. Mackenzie used what she needed, made sure her car was serviced, then stashed the rest for law school.

Her class load was only nine hours this semester and each class met on Tuesday and Thursdays. At least she could work more hours and save money for law school just in case she didn't get into that program.

The Super Bowl was coming up and Mackenzie promised Nick and Tiphane she would come to the Caribbean Bar and Grill to watch. They had big screens installed for the Super Bowl. Nick was so excited he told Mackenzie she had to be there.

Although she wasn't in a festive mood, she promised herself she would stay for an hour, then make up some excuse about school, so she could leave.

Green Bay and New England were playing, so she knew she could always use the excuse that, since neither Dallas, nor New York was playing, why even bother to watch.

Mackenzie wore the usual football attire a sweatshirt and jeans with tennis shoes and a baseball cap, pulling her ponytail through the back.

The Caribbean Bar and Grill was crowded and filled with cheerful fans shouting. Many of the fans, both black and white, sported cheese heads and were drinking beer as they shouted.

Nick and Tiphane were both working, so Mackenzie just found a seat at the bar where Nick was serving. She sat there and watched her good friend make drinks and jokes for his customers until there was a huge play, then he came over and gave her a hug over the counter.

"Did you see Tiph?"

"Yeah, somewhere around here buzzing through the crowd, Mackenzie said, as she motioned her hand in a zigzag.

"She said she needs to talk to you. Make sure you get her attention."

"Well, we waved when I came in. I'm sure she'll find me."

"Just make sure you see her before you do your little Brooklyn Dip and creep out."

"Ha, ha very funny."

"You know it's true."

Mackenzie half smiled and ordered a pineapple soda.

"Thanks, big head."

She moved through the tables and folks standing around and made her way to the outside patio. It was empty and cold but all the noise inside was driving her crazy. Mackenzie sat outside and thought about how far she had come after trying to end her life. She was so glad that her past was finally behind her. She had stopped having most of the flashbacks and nightmares about the clubs, drugs, and her past partners. Thank God she was finally free.

"Well, well, well, if it isn't Ms. Mackenzie."

Mackenzie turned around and saw Julian dressed in his Green Bay paraphernalia.

"Hi Julian. How are you?"

"Pretty good, and yourself?"

"Ready to graduate in four months."

"That's right. You'll be finishing up soon."

"Yes, thank God, and I can't wait."

Julian smiled and sat down beside her. "So what have you been up to besides school?"

"Studying," Mackenzie said calmly.

"Why did I even ask?"

They both laughed for a second or two, then Julian spoke. "You know, I've been wanting to call you. I just didn't know what excuse I would use."

Mackenzie repositioned herself out of awkwardness and replied, "Oh yeah?" She felt the nervousness creep into her stomach and hands, so she put down her pineapple soda and folded her arms up against her stomach.

"Yeah. I enjoyed talking with you and wanted to do it again. Or maybe take in a movie."

"Well, with school and all, I really don't have much time."

"I know you keep reminding me."

"Julian, the timing is just not right. There is so much I'm doing right now. I took the LSAT a week ago, and if my scores are good enough, I have to work twice as hard to save up this summer."

Julian looked disappointed and didn't say anything.

"Look, it's getting late. I have some stuff to do, so I guess I'll see you around." Mackenzie stood up and walked off, leaving her pineapple soda and Julian on the patio.

She was walking through the crowded bar and towards the exit when Tiphane stopped her. "Are you leaving already?"

"Hey Tiphane. Yeah, I'm tired. You know football really isn't my thing. Now basketball is another story." They both laughed.

"Listen," Tiphane said, "that guy called Ken and asked about you. So then Ken called me."

"What guy?"

Tiphane looked at Mackenzie like she was crazy. "The lawyer, girl. You know, green eyes, nicely built, dresses well."

"You mean Julian? You are still Nick's girlfriend, right?" Mackenzie asked, poking fun at Tiphane's obvious infatuation with Julian.

"Yeah, I just spoke with him on the patio. How's Ken doing?"

"Girl he's fine, living in Houston now, making extra long money."

"Oh, I'm sure."

"Yeah, he told me to tell you hi."

"Yeah, well tell him I said hey."

"Okay, well I'm glad you talked to Julian."

"You're so funny, Tiphane. I'll see you guys later. Tell Nick I said bye."

Mackenzie walked down Elm Street to her car parked on the street and drove home to the smooth sounds of the best of *Sade.* Julian was actually asking her out. He was good looking and had his profession together, but surely he couldn't be interested in her. Mackenzie wasn't looking for any casual sex. She had had enough to last a lifetime.

Mackenzie pulled up into her driveway, got out of the car, checked her mailbox, and went inside. Peeling off her baseball cap, sweatshirt, and jeans, she went into the bathroom to run some bath water. Tomorrow she would be working a double shift, so she needed her rest.

Her phone began to ring just as she was about to step into the bathtub. Her luck was not good tonight at all. First, she sees Julian, then Tiphane tells her that Ken is doing well in Houston, and now her bath was being interrupted.

"Hello," she said sharply.

"Mackenzie. Hi, this is Julian."

Ah, damn, she thought, *persistence is not a good thing.* "Hi Julian. What can I do for you?"

"Umm, well I uh, I don't want you to do anything. I just wanted to know if you wanted to workout with me next Saturday."

"Workout at the gym?"

"Yeah, there's a facility in my building, well actually on my floor, that we can use. Ken said you were in the military, so I figured you worked out still."

"I wouldn't say that. I may do some crunches every now and then to keep my stomach flat, but that's it."

Julian laughed. "Well, it's working."

There was a moment of silence, then Julian said, "So what do you say? You want to get your workout on with me or what?"

"You're so corny, Julian. Yeah, I can do that. Should I meet you there?"

"No, I'll come pick you up, say about nine, nine thirty?"

"Nine thirty would be fine."

"Okay. Well, I'll see you then. Have a good week."

"Thanks, you too."

Mackenzie hung up in disbelief, wondering what she'd gotten herself into. A workout date was all she needed these days. To see Julian in shorts or sportswear was probably going to drive her up the wall. But if she said yes, maybe he would leave her alone.

She soaked and meditated, and thanked God for peace in her life. Then she rubbed her feet and relaxed to no end, dozing off.

When she woke up, the water was freezing so she added more hot water, washed up, and went to bed.

When she woke up, she felt like a million bucks. She dressed quickly, ate a bagel with cream cheese, talked with Amos over the phone for a minute or two, then dashed off to the shelter for a double day's work.

Mackenzie drove down Central Expressway and made it to work without any major delays. Central was notorious for delays. When she arrived at the shelter, she started breakfast and made sure the overnight staff was passing out medication.

After the residents ate breakfast, Mackenzie drove them to the various schools that they attended in the area. Behavior was good, and there were no major incidents.

In fact, the entire day was great. All of the group sessions went well, phone calls were done, and by the time her shifts ended, she still had enough energy to go home and look over schoolwork.

Her entire week seemed to go in a peaceful manner. It wasn't until Friday that she started to get nervous about Saturday.

When she made it home Friday night, she pulled out a Nike outfit that she had bought at the mall while taking the residents to the movies.

Mackenzie had splurged that day because she'd even bought tennis shoes to match. After she tried the outfit on and modeled in front of the mirror a half a dozen times, she took her bath and fell asleep.

Mackenzie woke up around seven, took another bath, then did some stretches. She stretched out across her bed and dozed off until her phone rang.

"Hello?"

"Hey Mackenzie. It's Julian. I'll be there in about fifteen minutes. Are you ready?"

"Yeah, I'm ready. I'll see you when you get here." They hung up and she went into the bathroom to re-tie her hair and put on her deodorant and chapstick.

Julian arrived within fifteen minutes, knocking at her door. He was dressed in a black and red warm-up outfit with a black fitted shirt underneath. Her red, Nike Capri tights and fitted red shirt matched well with Julian's outfit.

When she looked outside, she didn't see Julian's Mercedes. "Where's your car?"

"Well, I thought we would ride back instead."

"Ride. Ride what?"

"My bike; it's right there."

She had looked right past his silver and black BMW motorcycle. It was clean and sparkled in the early morning sun that reflected off of the silver.

"Oh, I didn't even see that. What about a helmet for me?"

"I have an extra one underneath the seat. Come on, you ready?"

"Yeah, let me grab my keys, backpack, and a towel."

They drove down the back streets towards downtown until they stopped in front of a tall building on Main Street. Julian drove underneath to the parking garage and cut off his bike.

He helped her get off, and then took her helmet to put it away underneath the seat.

"Is this where you live?" she asked.

"Yep, this is my place. It's not quite a home yet though," Julian said, winking and smiling at her.

Chapter Nineteen

They took the elevator up to the tenth floor of a somewhat historic building with tall ceilings in the lobby, marble floors, and nicely designed art fixtures throughout. Once up in the tenth floor, Julian led her down the hallway to the gym.

The gym was absolutely wonderful, with state-of-the-art equipment, clean floors, steel that sparkled, and several pristine water fountains.

"So what do you want to do? Legs, arms, or a combination?"

"Let's do a combination. At least if I don't work out for a while, all of my muscles will have been used today," Mackenzie said with a smile.

"Well, let's stretch or you can do whatever you do before you work out, then we can do circuits."

Mackenzie stretched while Julian came out of his warm-up, flexing tight abs, arms, legs, and behind. She knew she should have said no to the workout; watching his body move was only going to intensify her dreams.

Ignoring her thoughts, she took off her sweatshirt after she stretched, then they worked out non-stop for about an hour and a half.

When they finished, Julian offered to let her freshen up at his apartment while he changed. She let him know that she'd brought a change of clothes, too, so if he didn't mind, she'd like to take a shower. Saying yes without any hesitation, Julian led Mackenzie out of the gym and past the elevators to a corner apartment.

Convenient, she thought. *That explains the nicely built body.*

Julian opened his door and Mackenzie had to hold back her amazement. His apartment could have been on an episode of *The Rich and Famous.*

Julian's apartment was flawless. He had a stainless steel kitchen, with marble slated counter tops that matched the floor. The living room had thick, plush, off-white carpet with a cream leather sectional accompanied by nice architectural tables with glass tops.

There were two rooms that seemed big enough to be a separate apartment one was his office space, and the other was his bedroom. He had a king-sized wooden bed that gave his room an authentic country feel. But then there was a huge, 72 inch TV and entertainment center, fully equipped. She could definitely tell that his law career was doing well for him.

Julian showed her to the shower in his office space, and then disappeared into his bedroom. His shower was hypnotic, relaxing, and transforming, taking her into another world. She took her time, shaving her legs and massaging her shoulders in this pleasure palace that helped her forget about school and everything else.

After the long, much-needed shower, she dressed, putting on some denim blue jeans, a blue turtleneck, and a pair of black boots. She was still ignoring the thought of Julian in his workout clothes and the way the sweat formed on his head.

Mackenzie sat in the living room and waited for Julian to finish his shower. When he emerged from his room, Julian also had on a pair of denim blue jeans and a denim shirt to match his brown, Cole Hahn boots.

"Do you want to grab something to eat?"

"Sure. After a workout I'm usually starving."

"Okay, let me grab my keys and jacket. Be right back."

She pulled out her black jacket from her backpack and waited on Julian.

When he returned, the living room quickly filled with the scent of masculine cologne, which aroused her pheromones.

"You can leave your stuff here. We'll just come back and get it before I take you home."

"Okay."

They grabbed the elevator and went downstairs to the dimly lit underground parking area. "Come on, we'll take the bike and just go somewhere that requires a little riding." Mackenzie raised her eyebrows and started putting on the helmet that Julian was handing her.

Once on, she held on tightly to Julian as he proceeded to take off through the parking lot, zipping through and around corners until they were on the street. They headed towards Deep Ellum and got on the freeway.

Julian drove the bike fast and controlled as they cruised the freeway for what seemed to be hours. Holding on to Julian seemed to make her feel a sense of security. For the first time in a long time, she just felt safe and happy.

When they finally stopped, they were in the middle of Austin. Mackenzie looked and saw the capitol building and several large office buildings and hotels. She smiled at Julian's sense of spontaneity.

She really didn't mind where they were, she just wanted to take off that helmet, which was starting to get on her nerves, and fill her desperately empty stomach. She'd eat anything right now.

Julian drove around for a couple of minutes before finding a parking lot with an attendant. They parked and Julian paid the attendant. Out of nowhere, he grabbed her hand.

"You ever been to Austin before?" Walking hand in hand, Mackenzie told Julian no. She'd figured that's where they were because she had seen the capitol coming in. Julian assured her that she would like it, and he told her about a down-home restaurant that had the best vegetables. Everything, he said, was grown out back, so it was fresh.

Julian flagged down a cab, which took them through Austin's neighborhood area, which was eclectic and hippy, to an old house that had walkup stairs and glass doors. Julian paid the driver, and they walked upstairs where the hostess led them to a back area that was cozy and filled with plants and bistro tables with fresh flowers on each one.

They took off their jackets and sat down. The place was warm, which helped Mackenzie's feet to thaw out. After the long ride here with wind slapping her around, she was pretty cold.

"You like it?"

"Yeah Julian, this is really nice. How'd you find this?"

"I met one of my clients here a few years back, and ever since, I try to get here at least once or twice a year."

The waiter came over and asked what they'd like to drink. Julian ordered an orange juice and she ordered hot lemon tea. "Are you cold?"

"Just a little, but I'll be fine after I drink some hot tea."

They sat and talked, drinking their tea and orange juice. Mackenzie asked Julian why he'd chosen law and not some other field, and he asked her the same thing. Their responses were identical they both felt as though there was not enough African-American representation in the field of law, and if they, as African Americans, understood the law, perhaps they could change why, as African Americans, they kept getting the short end of the law.

After a while, the waiter bought them menus, and they took their time reading them. Julian was right the restaurant offered a wide variety of fresh vegetables. Mackenzie ordered fresh broccoli, corn, and smothered baked chicken over white rice. Julian ordered fresh sweet potatoes, green beans, and fried chicken.

They ate and talked like two old friends, sharing childhood stories and discussing their fathers. Julian's father was white and a service man at the time he'd met his mother. He wanted her to marry him and go back into the service with him, when her parents told her that if she left they would disown her, she decided to stay, and his father left before Julian was born.

Mackenzie told him about her father and how she'd never forgiven him for leaving all five of them and their mom with nothing. As a result, her mama had turned to drinking, married a mad man, and died shortly after that. After fighting back tears and having to excuse herself from the table, Mackenzie returned and they shared an apple a la mode and had some coffee before they decided to leave. They walked hand in hand back to the parking lot, enjoying the nippy winter air.

"Are you ready to go back to Dallas?"

"No, I'm fine. We can do whatever you want."

"Cool, I have an idea. Come on." They got back on the bike and put on their helmets.

Julian moved through the Austin traffic and onto the freeway to the Mall. They parked, put up their helmets, and went into the mall. Julian bought himself some cologne that Mackenzie picked out, then she bought some perfume that he picked out. They also bought matching brown timberland boots that were on sale at Foot Locker and tried on leather pants that they both felt too shy to buy.

Mackenzie then bought herself a black dress the Gap had on sale that Julian liked, and he purchased a casual outfit that he saw at the Banana Republic. Although she enjoyed his company, Mackenzie knew she had to remain mindful of her expenses and the small budget that she was on.

They continued on their shopping spree, occasionally touching like a couple, walking closely together. They went to Neiman Marcus, where Julian bought a black suit that she liked and some shoes. Mackenzie tried on a few Donna Karan sweaters and dresses, and then talked herself out of spending money from her savings.

So Julian bought her a couple of outfits, new shoes, and some Cole Hahn low riding boots. Mackenzie felt spoiled by a man for the first time in her life, and it felt good.

With all of their shopping bags, they were faced with the dilemma of getting all of the stuff back to Dallas. Julian suggested that they rent a room at the courtyard Marriott and relax before they made any plans.

With some reservation and concern, Mackenzie agreed, tossing caution to the wind. She allowed him to rent a room for them.

Mackenzie was exhausted and Julian was, too, so they took a nap. Julian held her from behind and they fell asleep like time was on their side. Mackenzie drifted off to sleep, feeling comfortable. To her, he was the perfect gentleman with no expectations, only an extension of kindness.

When she woke up, the sun had gone down and the streetlights lit up the room. "Julian, are you awake?" Julian was sound asleep, so Mackenzie moved from underneath his arm and went into the bathroom to clean her face. She noticed a set of toiletries that Julian set out for her and brushed her teeth and proceeded to lie back down.

When she went back into the room, Julian was awake and motioned for her to come back to the bed. Mackenzie sat down beside him, feeling a little nervous and fidgeting with her hands. He sat up.

"Mackenzie, I need to ask you something."

Mackenzie was beginning to think of anything to say to avoid the conversation.

"What is it, Julian?"

"I've enjoyed you today. In fact, every time that I've been around you, I've had a great time."

"Thanks."

"No listen, let me finish. It's been a long time since I've been involved, and quite honestly, I haven't wanted to be in a relationship."

"Julian, you don't have to explain today or any day. Let's just enjoy being friends. I'm not asking for more."

"But I am. I want to be in your life and you in mine and not in a platonic way. I want you to be my girlfriend, my woman, someone significant. I know this may sound silly, but I'm serious."

"Julian, you know what I'm trying to do. I don't have time for a relationship. I just don't."

Julian sat up closer to her and pulled her face into his, kissing her passionately. She couldn't hold back the passion she was feeling and kissed him back. They kissed passionately as Julian untied her hair, pulling it down her back and playing in it.

"I want you, Mackenzie. Say yes. Tell me we can give it a try."

She kissed Julian again and kissed him on his ear, whispering a soft, "Yes."

He pulled her on top of him and gave her a big hug. They laughed, then started kissing again.

Mackenzie was wet and filled with the need to make love to Julian. Since Demarcus, she hadn't felt the need for a man to be inside of her, until now.

Julian rolled her over and intertwined his hands with hers. He looked at her and told her she'd made him feel happy and complete. He went on to say that he wanted to be with her as long as they could be.

As hard as it was, she told him that he made her happy as well, and that she needed a man like him in her life.

Mackenzie lifted up his shirt and undershirt and traced the hair on his chest, which was fine and slightly curly. They sat up and she straddled him. He took off her turtleneck and bra and outlined her breasts, giving them gentle strokes. She felt the rising of his nature and smiled at him.

They kissed again until they were overtaken with passion. Julian stopped, and she got up so they could undress. Julian went over to his jacket and pulled out a rubber.

When he walked back over, Mackenzie unbuttoned his pants and took them and his boxers off as he sat on the bed. She took his rubber and placed it on, as his penis stood erect.

He pulled her onto him and pulled off her jeans and panties, pulling her down on him as he slid inside comfortably. Mackenzie bit her bottom lip in ecstasy as they moved in a rhythmic motion, staring into each other's eyes as Julian held onto her hips.

Passionately moving and panting, she gripped Julian's face and kissed him as he continued to move with her. Unable to hold back any longer, they both cried out and climaxed together.

Both shaking, they smiled and kissed until Julian stopped throbbing enough to pull out.

The two sat and talked about her plans to finish school that semester and then attend law school. They discussed the possibility of her having to go out of state to law school if she didn't get into SMU.

After deciding to be supportive and work for the relationship either way it went, they made love a couple more times before falling asleep in each other's arms.

Mackenzie, sound asleep, dreamt of a horrible past and trying to hide it from Julian. Would he still look at her the same if he knew about Erasmus, the drugs, and what had happened with Demarcus? She hoped that he would never find out.

Chapter Twenty

After their time spent in Austin and a commitment for a relationship, Julian and Mackenzie became close and exclusive. When she received her test results followed by a letter of acceptance to SMU law school, Julian and Mackenzie celebrated by exchanging keys and spending spring break in Canyon, Oklahoma with his mom.

Julian and his mother resembled each other, and she was just as down-home as he was. The first night they were there, she baked chicken smothered in gravy, onions, and peppers with wild rice and green beans.

After dinner, she fed them homemade apple pie, Julian and Mackenzie's favorite, topped with ice cream. Then Mackenzie and Iris, his mother, watched movies and talked while Julian washed the dishes and cleaned up the kitchen.

His mother was a rare gem and made Mackenzie feel at home. She thought of her own mom and how she knew she would have loved Julian to pieces.

Mackenzie slept in Julian's old room while he slept on the couch. Occasionally, they would meet in the bathroom and steal kisses and touches.

That week, Mackenzie saw a new side of Julian. He was down-home outside of his attorney image. In fact, he even fished for the three of them and fried the fish, too. To Mackenzie, he was perfect, with no flaws that would drive her crazy.Once spring break was over, Mackenzie began to prepare for graduation. Once it arrived, Julian, Amos, Nick, Tiphane, Aunt Cecile, and the twins accompanied her there and sat in the audience while she accepted her Bachelors in Social Work with a 3.8 GPA.

They all went to dinner afterwards and laughed and talked for a couple of hours. Lena and Lannette were looking for eligible bachelors while everyone else ate and sipped lemonade.

When they made it back to Julian's place, he surprised Mackenzie with a two-week vacation in St. Croix. Mackenzie was shocked to say the least. No one had ever given her so much and or showed her things like this until Julian. They left the following morning.

Julian said that a client had given it to him for winning a high-profile case, and it was all-inclusive; all they needed to bring was their selves. Julian said just leave everything else up to him. Mackenzie was ecstatic, realizing that she had finally found someone to experience true love. She knew that telling Julian about her past could wait until they returned.

Mackenzie phoned her job and asked if she could take the rest of the month off. They agreed because things were actually slacking off. The government had cut some of the funding for the year, so it was actually good that they didn't have to pay her. *The joys of working non-profit,* Mackenzie thought.

Down in St. Croix, Julian and Mackenzie were in love. They woke up to the sounds of the ocean and took long walks on the beach each morning before breakfast. During the nights, they skinny-dipped a few times, made love on the beach, and counted the stars. Some nights they went dancing, grinding on the dance floor, then rushed home to make love in the middle of the living-room floor.

Mackenzie experienced orgasm after orgasm with Julian, and each time they made love, he made her feel special and appreciated.

"Let's go jet skiing," Julian asked a terrified Mackenzie, as they walked along the beach one afternoon.

"Oh honey. I am scared to death of water sports. I don't swim too well," she pleaded with Julian. "Since I was old enough to remember, I've had a reoccurring dream of drowning in the middle of the ocean."

"I'll protect you, sweetie. I promise you will be safe," Julian said, as he laughed at Mackenzie's nostalgic moment.

After Julian finally convinced Mackenzie that she would be safe, she agreed. After a few unsuccessful attempts, she managed to get a handle on the skis.

Afterwards, they rode scooters up along the roadside of St. Croix for the remainder of the day. The scenery was beautiful and romantic. As nighttime approached, they shared their first full moon and made love underneath it while the ocean roared in the background.

When they made it back to Dallas, they were both deeply tanned and relaxed. Mackenzie decided to let go of her job at the shelter and began preparing for law school after Julian told her he would make sure her bills were paid.

She was also notified that she would indeed receive the incentive of seventy-five percent tuition assistance if she did accept being a part of the program that placed new lawyers at a firm of the school's choice.

The other twenty-five percent, Julian said, he would help her with if she needed it. Mackenzie told him about her little savings, and he admired her planning.

When law school started, Julian took time to help her study and on many occasions, stayed up late into the night to prepare her for the many tests she took.

Their romance wasn't as intense due to her studying, but they did their best to share love when they could. When Mackenzie needed her space, Julian knew and understood. He also knew when she needed his company.

On his lunch breaks or in between court, Julian would bring her snacks or lunch that he would either sneak into the library or leave in the car until she could come down to eat.

When the first term was over, Mackenzie was third in her class. She and Julian celebrated her twenty-fifth birthday and the good news with some glasses of Kendall Jackson wine, feeding each other grapes before making love by his fireplace.

By the time her first year of law school was over, Mackenzie was number two in her class and madly in love with Julian. They never argued and seemed to sense each other's needs naturally. He knew mornings were hers, the time she used to meditate and prepare for her day.

Sundays, he liked to hang out with his boys to watch any type of sports that was on while she stayed in the library.

He would cook some Sundays before his boys came by or before he left to meet them, and the two would do their best to eat together around seven.

Each year, law school became tougher and tougher. Some days, Mackenzie just wanted to quit, but Julian always knew what to say and helped her when things were rough.

Mackenzie admired his calm disposition. She wanted to scream at the top of her lungs some days, and he would calmly put things into perspective about her teachers and why they did some of the things they did.

The competition was also wearing her out. No one there seemed friendly, just cold-hearted and trying to get to that number one spot. Her being number two drove her white, male competitors crazy.

She received so many hard stares and cold shoulders, it wasn't even funny. Mackenzie just kept to herself and tried to stay a step ahead just as Captain Lockley had told her so long ago.

By the start of her third year, Mackenzie was ranked number one in her class and envied by even the three other blacks that had managed to survive as long as she had.

Julian and Mackenzie celebrated via the phone because he had to go home. His mom was ill. "Give Iris a kiss for me, and I will keep her in my prayers. Tell her I will see her this Christmas."

Julian was there for two weeks before he called her in the middle of the night and told her, his mom had passed from complications of a bacterial infection, which had spread to her brain before doctors could catch it.

Mackenzie drove up that weekend for the funeral and did her best to hold Julian together. He was a wreck. He hadn't shaven, and his green eyes were rimmed by redness.

After the funeral and burial, Julian and Mackenzie went back to his mom's, where she entertained some of the neighborhood guests with his best friend and a few family members while Julian stayed in his mother's room alone.

Once everyone left, Mackenzie went in to find Julian lying in his mom's bed. Lying beside him, they held each other, cried, and fell asleep. When they awoke that morning, Mackenzie shaved Julian's face and washed him up in the shower, wiping away his tears. After their shower, Mackenzie ironed him an outfit she'd brought from home and made them breakfast.

Julian convinced Mackenzie that she should be headed back before it became too late, so she would be rested for class in the morning. But she told him she would stay with him and come back when he did. He convinced her that she was too far along to mess up her attendance now. He assured her that he would be home by Tuesday at the latest. He just wanted to tie up some legal matters and do something with his mother's things. Mackenzie finally agreed.

Mackenzie drove back home and talked to Julian on the cell phone he had bought her. He sounded a lot better and thanked her for being there, so willing to mess up her class rank for him.

Missing Julian, Mackenzie went by her apartment only to check her mail. She went to Julian's to sleep in his bed and hold his pajamas. He called to wake her up that morning to tell her that he loved her and that he had a surprise for her when he got back.

When Tuesday came, she was so excited she skipped her library session and hurried home to meet Julian. They met at her tiny apartment and made love as soon as she walked through the door. After they finished, Julian pulled out a ring box, popped it open, and asked her to be Mrs. Julian Taylor.

Mackenzie hugged him, crying and telling him "yes" over and over. At twenty-six about to be twenty-seven, someone actually wanted to marry her. Her past was over, and she was experiencing love like never before. Mackenzie knew with the engagement, she was going to have to tell Julian about her past.

He was everything she'd ever wanted in a man. He had no flaws; he was the perfect friend and lover, and surely he would understand her past and love Jay-Jay as much as he loved her. Julian said he'd wanted to wait until her birthday in two weeks but couldn't after seeing how, so soon, someone you loved could be gone so quickly.

"Mackenzie, will you consider moving in with me?" he asked.

"Are you sure?" Mackenzie replied. Law school was under control by now and she was actually studying her specialty, Civil Law, so it was interesting. But she didn't want to rush anything without telling Julian about her past.

"Baby, we're going to do this. Nothing's going to prevent us from getting married moving in will just speed up the process," Julian said, reaching out to hug Mackenzie, who realized that now was the time to tell Julian about her past.

But instead, she agreed to move in, putting off their conversation.

Mackenzie informed her landlord about her plans and broke her extended lease, moving in with Julian. Most of her things were there already, so the move was easy. The things she didn't plan to take, she donated to her old job and to the Salvation Army.

On Christmas, after exchanging their gifts, they spent the day with Aunt Cecile and the twins. Aunt Cecile was happy for Julian and Mackenzie. She thought the world of him. The two of them listened to old records while Mackenzie and the twins swapped beauty secrets and cracked-up laughing about their horror stories of the sorry guys they'd dated.

Later that evening, they went by Nick and Tiphane's to tell them the news and celebrated, playing charades in between glasses of Kendall Jackson and Nick drinking his Heinekens.

They finally made it home by midnight and fell asleep after making love in the shower, on the floor, and in the bed. Mackenzie held Julian as he cried, missing his mother for the first time on Christmas. That's where they usually spent Christmas.

With no class or work the next day, they slept in and then went to North Park Mall to get her watch resized. It was a sterling silver Mavado that Julian had bought her for Christmas. His gift, a tailored beige Armani suit, which lit up his eyes, fit him perfectly as he modeled it for her before jumping out of it to make love to her.

They walked through the mall up to Neiman's and went to the counter when Mackenzie saw this red head go up the escalator. Chills ran through her because she could have sworn it was Erasmus.

"You okay, hon?"

"Yeah, I must be catching a cold or something."

"Well, this shouldn't take long. We'll get you home and I'll give you some of my homemade medicine," Julian said, giving her his sex look.

When they made it home, Julian finalized their plans for the upcoming Millennium get-away in Austin, and they took extra precautions concerning Y2K.

Julian went to the store and stocked up on the necessary items such as water and canned foods. Mackenzie picked up their hygiene items and magazines for them to read just in case they were stuck inside for a long period of time.

Julian had the computer and laptops serviced the week before, so they were now ready to bring in the new Millennium. They decided to go to Austin by car and take a chance. They both said that if nothing happened, they would have missed the New Year out of fear and that wasn't of God.

In fact, at church the Sunday before, the Minister said that Christians ought not be afraid at this time; this was a time for sinners to be afraid because they didn't know God.

So for the New Year, they went down to Austin and brought in the New Year with no problems, just tons of love-making and eating at some of the finest restaurants in Austin, as well as their favorite down-home restaurant.

Chapter Twenty-one

ackenzie was winding down to her last semester of classes and beginning to prepare for her assignment. Julian assured her that he would go wherever the school sent her and just take the bar exam there so he could practice.

In the meantime, he helped her study for the bar exam, and she quizzed him on his bar exam in between making wedding plans. Mackenzie told Julian that she wanted a small ceremony in St. Croix, and since neither of them had parents that would be there, he agreed. They set their wedding for June 22nd.

"I want my sister Lauren to be my maid of honor," Mackenzie told him. And after recounting some of their childhood stories and sharing some laughs, he agreed.

"Walter will be my best man; we already talked about this."

"Really?" She laughed. Mackenzie liked Walter. She'd talked to him at the funeral, and when she went home to meet Julian's mother for the first time, he had been very friendly.

Mackenzie met with the law department two weeks before commencement, and they informed her that a law firm in Atlanta, McIntrye, Jones, Larue & Associates, wanted her. They were not a part of the program, but the school would approve them because it was a black firm that met many of the qualifications.

After graduation, she would need to report within three weeks. Mackenzie told Julian the news, and he was excited. Atlanta was a hot spot for black celebrities and athletes. In fact, Julian said he had plenty of connections there already, so this would be great.

They made plans to go for the weekend and look for a place. They decided not to purchase a house; they would rent a condo downtown so when her year was up, if they wanted to move, they could.

The Atlanta area was indeed busy, and there were black people everywhere. The airport was so crowded it took them at least an hour to get a rental car and make it out.

Julian had already spoken with a few agencies that helped find condos for rent, so all they had to do was select which one they liked after viewing them. After looking at as many as ten condos in the downtown and midtown area, they selected one on Peachtree in the middle of everything. It was on the top floor and had a pretty view of the Atlanta skyline. They put down a security deposit, and then checked in at the luxurious hotel down the street.

After showering and fooling around, they drove around downtown Atlanta, then parked in a lot with an attendant and walked to the underground mall. They looked through the many stores and vendors before walking to Sylvia's Restaurant for some southern cooking.

They both ordered fried chicken, greens, macaroni and cheese, and iced tea. After dinner, they had sweet potato pie and ice cream. It's a wonder they weren't as big as houses. But in between their splurges on southern favorites, they ate health foods and worked out together in more ways than one.

That night, they went to listen to a jazz set that was playing at an eclectic bar in Decatur that Julian had found in the weekend newspaper. Taking in a little music with the Atlanta southerners was quite relaxing to Julian and Mackenzie, sipping on their favorite wine and enjoying the soothing sounds in between kisses.

On Saturday, they drove to Stone Mountain and browsed around like two love struck teenagers. After that, they were both exhausted, so they headed back to the hotel room and took a nap.

"Mackenzie, do you want kids?" Julian asked, as they lounged around the hotel room upon waking up.

"We never talked about kids. I guess I never thought about it."

"Yeah, I never thought about it either until now. Should we start planning for some?"

Mackenzie thought about Jay-Jay and wanted so much to tell Julian, but she couldn't; the words wouldn't come out of her mouth.

"I'm okay with kids. I just wasn't sure if you wanted any since you never talked about them. And I got on the pill shortly after we started seeing each other. I figured we weren't planning on having any."

"I always wanted kids, but I wanted you to accomplish your dreams and not do something for me if you didn't want any."

"Well, I think we should wait on kids and enjoy married life for a while. Maybe do some traveling in between work."

"Really? I thought you would want to have kids right away the way you talk about the kids at the shelter, wishing that their lives could be better. It was like you had this motherly instinct already in place. Like you were a mother already."

"I do love children, and as for the teens at the shelter; I understood them because of how I grew up."

"Yeah, I guess that makes sense. Well baby, whenever you want to start, I'm ready." He smiled, stroking the side of her face.

Jay-Jay, Demarcus, and Erasmus were something that she needed to discuss with Julian, but she continued to put it off. She would wait to tell him until the time was right.

They stayed in on Saturday and gave each other back massages and other things, then fell asleep listening to Enya on their portable CD player something new Mackenzie had hipped Julian to.

They woke up and went to the gym on the top floor, worked out, took showers, and then packed to get back to Dallas. As usual, the airport was a headache, but they got their first class seats and played tic-tac-toe on napkins in between canoodling until they landed at DFW airport.

Mackenzie had less than a week to go before commencement, and she couldn't wait. Julian had to tie up many loose ends and cases before they left, so he was pretty busy for the most part.

Mackenzie had finals to take, but she wasn't worried. She was so interested in this stuff she could recite the laws backwards.

She was leaving school on a typical day when she decided to stop at Jason's Deli on Mockingbird by Central Expressway for take out lunch.

Mackenzie stepped into the to-go line and ordered a half spud with chopped beef and some lemonade. She waited patiently for her order, although her stomach was doing backflips because she was so hungry.

After she finally paid and proceeded to the exit, she was faced with her worst nightmare.

"Hey, Mackenzie."

Shaking and speechless, she stood there with the door still open. Mackenzie stepped outside of the deli, and cleared her throat.

"Hi Erasmus," she said, looking at her and Jay-Jay.

They stood there, just staring for a moment, until Mackenzie spoke. "How have you guys been?" she asked, not paying attention to the obvious state of their condition. It was like a scene from a movie and a definite reversal of fate. Erasmus was nothing like Mackenzie had known. She was much thinner, her hair was nasty and frizzy, and she needed a bath. Jay-Jay was also thin with filthy clothes and unmanageable hair.

"We've been trying to find you. Say hi to Mackenzie, Jay-Jay. Come on, say hi." Jay-Jay stared at Mackenzie but didn't say a word.

"Hello Jay-Jay," Mackenzie said, extending her arm to the tiny girl.

"She doesn't talk much, but when I ask her to she does."

"That's okay. You guys hungry?" Mackenzie asked, attempting to change the subject and hide her concern for Jay-Jay and Erasmus.

"Well, we could actually…"

Before Erasmus could finish her statement, Jay-Jay responded. "Yes."

"Come on. We don't stay too far from here." She grabbed Jay-Jay by the hand and the three walked to her Honda accord.

"I like your skirt," the little girl said, smiling at her mother.

"You do?" Well thank you, Jay-Jay."

"Yeah, you look real nice, Mackenzie. Real nice." Erasmus smiled and Mackenzie smiled back.

They drove quietly as Mackenzie trembled behind the wheel. The sweat was dripping from the center of her back and on her nose.

She was worried because sooner had come quicker than she'd wanted. It was time that she told Julian about Erasmus and Jay-Jay and everything else that she'd kept inside. She'd convinced herself long ago that he would understand. He was her friend and loved her. Why wouldn't he? In fact, she promised herself that she would tell him today.

Mackenzie drank some of her lemonade when she stopped at the light and wiped the sweat from her nose.

"Erasmus, so where have you guys been staying?"

"Well, right now we're in between places. We'll probably go back to my moms." Erasmus sounded a little sad. It was obvious that she was hoping for more than just dinner with Mackenzie.

They continued on quietly as Jay-Jay slept in the backseat while the wind whistled a soft tune. Mackenzie's mind drifted back to her past life, then thought of the life she now had. It was obvious that she was torn.

"We stay here. I'll just park on the street."

"Wow, this is nice. So whose we? You have a roommate?"

"Not exactly," she paused, then looked at Erasmus. She saw what she'd once loved and the familiarity in her eyes. "So much has changed, Erasmus. I don't even know where to start."

"I have time."

"Do you?" It's quite a bit."

She smiled at Mackenzie and replied, "I have time."

"Well, let's get Jay-Jay upstairs and lay her down, then let me start something for dinner."

"Okay." Erasmus picked up Jay-Jay as she slept peacefully on her shoulder and the three took the elevator up to Julian and Mackenzie's apartment.

They entered the apartment and Mackenzie led Erasmus to the guest bedroom.

"Jay-Jay can sleep here, and we can get started on dinner."

Mackenzie ignored the concern that loomed in her mind. She was happy that she was with her family again, and although things had ended on harsh terms, she was happy to see Erasmus.

"So, this is your home? This is something that belongs in a magazine. How do you afford this?"

"Very carefully," Mackenzie smiled, trying to downplay the extravagance.

"Do you think I can shower and change? I mean, that is if you have some clothes I can borrow? If it's not too much to ask."

"Of course. Come follow me." They walked into the bedroom and Mackenzie laid out fresh towels, underwear, toiletries, and a clean outfit.

"I can wash your things while you shower."

"I have my toothbrush and some toothpaste." She laughed. "I need everything else." They both laughed.

"Thanks Mackenzie. We really appreciate this. Let me check on Jay-Jay before I shower."

"Oh, I'll check on her. You go ahead and take care of yourself."

"Are you sure?"

"Yeah, go ahead. I'll be fine." Mackenzie said, because a part of her wanted to be close to Jay-Jay. She wanted to see her sleep and touch her tiny body, listening to the sounds of her breathing.

She left Erasmus to shower, started to reheat some lasagna that she and Julian had fixed together, placed Erasmus's clothes into the washing machine, then hurried to the guest-room to check on Jay-Jay. Her heart filled with excitement as she walked into the room and gazed at Jay-Jay sleeping.

The dirty clothes and frazzled hair was a mirror image of Mackenzie, Pat, and the struggles that they'd once faced the poverty, the substance abuse, and apparent signs of a broken home.

Mackenzie sat beside Jay-Jay, then outlined her tiny pink lips and began counting the freckles perfectly placed on her face. She was overwhelmed with joy at seeing Jay-Jay, and touching her, she wanted to forget her absence and irresponsibility for leaving her with Erasmus.

She picked up her daughter and held her in her arms, inhaling her scent and savoring motherhood. She placed her lips on the side of her faced and slowly kissed her as tears filled her eyes. Her body was warm and together their heart's beat as she held her beside the bed.

Mackenzie realized that her two worlds would have to collide and some how co-exist. Today, she was going to brace herself and finally come forth and tell Julian everything because telling him meant saving her daughter and giving her a life she deserved with her real mother.

She continued to hold Jay-Jay until Erasmus returned from her shower. "You okay?" she asked, as Mackenzie daydreamed about a better life for Jay-Jay.

Placing Jay-Jay back on the bed, she replied, "Yeah, I'm fine. How about you, do you feel better?"

"Yeah. Thanks so much. I really needed that," she said, in between coughs.

"Come on, let's allow her sleep." They walked into the kitchen as Erasmus towel dried her hair and observed the many photos of Julian and Mackenzie.

"A lot has changed," she said softly as she pulled her hair up in a bun.

"Yes it has, Erasmus." They sat at the kitchen table, both unsure of what to say to each other, until Mackenzie spoke first.

"So what happened?" she asked, searching her eyes for the truth.

"Where do I start? So much has happened I don't know where to begin."

"Why don't you try starting where we left off, when you left."

"Mackenzie, I'm not here to fight with you. I just wanted to bring Jay-Jay by so you could see her and maybe be with…"

"After all this time?" she said, shaking her head. "You guys should have never left."

"I know, but you and I both know what it was like then. We were both pretty messed up, someone had to leave, I guess."

"You guess? Things were pretty bad, but"

"I've been sober for almost a year. I know you can't tell now, but I have. It's just so hard to make a fresh start. But look at you," she said, smiling at Mackenzie, "you did it."

"What made you stop?" Mackenzie asked her.

"She did," Erasmus said, looking towards the room that Jay-Jay was sleeping in.

"What happened? Is she okay? She's not sick or anything is she?"

"Nope, she's pretty healthy, strong, too. But one day she made a real difference in my life."

"What was it?" Mackenzie asked with concern.

"I was doing my usual routine, you know, hanging out at the apartment with some friends. She had been sleeping all morning even with all the noise and music. I guess she woke up from a bad dream; she walked over to me with hair everywhere and crying. At first I didn't see her little self, but she pushed her way over to me and said, "Mommy, I'm tired.""

"Her face was so miserable and sad. Like she was so hurt. Of course, I was high as a kite, but in my heart, I knew how she felt. Hell, I was tired, too. She climbed on me and just curled up on my lap, hugged me hard, and fell sound asleep. That hurt my heart. I couldn't even get high anymore. But that didn't stop my "so-called" friends; they just kept getting high like she wasn't even there. And that was it; I just lost the taste for it. The so-called friends, the scene, everything.""

"Wow. That would have been hard for me, too. Believe it or not, I stopped the day after you left with that girl and Jay-Jay." Mackenzie grew silent for a moment.

"So Jay-Jay calls you mommy huh?"

"Yeah, I wouldn't let her call Nia that."

"Who's Nia?"

"That girl you referred to."

"The one you left with," Mackenzie said with a sarcastic grin. "You guys stayed together for a long time I see."

"Yep, until she just left one day, and I realized that I didn't care enough to go after her."

"That's pretty harsh," Mackenzie said, lifting her eyebrows.

"She wasn't who I wanted to be with. She never was," Erasmus said, looking deep into Mackenzie's eyes.

"Well, I'd better check on the lasagna and put your things in the dryer. Do you guys want some garlic bread?"

"No, we'll just have some lasagna."

Mackenzie stood, sashayed to the stove, and took the hot casserole pot of lasagna out. In a world of her own, she took out three plates, three cups, and grabbed some lemonade. When she turned to look at the table, now covered with food, cups, and plates, Erasmus stood there in her path.

"What's wrong, Erasmus?" she asked.

"I've missed you so much. We've both missed you."

Mackenzie closed her eyes, then looked back at Erasmus. "I've missed you guys, too."

"Can I give you a hug? I mean, I just feel like this is a dream or something."

"It's not a dream, Erasmus," Mackenzie said, as she reached out to hug her. They held each other in between sighs.

"I still love you. I've never loved anyone the way I loved you."

Mackenzie pulled back to look at Erasmus. "I guess a part of me still loves you, too," Mackenzie said, then realized the words and their impact.

Erasmus pulled Mackenzie close and they shared a warm kiss that reflected what they'd once been, when the phone rang.

"I better get that." Mackenzie let go of their embrace and answered the phone as she sat at the table, motioning for Erasmus to sit and join her.

"Hi Julian. Oh just heating up the lasagna." She smiled at the phone. "Yeah, school was fine today. I have a quiz tomorrow; will you have time to help me prepare?"

Erasmus knelt down in front of her, ignoring her phone conversation, and placed her hands on her legs, massaging them and looking into Mackenzie's eyes.

"Sure, sweetie, we can go on Sunday," she replied to Julian. "Okay, that would be fine…No, I'm fine, just about to eat a little dinner."

Erasmus, still on her knees before Mackenzie, pushed up her skirt and massaged her thighs, placing one of Mackenzie's legs on her shoulder. She let her hand go up her skirt to her panties and slowly took them off.

"You'll be home when?" Mackenzie asked, as though anticipating a rendezvous with Erasmus. "Okay, yeah, you can get some wine; I'll have a little before bed," she responded, looking back at Erasmus who was tracing her hair-line and her lips before parting them and placing her mouth there.

"Okay. Bye, honey, see you soon," she said, hanging up the phone before pulling Erasmus into her, enjoying a moment of ecstasy.

Within moments, she climaxed, arching her back and biting down on her lip. As guilt filled her entire body, she flashed back to church, the first time she'd met Julian, the first time they'd made love, and the day he'd proposed.

"That shouldn't have happened," she snapped, pulling down her skirt, reaching for her panties, and avoiding eye contact with Erasmus. "Move please," she said, with a hint of anger.

"You're right. I'm sorry. We should be focusing on Jay-Jay." Erasmus quickly moved out of her way, standing back to give her room.

"Oh my god, I hope she's still sleep," Mackenzie said, as she got up, fixed her clothes, and headed to Jay-Jay in the backroom. She tried to escape her own shame while Erasmus followed.

"She's still asleep. You think we should wake her so she can eat?"

"Whatever you want to do."

"Erasmus, you know her sleeping patterns; why can't you just give me a straight answer?" Mackenzie was angry with herself for allowing anything to occur between her and Erasmus. She needed a target to vent because she was on overload and filled with guilt.

"And why do you keep looking at me like that?"

"Like what? And if we don't calm down, we'll wake her."

Jay-Jay moved slightly, as they both watched hoping not to disturb her.

"Come here. We need to talk."

They walked back into the kitchen area, which in Mackenzie's mind was the scene of the crime. "No, let's go into the living room. I want you to see something."

Walking into the living room, which was filled with pictures, mementos, and furniture that Mackenzie and Julian had spent plenty of cozy nights on, she knew that it was time for her to make some decisions.

"Do you see all of this stuff? We have to forget what just happened."

"Mackenzie, I can quite well see that things are going well for you, and I'm happy for you."

"That's not what I mean. I'm talking about the pictures. I'm engaged. My life isn't the same, and I like it this way. I don't want to ruin it for any reason."

"I know things have changed, and I'm not going to fight you about this. That's not why I'm here. We need to make some decisions concerning Jay-Jay. Mackenzie, it's hard taking care of a child without stable income.

"Without sounding harsh, this is your child," Erasmus said, sending an earthquake through the apartment.

"I know this is my child, and I have no problems taking care of her, but she doesn't even know me. What am I supposed to do? Just expect her to love me? Erasmus, she's seven years old."

"She's eight, Mackenzie. And believe me, she knows that you are someone special. I talk about you all the time. She knows that you are no stranger."

"So just like that, you want to drop her off and leave her? That sounds familiar. You haven't changed one bit."

"Wait a minute, I thought this was something you wanted, but obviously it's an inconvenience for you to take care of your child. YOU are still the same: selfish." There was a moment of silence.

"I love that little girl as though I'd had her myself. I'm trying to do what's best for her. I have nothing, and I'm struggling. What am I supposed to do? I have to scrounge for food on a daily basis to feed us. Can you imagine what that feels like?"

Mackenzie was reminded again about her childhood, causing chills to crawl down her spine. "Erasmus, I know all too well about an impoverished childhood. So, give me a break."

"Okay, one thing is for certain here, we both want what's best for Jay-Jay. How we do this is what's going to be crucial. I have a situation here, which Julian knows nothing about. He knows absolutely nothing about you or Jay-Jay. I want to tell him on my own terms and in my own time. But in the meantime, we can find a place for you and Jay-Jay, and I'll take care of you until you get back on your feet. Then we can split the cost. I have some contacts on jobs. She's in school, right?"

"Not for the last month. We've been transient, but she's smart as a whip. I'm sure she can get back into the hang of school and such."

"Okay, well that's a priority we need to handle ASAP. But first, we need to find an apartment. We can check online after that, and then we can locate a school."

"Are you serious? I mean, you're going to put us up and do what? Make monthly visits and pay the bills?"

"That's not what I said. You're going to pay half once you get a job, and you *will* get a job. I'll be actively involved in her life, Erasmus. What's the problem?"

"This is just a convenience for you; what about me? Who says I want to do this? And why are you calling the shots, because you have the means? That's not fair."

"Erasmus, if the tables were turned I would do this for you. How am I going to tell him about you and Jay-Jay? He has no idea about my past."

"But you're going to marry him?"

"Erasmus, just let me handle this my way, please. Now let's get online so we can find you guys a place that's cozy and comfortable. Maybe we can get a one bedroom with a den that we can make into her room. Do you think that would work?"

"It's whatever you want to do, but what about the furniture? I told you, we have nothing."

"Just leave that to me. I have a little savings that I can dip into. It will be my gift to you both for lost time, and it will come with a lot of love." She smiled at Erasmus, hoping that she would agree to her idea and give her time to tell Julian.

"Well, we can definitely use all the help we can get. I have got to find a job to make this work though."

"Which reminds me, let me make a quick call." Mackenzie hurried to the phone while Erasmus went to get Jay-Jay.

Moments later, she returned to Erasmus and Jay-Jay in the spare room with news for Erasmus. "Okay, tomorrow do you think you can make an interview around lunchtime?"

"It depends. Can you keep Jay-Jay?" she said, as she played in her hair, attempting to wake her.

"Sure, she can tag along with me to class and you can drop us off, then pick us up when you're done."

"We need a place to stay tonight. Do you think you can help with that, too?"

"Of course, that will give us time to look online and get you ready for your interview and you guys can meet Julian. I have to ease him into this." She winked at Erasmus.

"So where is this interview?"

"It's my old job at a homeless shelter for teens. You're going to love it."

"Well, I have to get the job first."

"You already have the job, they just want to meet you and then let you fill out some paperwork. Come on, let's talk in the kitchen; she's probably still tired."

"I do have my license, birth certificate, and social security card on me," Erasmus responded, as she followed Mackenzie into the kitchen area.

"Okay. We'll see, you'll have a job and an apartment by tomorrow this time. You still have Jay-Jay's things, right?"

"Yep, it's with mine."

"Are you ready for her documents; I mean, do you want them? I can hold onto them if you want me to."

"Erasmus, I'm not scared to be her mother if that's what you think."

Erasmus sighed. "That's not what I mean. I just don't want you to think that I would ever try to replace you and whenever you want to make a transaction, I will understand."

"Well, she's not a piece of clothing that can be exchanged at a store or something, she's my daughter, and when the time is right, I will make sure that she is with me."

"That's what I mean. Your attitude about all of this, Mackenzie, it scares me, but if that's what you want, I understand," she said, shrugging her shoulders and then looking away.

"I'm doing what I can given the situation, Erasmus. I said I would pay half of the rent, take care of any financial concerns for her, what more did you want? That's what I can do right now."

"She's your child, you're her mother. It's not like it's some charity case. Nothing should stop you from being her mother."

"What's that supposed to mean? Are you trying to pick a fight with me?"

"No, Mackenzie, I just think you're not being realistic right now."

"So because I finally have myself together, you want to tell me how I need to decide what's best for me. What's that about? Now I'm the bad guy? You left and took her; I did what I had to do to survive all of that. I've been fighting just as hard as you to fix my life; you show up with Jay-Jay, and I'm supposed to drop everything?"

"She's your daughter why not?"

"Because it's not that simple. I told you, he doesn't even know."

"Know what?" Julian asked, as he walked into the kitchen without either of the two women noticing.

Chapter Twenty-two

"Oh hey, sweetie. I didn't hear you come in."

"Hello beautiful. How are you?"

"Just fine, especially now that you are here. I was wondering when you would get in."

"Yeah, we had a tough day at the office, but everything is okay now, just needed some extra attention that's all. You would have loved all the commotion, though it was pretty intense for a moment."

"Really. What happened?"

"Oh just one of the football clients getting caught up with some groupie who then tried to blackmail him. He wasn't coming clean with us about his part in their rendezvous, so when her lawyer dropped a bombshell on us, it seemed like we'd dropped the ball until he confessed to me privately about the whole situation. It was pretty bad. But we got them to settle without bringing the "details" to light."

"Wow, I can only imagine."

"Yeah, it was pretty bad for him. I felt bad for the guy and his situation, but I told him, dude you can't get involved with just anyone with your status. He agreed but went on to tell me she was a friend of a male friend. And that's what the problem was. He was gay and the girl was gay; she was only threatening him with going to the public about him and her because she knew that he was gay. And if he didn't make some financial agreement, she would continue with her lawsuit, claiming that he'd assaulted her."

"But couldn't it be proven with tests that he didn't assault her?"

"In the real world of law, but we received some interesting photos, and that pretty much put us up against the wall."

Mackenzie glanced back at Erasmus, attempting to hide any visible association to gay people. "Well honey, you have had a tough day. Are you hungry or did you eat at the office?"

"Baby, I'm starving. That case didn't leave much time for anything." Julian was so caught up in office jargon with Mackenzie that he'd forgotten about the conversation he'd walked in on.

"Sweetie, this is Erasmus."

"Hello. How are you?" Julian said, extending his hand.

"Hello sir. I'm doing fine, and you?" she replied, as she shook his hand.

"Pretty good now that the case is finished."

"I can imagine."

"So you go to law school with Mackenzie?"

"Oh no, not me."

"Sweetie, this is an old friend that caught up with me. We were just talking about what ideas I had about the ceremony."

"Oh, so what did you decide? Hawaii, or are you going to consider traditional, and pardon me dear for entertaining you with all the pitfalls of law. I thought you were a classmate."

"Oh, no problem. It was actually pretty interesting, sounded like something on television."

"It did. But unfortunately, we see a lot of this; usually the clients tell us up front." Julian laughed a bit and walked to the refrigerator.

"Really, I didn't know that?" Mackenzie said, sounding surprised.

"Yep, it's a pretty big thing in Dallas. With the type of clients that we have, I don't talk too much about it. Some of these guys are married, in top positions, or in the limelight all the time saying too much to anyone could cost the firm a lot of money.

"Attorney client confidentiality, right?"

"Exactly Erasmus. It could get real bad, real quick."

Mackenzie agreed with a nod. "Well, let me fix you a plate. Afterwards, I'm going to take Erasmus to run a few errands. But we'll be back. She's going to need our help through the night."

"Sure. What's up?"

"Just a little transitioning, but with a little help, they'll be fine."

"Anything in particular that I can do?"

"Oh no, sweetie, but if we do need you, you know I will let you know. Kiss kiss," she mouthed to Julian and went to wake Jay-Jay as Erasmus followed.

"So you're not going to tell him?" Erasmus asked, as they entered the room where Jay-Jay was sleeping.

"Erasmus, let it go."

"Jay-Jay sweetie, it's time to wake up. Come on, sweetie, we're going bye-bye." Mackenzie stroked the side of her face and kissed her until she stretched and opened her eyes, smiling.

"Hey there, little girl. You ready to go?" Erasmus said, smiling with Jay-Jay. "Come on, let's put your shoes on. We're going bye-bye."

"Are we coming back?" she said softly.

"Yes, you guys are coming back."

"Can I sleep with you, Mackenzie?"

"Well, maybe I can sleep in here with you."

"You can. Can we watch movies and eat popcorn?"

"Sure, we can watch it on the big television."

"Can we?" she asked Erasmus.

"Of course, but right now we have to go."

"Okay." Jay-Jay helped with her shoes and let Erasmus comb her hair, then politely asked if she could wash her face and hands. Mackenzie was proud to see that she was soft spoken, with manners, and a lady waiting to happen. Mackenzie wasn't sure if she looked more like her or Demarcus, but seeing her in action made her feel warm on the inside.

"Julian, we'll be back shortly."

"OK."

"Well, …who's the pretty young lady?"

"Jay-Jay," she said softly, smiling at Julian.

"Well Ms. Jay-Jay, you are adorable. If I had known we had such a special guest, I would have brought something special home."

Jay-Jay continued to smile at Julian. "What's your name?"

"Julian, but some of my friends call me Jay. Would you like to call me Jay?"

"Yes. Are you going to watch a movie with us?"

"Sure, what are we watching?"

Jay-Jay looked up at Mackenzie to see what she would suggest as she and Erasmus stood quietly, listening to Jay-Jay and Julian converse.

"Well sweetie, we can pick up some movies at the store if you like."

"Can we?" Jay-Jay asked.

"Sure. Now let's get going. Tell Julian goodbye."

"Goodbye Jay," she said with a smile.

"Goodbye Jay-Jay. See you in a little bit," he replied, tickled to death at the little lady.

The three of them left to pick up some things for Erasmus to wear for her interview and bought some videotapes for Jay-Jay. It was a crisp evening that the three of them shared, holding hands and shopping throughout North Park Mall.

It was a dream come true for Erasmus and the brink of destruction for Mackenzie. Her two worlds were on the verge of a serious collision that she wanted to ignore. Her heart was deeply moved by Jay-Jay and spending quality time with her. It was all that she could think of outside of her law education, but even that, for this moment, was second.

Chapter Twenty-three

Mackenzie waltzed in her fairytale world helping to relocate Erasmus and Jay-Jay. She also helped to enroll Jay-Jay in school, and furnished the two-bedroom apartment in far North Dallas right off of the toll-way.

During her free time, Mackenzie spent endless hours there helping Jay-Jay with homework, cooking with Erasmus, and studying when she could. Julian was caught up in another high priority case that kept him flying back and forth to Houston. They talked often, via cell phone, and continued making plans for their wedding, although this information was something Erasmus had to get used to.

It was a typical afternoon after Mackenzie's class. She and Erasmus had decided to meet for lunch before picking up Jay-Jay at school.

"So where shall we meet?" Mackenzie asked Erasmus, as they talked over the phone.

"Well, let's meet close to the school. It's around 12:15 now; I could be on my way in about ten minutes. I think there's a Subway over there."

"Okay. I look forward to seeing you. Will you have time to look over one of my case studies?"

"Yeah sure."

"Okay, sweetie, I'll see you soon…Love you, too, sweetie. Bye."

Mackenzie grabbed her notes, backpack, and some bottled water before hurrying to meet Erasmus. She jogged to her car and hopped in, driving to what would hurt her most. Julian had walked in on her conversation, hiding he'd overheard the terms of endearment that she'd used. His only question was who had been on the other line? He already had an idea. He'd come home early to discuss some information that was delivered to him at the office.

He had questions for his fiancée, and he wanted answers now. He followed close behind her, watching her talk on her cell phone. He knew she was talking to someone else because she hadn't answered his two calls. His temperature was rising, and he was running out of patience with Mackenzie.

He pulled into the Subway on Preston and Campbell and watched as Mackenzie hurried into the subway all smiles with her schoolwork and embraced Erasmus.

Julian's heart sank, and he was confused as he remembered quite clearly the phone conversation that he'd overheard, but what he saw he could not register. Even the contents in the envelope didn't register. Mackenzie had kissed Erasmus on the mouth after they'd hugged. And when they sat close beside each other like two high school sweethearts, he couldn't bear to see anymore.

He left the two of them and went home, trying to figure what he'd had just seen. Part of him wanted to know what was going on, while the other part of him wanted to throw all of her things out and never look back. But she had a piece of his heart, so he had to know why.

"What's going on?" Julian asked Mackenzie sternly as she returned from lunch.

"Hey sweetie."

"Don't call me that, and I asked you a question."

Julian's tone was different, one Mackenzie had never heard before. "Umm Julian, what's with the attitude? Is there something wrong?"

"Obviously you don't want to be with me anymore!" he said.

"What?" Mackenzie responded, as a perplexed look covered her face.

"You heard me. The wedding's off, so you can do whatever it is that you want to do."

"Excuse me. What are you talking about, Julian?" Mackenzie was beginning to feel a little nervous about Julian's tone. She knew that she hadn't left anything to be questioned concerning her and Erasmus; she had covered everything.

"I saw you this afternoon. I saw you and Erasmus. Do you think I'm stupid, Mackenzie?"

"You followed me?"

"Is that all you can say? You're not going to try to explain?"

"I thought you trusted me, Julian. I can't believe this."

"Mackenzie, don't put this on me. I saw you with Erasmus. I saw you kiss her on the mouth. Explain that to me because I'm having a hard time trying to understand this."

"Julian, she's a very good friend of mine; we've been doing that for years."

"Mackenzie, just stop. And we're not in Europe! Just stop lying to me. That was not a friendly kiss." Julian raised his voice, stressing his impatience with Mackenzie and her inability to come clean.

"First of all, they kiss on the cheek in Europe. And Erasmus and I have been friends for years. It's just something that we do!"

"Mackenzie you're not telling me the truth; I know what I saw!"

"I am telling you the truth."

"Are you?"

Mackenzie was frozen with fear. It was now time to tell Julian, the man she was to marry, everything, but she just couldn't do it.

"I'm telling you the truth."

Julian walked out of the kitchen area and returned quickly with a large envelope. He placed it on the table in front of Mackenzie. "Open it," he demanded.

"What is this?"

"Open the envelope, Mackenzie."

Mackenzie struggled a little with the large envelope, then opened it and retrieved the many items inside. Photos, a phone bill, and copies of a lease agreement that Mackenzie had co-signed for Erasmus filled her two hands. Mackenzie's flesh began to crawl.

"I want you out of here, now."

"Julian wait, let me explain. Please."

Julian turned and walked away as Mackenzie quickly followed, attempting to plead her case.

"Julian. Julian. You have to listen to me. That's the past. It doesn't mean anything to me absolutely anything. It's Jay-Jay."

"Look here, you damn lesbian, I said I want you out of here now."

His words pierced Mackenzie like thick swords, tearing at her and all that she'd worked so hard to overcome. She pulled back and looked at Julian, but she wasn't about to lose the only man she'd ever loved. She lowered her voice to speak calmly.

"Julian, I know I should have told you. That was a very long time ago. I am free from that. I promise you. She's just been having hard times. I couldn't let them suffer any longer."

"It looked like more than helping someone that was in a bind, Mackenzie. You two were lovers."

"No Julian, that's not what it was. She needed help. She found me so I could help them. That's all it was."

"Mackenzie"

"Julian, I'm talking about right now. She needed help; I helped her."

"But she was your lover. Right?"

"Yes she was, but that was a very long time ago. Demarcus and I broke up. I was going through a lot of things at the time, and she was there for me. Jay-Jay"

"You've said enough. I just want you to leave. I've never been so humiliated. You weren't even going to tell me. I received an anonymous call. Can you believe that? Someone called me and told me that they had some interesting information about my soon to be wife. I thought it was a prank until they delivered these photos to me. Just go, Mackenzie."

She grabbed Julian and tried to make him look at her, but he pulled away. She kept trying to hold onto to him, but he pushed her away harder and harder. She grabbed at him again, and he shoved her to the floor.

"You're sick, you fucking lesbian. I DON'T EVER WANT TO SEE YOU AGAIN!"

Still fighting for the only man she'd ever loved; she grabbed him by the heels of his pants. He kicked at her and wiggled free. Walking out, he slammed the door.

She lay there screaming and crying until no more sounds would come out. When she found enough energy to get up, she remembered Erasmus and Jay-Jay and wondered what she would do next.

Mackenzie cleaned up the mess that now filled their kitchen and called her old friend Amos. She told him what had happened, and he offered to let her stay with him until she left for Atlanta in a week or so.

She packed up her stuff, wiped the tears that poured from her eyes, and promised herself she wouldn't crack under pressure. God had brought her too far to desert her now. She knew that more than anything right now. Her past was over with, and without it, she wouldn't be where she was today. She was a survivor and an inspiration to many others that would face similar issues. She had to be strong because this was just the beginning process to getting Jay-Jay back.

She phoned Erasmus to tell her what had happened, but there was no answer. She made plans to swing by and see what she needed to do to take Jay-Jay with her. She was ready now to take full responsibility.

Mackenzie also knew she had her finals and bar exam in Atlanta to take, so she had to stay focused. She knew she could handle it because it had happened, and if she couldn't handle it, God wouldn't have allowed it.

Loading her stuff into her Honda and Amos's truck they headed over to Erasmus's apartment. When she arrived, things just seemed to get worse. There were police officers surrounding the apartment with yellow tape blocking the stairwell.

"What's going on?" she asked, alarmed.

"And you are, ma'am?" the oversized police officer asked.

"Mackenzie Kennedy. I'm looking for Erasmus Palonski."

"This apartment rented to you, Ms. Kennedy?"

"Yes, but my friend and a young child, Jasmine, lives here. I was helping them out."

"Do you know where we can locate her next of kin?"

"Can you please tell me what's happening, and where's Jasmine?"

"Jasmine is in child protective services. Ms. Palonski is in custody right now, that's all I can tell you, ma'am."

"I don't understand," Mackenzie said, bewildered.

"That's all I can tell you."

Mackenzie turned to walk away in disbelief, wondering how she was going to get to Jay-Jay.

"Ma'am, you may want to let her next of kin know that's she in custody down at Lew Sterret."

Mackenzie nodded and walked back to her car, motioning to Amos to head out. She followed Amos to the south side of Dallas where Amos stayed.

Not only was she forced to leave behind the platinum, diamond-filled engagement ring and the cell phone Julian had bought her but today, she had to leave behind Jay-Jay and Erasmus too.

Back at Amos's they unloaded her things and made several trips up and down the stairs of his three-story apartment building, dodging blunt smoking neighbors and women braiding hair while sipping on beer.

Chapter Twenty-four

After the most hurtful moment in her life, Mackenzie went on to finish up law school. She passed her finals and prepared to take the Georgia State bar instead of the Texas State bar. She figured since she was leaving Texas and probably never coming back there was no need to put herself through it.

Erasmus's family had taken on full responsibility to clear her name and get the 1st degree murder charges against her dropped. After all, Erasmus had an alibi at the time the murder had taken place; she'd been either working at her new job, or having lunch with Mackenzie. The Palonski's had vowed to fight Mackenzie for custody of Jay-Jay, which Erasmus supported. It was the only appreciation she could show them for their help in clearing her name. Mackenzie decided to leave Texas quietly.

Mackenzie knew her decision wasn't the best, but given her background, she felt it was her only solution. She thought about her own childhood and losing Pat at an early age, and the anger that she'd experienced. She didn't want Jay-Jay to lose Erasmus if that was the only mother she'd known. She prayed that one day Erasmus would bring Jay-Jay back for good once everything cleared up. She could only wait.

She contacted her employers in Atlanta and got all of the pertinent information she needed to get her things there and a flight out.

She didn't go to her much-anticipated commencement ceremony. She said her goodbyes to everyone over the telephone and promised she would call as soon as she was situated.

She told Nick and Tiphane that the engagement was off.

"Why," they asked, confused. "I thought it was all good with you two?" Nick said, then apologized for things not working out. Mackenzie assured them both that it wasn't their fault, just her fate.

"It's a long story, but it's for the best," she told them she would tell them everything some other time. She just wasn't in the mood to hear anyone's comments right now. It was time to put Mackenzie first, not love, or anything for that matter, and as hard as it was, she had to let go of the idea of getting Jay-Jay back now too.

Upon arriving in Atlanta, her firm sent a car for her and put her up in a hotel when she told them her living arrangements had fallen through.

They helped her find a loft in the midtown area not too far from where Julian and she had been planning to move. She took it because she wasn't about to let him win and make her go back into some shell with no confidence. She was where she wanted to be; a Civil Law Attorney in a new town and ready to kick ass in the courtroom.

Mackenzie traded in her Honda and purchased a new 2000 Z3 BMW black convertible with black leather seats and a beige top, loaded with all the toys. She'd been waiting for the moment that she could let go of that Honda and buy another car. For a moment, she thought about her struggles of finally getting here. She smiled at the taste of victory and took her new car for a drive around the city.

Her loft was fairly reasonable. In fact, her firm said they would foot the bill for her first year. If she decided to stay with the firm after that, she would then have to pay her own rent.

It was a cute loft with a 17ft ceiling, set in an old gymnasium, with hard wood floors, new appliances, a built in microwave, and walls painted in bright yellow. It was contemporary and a dream come true to Mackenzie. It was spacious with tall windows that had a view of the city lights of downtown Atlanta.

That weekend, she drove her BMW around town and purchased her very first set of art deco, baby blue leather chairs and sofa with stainless steel tables that came with the set. She also bought a oak sleigh bedroom set, a funky shaped stainless steel dining set that had a glass top, and a top-notch desk and computer.

Her firm said they would introduce her to the other employees on Monday and to come ready. She found the Phibbs Plaza on Lenox Road and went on a shopping spree for her new job. She had always taken good care of her credit and as a result, she had quite a bit on all four of her credit cards.

She bought plenty of power suits, shoes to match, and a couple of bags. When she made it to the firm, McIntyre, Jones, Larue, and Associates, located in the heart of Atlanta, she was sharp.

She met the partners, who were all handsome African-American men in their early forties. Each was from a different place. Dervin McIntyre was from New York, Adam Jones was from Chicago, and Manuel Larue was from New Orleans. They'd started the firm in the early nineties when the big pilgrimage of African Americans headed there to provide service to minorities that had civil claims. They fought racism, discrimination, and other civil liberties.

The five other associates were Ernie Neal, Ananda Blake, Darious Smith, James Hopkins, and Tiffany Wellington. Then there was her personal secretary, a Jewish woman with a Northeastern accent that sounded like every word was coming from her nose.

Her office was adjacent to Ernie's and down the hall in front of Ananda's. Ernie and Mackenzie would be working together for the most part and collaborating when they needed too.

All of the associates were broken up into pairs and overseen by one of the partners. Ernie and Mackenzie were supervised by Mr. McIntyre and were responsible for the many discrimination cases.

Ernie, also from New York, got along well with Mackenzie. He hipped her to the nice places to shop and eat and helped her become acclimated to Georgia laws.

It was obvious that he was gay because of the way he sashayed through the office when he became too comfortable. No one ever said anything; it was just understood.

The rest of the associates were pretty nice, except Ananda. She was a light-skinned, green-eyed, pretty-hair sister who acted like she was "the baddest bitch." She dressed wonderfully, Mackenzie thought, but it was obvious she couldn't stand her. She always stared at her from her office or when she was walking by. Mackenzie felt it only meant one of two things: Ananda was either jealous or gay-two things she didn't want or need right now.

That year, Mackenzie had to prove herself and bust her ass as an attorney. Ernie and she were a successful team and won plenty of civil cases and settlements. And each win called for a mini-celebration at Ernie's home in Grant Park filled with lots of laughter and good food.

Ernie enjoyed the company because it kept him from running the streets of Atlanta when he wasn't working. Mackenzie knew he enjoyed the nightlife from time to time because he'd called her for a ride home a few times when he was too wasted to drive. The Georgia police loved arresting young black males, and with his prestige as a lawyer, he didn't need that.

For their company Christmas party, which was held at a downtown hotel, Ernie and Mackenzie went as a date and danced the night away, laughing and enjoying themselves.

Everyone was there with a date including the partners, who had beautiful wives. Right before Ernie and Mackenzie decided to leave, she went to the restroom. As she was standing at the mirror re-applying her lip liner and gloss, Ananda walked in.

"Hey Mackenzie."

"Hey girl, how are you?" Mackenzie responded, trying not to sound fake because Ananda never spoke to Mackenzie around the office.

"I'm doing fine, now."

"I beg your pardon?"

"Do you want to go somewhere for drinks after this or catch a nightcap?" Ananda asked with a sheepish grin on her face.

Mackenzie shook her head and frowned. "I'm sorry, but I'm not into women at all. If you'll excuse me, I need to get back to Ernie." Mackenzie, with a sense of embarrassment, walked out.

Briefly, she thought about Ananda, who was so pretty and surely had men throwing themselves at her. To Mackenzie, she was another reminder of the many beautiful women that Mackenzie had often been involved with, but this time she wasn't interested. Walking calmly to her car, she smiled to herself because she was finally free.

When Mackenzie made it to work that Monday, after working out in the company's workout area, she was shocked when she received a dirty look and a slammed office door from Ananda as she passed by her office. Luckily, no one said anything. She decided that that woman really had some issues, and as far as she was concerned, none of them concerned her.

Ernie and Mackenzie finished up a case, and she took off the next four days for her twenty-eighth birthday. She was planning on going to a spa on Miami Beach to get pampered.

Mackenzie flew instead of driving because she was desperate to relax and unwind. Her workload, even with Ernie there to help, was tough. She rented a Volvo S80 from Hertz at the airport, drove to South Beach, checked into the Eden Roc Resort, and enjoyed the next five days filled with facials, massages, and intense workouts.

Going back to work was difficult after her time in South Beach. Nevertheless, she went back. The mood was icy, to say the least. Mackenzie went into Ernie's office and asked him what was wrong. When he wrote on a pad, "We will talk later. I will meet you at your house at seven," she knew something was up.

Following his lead, she started talking about an upcoming case and then left. When Ernie made it to her house that night, what he said shocked her.

"Mackenzie, we work for a gay firm in one of the gayest cities in the world. What you did to Ananda was not very good, as far as the partners are concerned," Ernie said, sounding more and more, like a woman as he spoke.

The firm that she'd been recruited to work for was a gay firm with gay employers, as well as employees. That is the only reason they'd recruited her. Mackenzie couldn't believe it.

"They checked into your past and believed that you'd fit into the firm."

Which she didn't understand, because for the last three years, she had been with Julian. He asked her if she knew someone by the name of Richard Lockley. When she said no, Ernie said he'd pretty much confirmed her as a choice for the firm through some contact at her old school. Then she remembered Captain Lockley, and everything started making sense.

More than likely, he was gay, too, because she couldn't remember ever having seen any women around, just an occasional male friend that Captain Lockely said he went fishing with from time to time. But now that she thought about it, the two seemed to communicate secretly whenever she was around.

The partners were questioning their decision to hire her since she'd turned down Ananda's proposition. She explained to Ernie that she was not gay, and furthermore, she was insulted that they hadn't recruited her because she was good enough to be there.

Ernie and Mackenzie sat up most of the night discussing the firm and the facts lying behind the name McIntyre, Jones & Larue.

Ernie even told Mackenzie that he and McIntyre were a secret item because Larue and McIntyre lived together. When she asked about the Christmas party, Ernie said that was something the company did in order to keep down the scandals. Mackenzie was floored. It was obvious that she would have to quit because she didn't fit their profile, at least not anymore.

Mackenzie told Ernie about her past and Julian, and they both figured they'd probably made their decision based on her life before she'd met Julian. What she didn't understand was how Capt. Lockley had known. It had happened *after* she'd left the army.

Mackenzie didn't mind fighting for the rights of gay people; she just wanted it to be clear that she wasn't gay anymore. How would she ever explain this to Aunt Cecile if she found out why they'd hired her? What about her family in New York so many people lived in New York from Atlanta. How could she hide?

"Just keep quiet and keep collecting a paycheck for the next six months, then bounce. Don't throw away the money for any reason, girl," Ernie said, as he tilted his head to the side.

He was right. It would make no sense to blow a six-figure income when she knew the truth. Ernie suggested that Mackenzie start being a little more gay friendly though and accompany him out on occasion or show up from time to time at a lesbian bar. So, she agreed and kept her mouth shut. In a year's time, she would have saved up quite a maybe enough to go into private practice.

Surprisingly, the tension eased up when Mackenzie returned to work the next day. Mackenzie figured Ernie must have given the all-clear signal. Mackenzie just shook her head.

Ernie and Mackenzie went out on every other Friday to either *Bulls* or *Tier II*. On occasion, they would catch a drag show at *Jake's* on Sunday's. Mackenzie remembered the days of the past. The many faces that she saw there, were sad reminders. The kids seemed younger and younger, and the substance abuse was written on so many of their faces. Mackenzie was glad that drama was over for her.

On one Saturday in February, on a cold winter's night, Ernie convinced her to go to *Tier II because* he was supposed to meet a guy there he'd met online who was in town to visit a female gay friend. After much coercing and a promise to bake her some of his turkey lasagna, Mackenzie agreed.

She put on her dress down, Armani jeans, a black Armani sleeveless tank, and some boots. She put on her black leather jacket. Ernie wore thug denim and she cracked up laughing because she'd never seen him in anything quite like it.

The club was packed with smoke and tons of lesbians standing around playing pool, talking, dancing, and drinking. Mackenzie told Ernie that they were only staying for an hour, and if he liked the guy and felt safe, she was going to leave him there.

Ernie met up with his online friend and they hit it off. Ernie gave Mackenzie the "You can leave" signal, and she said her goodbyes. Just as she was walking out, she bumped into Ananda and a group of her friends. They looked like they were fashion models with just the right amount of makeup and clothing, with everything perfectly in place.

"Guess I just wasn't your type, huh?" Ananda said with a sarcastic grin.

"Yeah, right," Mackenzie said, and walked to her car.

On the way home, driving up Ralph Mac-Gill road, Mackenzie kept going over in her head the talk she'd had with Ernie. She was in something she didn't need to be in, and if she had any faith, she was going to have to walk away. She decided she was going to call for a meeting with the partners on Monday and tell them she was resigning. She knew they would all be in the office because, on Mondays, they met and discussed the latest cases that the firm was working on.

She could stay for the next two weeks or leave now. She had saved up enough money, paid off what she'd spent on her credit cards, and really believed that she had to step out on faith. It was up to them either way she was leaving.

She didn't tell Ernie her plan for fear of the partners hearing it from him first. It was obvious that this was a *family* firm.

Monday morning, she skipped her workout and put on a killer two-piece, single-breasted skirt suit with a cream blouse and some black gator pumps. She grabbed her matching gator brief case and went into Mr. McIntyre's office, telling him she needed to meet with the three of them immediately. He then said he would speak with the other partners and get back to her. Mackenzie was nervous, but she knew she had to do it. She wouldn't keep her mouth shut again. It was time to tell the truth.

At about ten that morning, after pacing back and forth in her office, they called her into the conference room filled with eccentric African art and sat around a huge oval table that had glasses of water for all that were apart of the meeting.

"Ms. Kennedy, you requested a meeting, correct?" Mr. Larue asked.

Mackenzie sat up straight and responded, "Yes, I did, sir."

"What can we do for you, Ms. Kennedy?"

"Well, I need to clear something up. First of all, I would like to resign from your firm on the grounds that I was misled. I am not gay, and although I do not mind advocating for them or fighting for their civil liberties, I don't want to work for a firm that hired me because they think I'm gay. I want to work for a firm that believed I could win cases. Now, I've busted my behind here because it was the right thing to do in each incident and that's the only reason why. So, I would appreciate it if you would accept my resignation, effective immediately.

"And before you try to talk to me about contracts and cases, I want you to know that I have no problem going to the media with this story."

"Well, Ms. Kennedy, before you start making threats, perhaps you might want to take a look at yourself and your association with this firm. You knew what we were about after the Christmas party, yet you stayed and went out to lesbian clubs, socializing, dancing, and playing pool. Need I say more?" Mr. McIntyre said sternly.

"Sir, with all do respect, I'm not looking for any trouble."

"Neither are we. We do a lot for this community, and the last thing that we need is some "confused" lesbian to trash our image."

Mackenzie blew out hard, realizing this wasn't going to be as easy as she'd thought.

"If you trash us, I can assure you, you will never practice law again."

"I would just like to resign, sir, and move on. I'm not trying to ruin anyone. I just want to move on," Mackenzie said, hoping that the partners would show some sympathy.

The partners all sat there for a moment, then Mr. McIntyre told her that they would speak to her after lunch. Mackenzie excused herself, went back to her office, and declined lunch with Ernie. She just wanted to be alone and figure out her next move. She had been set-up to fail. All she could do was pray that God would see her through yet again.

"If I have to leave today, I will just clean out my desk and office, pack it up, and call it a day. If they make me stay for two weeks, I'll just do the exact same thing. And if they won't accept my resignation,

I'll just walk out," she said to herself, reaffirming that either way, she was leaving.

Mackenzie only had a little over four months left before her contract there was up, and she could wait it out. But she had come too far to lie about that. It just wasn't worth it. Being delivered meant she had to stand up and tell the truth. She couldn't be afraid to tell whom she loved, even if he was gone.

Mackenzie sat back in her chair and waited for them to call her back. Staring at an old picture of her parents, tears rolled down her face. She thought back to Pat and their rundown apartment, and she thought about how things used to be before Jun had left them. She thought about her long journey and how happy she was with her accomplishments. She had made it being a part of this firm was only a portion of what she had accomplished. She knew there was more to come.

Her phone rang, interrupting her thoughts. It was Mr. McIntyre who asked that she come back to the conference room.

Mackenzie straightened up her clothes, gargled some mouthwash, wiped her face, and went back to the conference room. The partners all stood as she entered, then sat back down after as she took her seat.

Mr. McIntyre said, "We understand your position, and we don't want to lose you as an attorney. However, if it's something you just couldn't do, we will grant your resignation in one month so that you can finish up the cases or settlements that you are working on. In addition, the firm is willing to pay the remainder of your contract as well as six months severance pay."

Mackenzie couldn't believe the news. She thought for sure that she would have to fight them or go to court for this. "Well, thank you for understanding."

Mackenzie agreed to all the terms, and they ended their meeting with handshakes and half smiles.

Part IV:
Reunions

Chapter Twenty-five

Mackenzie did as the partners asked and worked for the next month. She still didn't tell Ernie what she'd told the partners. She just told him she was quitting in a month because she felt burned out. The partners knew Ernie was a talker because they didn't tell him either.

They cut down on going out, and she worked endlessly to finish up things before she left. Some nights, she didn't even sleep. When the month was up, she received her severance money and her last paycheck and went on her merry way.

Since her loft was paid for one year, they let her stay but told her that she would be responsible for rent after her year was up. Mackenzie never understood why they were being so nice to her and why they offered to continue to pay her. More than likely, she guessed they feared the negative publicity that would come to the all-black firm if people knew about their hiring practices and charades. Mackenzie considered it a blessing from God and decided to move on.

She cut down on her spending and became economical because she had no idea when she would find work again or whether she was staying in Atlanta. She did sign up for a six-month membership to CR

Fitness so she could stay toned and in shape. She worked out daily, ran through Piedmont Park or Grant Park, and ran in 5K's whenever there was one close enough to her loft. Working out began to provide an outlet for her since she wasn't working and more importantly, it prevented her from thinking of Julian as much.

By May, she was bored out of her mind because Atlanta just wasn't appealing to her. She didn't want to date anyone and many of the women acted like you had to belong to this sorority or this organization to be accepted, and since she wasn't jumping through hoops to be in any clicks, she became a loner.

Mackenzie decided against any vacation time besides the media kept talking about an impending recession that was going to take place at any time. She was holding on to her money just in case.

Finally, she decided to call Nick and Tiphane to let them know she was okay. And after a few cuss words and name calling, Nick told her he and Tiphane were finally getting married.

"Yeah, we've been trying to find you but you know how you like to disappear. You have to stop doing this, Mackenzie. We worry," Nick said, sounding more and more like her older brother.

"I know. It's been a little tough for me, but I promise I will do better. I'll be there for the wedding."

"Be there? Baby Sis, you're in it. Tiph didn't tell you?"

"Uh no, she was so happy to hear from me and to say you guys were finally getting married. I'm afraid she left that part out," Mackenzie stated, sounding a bit sarcastic as usual.

"Yep, we want you be a brides-maid."

"Do I have a choice?" Mackenzie asked, as the two laughed.

"Nope. Give us your shoe size, dress size, and show up."

They laughed again, and Mackenzie told Nick she was sorry and blamed it on her workload. She promised she would be there come hell or high water. So they emailed each other back in forth with details and pictures of the dress and shoes. She made plans to be in a wedding in a month and a half. It was close to her and Julian's would-be 1st anniversary.

It felt so good talking with Nick, Mackenzie decided she would call her other friend Sam back in New York. When she reached his grandmother, they talked for a while, and she told her that Sam had moved out and was getting married in July. Mackenzie gave her the new number to give Sam, and they said their goodbyes.

Everyone was getting married. *It must be nice,* Mackenzie thought. She thought about Julian and how horribly he'd treated her when he'd found out about her past. Surely their love was much stronger than her past, sin? At least, to her it was.

Nick and Tiph's wedding was at the end of June. Mackenzie was planning on driving there but when the weather report said storms would be in Alabama, Mississippi, and Louisiana, she decided to log onto priceline.com and find a flight.

Blessed, she found a flight for $125 round trip and headed to Dallas. She arrived a week early so she could do last minute fittings, get her hair and nails done by this stylist, Raina, Tiphane had emailed her about, and visit with Aunt Cecile and the twins.

At the rehearsal dinner on the Friday before the wedding, Nick and Tiphane were glowing and happy. They looked so in love. Mackenzie remembered the day Nick had her talk to Tiphane for him and how his eyes lit up when she'd told him that Tiphane had invited them out.

After the dinner, the guys disappeared and many of the women of the wedding party, along with a few other of Tiphane's close friends, went back to her place to exchange last minute beauty tips, eat popcorn, and watch *Love Jones*.

Tiphane and Mackenzie went to her bedroom to talk and catch up while everyone else watched the video. Mackenzie told Tiphane about her past job at the firm in Atlanta and all the scandals. She thought Mackenzie was making it up. Tiphane told her that she and Nick were trying to have a baby.

When Tiphane asked about Julian, Mackenzie fought back tears and told her that he wasn't the man she'd thought he was. And what they had wasn't love. Mackenzie avoided eye contact as much as possible for fear that she would realize there was more to the story.

But that didn't work. "Mackenzie, can I ask you something?" Tiphane asked softly.

Mackenzie turned to face Tiphane, shrugged her shoulders, and replied "Yeah, what's up?"

"Did you guys call off the wedding because you're gay?"

Mackenzie couldn't believe her ears. Part of her wanted to bolt out of the room, while the other was torn with the association of the term "gay" to her life.

Pausing to wipe her face, Mackenzie knew she had to answer or allow speculation to win something an attorney never does.

"Tiphane, girl if you only knew," she responded.

Tiphane positioned herself on the bed and sighed in a friendly manner. "Well, I don't mind listening."

So, Mackenzie made herself comfortable, taking off her shoes, and sat Indian style on the bed. She intricately described her past life, her attempted suicide, and the time she'd been thrown over the patio, excluding only her daughter Jay-Jay.

"I've been with several women. When I met Julian, that life was over with. My ex-girlfriend showed up one day needing help. I was only trying to help them out, but he followed us one day and watched as we sat and ate lunch. He assumed we were back together. He said someone called him and told him that I was hiding something from him. He wouldn't allow me to explain. He called me all types of awful names and threw me out. No wait, he kicked me out, literally!

"And I understand that he was hurt, Tiphane, but he wouldn't even let me explain. It was so long ago, and I was trying to help her and Jay-Jay. That's all."

"So what about the hot checks? Did you ever figure that out? Do you think she would write hot checks? That's your old roommate, right? And she's Erasmus. Right?"

"Yeah, that's her. She didn't say anything about the checks. Do you think it could have been her?"

Tiphane looked with disbelief, furrowed brows, and a dropped jaw.

"Well, it's been on the news for almost a year. It's a murder case about some girl that blackmailed a football player. She was murdered, and at first, the police thought it was her ex-girlfriend, Erasmus Pola-something. Well anyway, she was cleared on the murder charge because it turns out the football player, or should I say ex-football player, killed her. But during the investigation, that Erasmus girl was found guilty of check fraud from the early nineties. I'm not too sure of all of the details though."

"You're kidding? I can't believe this. Did they say anything about her child?"

"They did mention that she had one but even that was questionable. It was crazy; they just finished the case."

"Unbelievable. Julian worked on a case similar to this. Something about some football player and a groupie blackmailing him. Do you think this is the same football player?"

"Julian worked a little on the case because he was the ex-football player's lawyer. He didn't talk too much about it with us. I guess I see why."

"Yeah, he probably wanted to throw away the key on Erasmus if he could. Is she still in jail?"

"Probably not. She's been in there since they arrested her, so I think she's been released with time served."

Mackenzie thought about contacting her to check on Jay-Jay, but then dismissed the idea in hopes that Erasmus would find her.

"So do you miss him? I mean, would you take him back if he asked."

"Probably not. What he did hurt. I'm not sure if I can."

"I understand. Seems like he would have let you explain."

"Yeah, that's what I keep telling myself every other day when I think about him. That hurt bad," Mackenzie says, as she wiped the tears that had fallen with her shirtsleeves.

They both keep silent and wiped away their tears momentarily before Tiphane went into their master bathroom and brought back a box of Kleenex tissue.

"You know, Mackenzie, I knew something was up when you disappeared the first time and a few of my gay friends that come to the restaurant said they saw you out with a bunch of gay guys and some girl. I guess I put two and two together."

"Yeah, I'm sure it was me. I was out there."

"So you're not into women anymore? Did you really love Julian?"

"Girl, if you'd been through what I've been through, trust me, you would believe without a shadow of a doubt that I'm through with the drama! And yes, I did love Julian, a part of me always will, but I don't ever see us getting back together again."

"Well, I believe you. I'm just sad that he didn't. You two were such a good couple, so promising. I'm here for you though, anytime you need to talk or whatever, you don't have to go through this alone." They hugged with more tears and promises to keep in touch before going back out to the living room with the other women.

Afterwards, some of the ladies left. Mackenzie excused herself to one of the guestrooms showered, and cried herself to sleep.

Tiphane's mom Marty was there at six that morning, buzzing around making everyone nervous. The rest of the brides maids arrived with their dresses and makeup bags around nine, and everyone started to get ready for the twelve o' clock wedding at the Botanical Gardens.

Nature was being kind and held back the forecasted rain. It gave just enough sun for Tiphane and Nick to exchange their vows, kiss, take pictures, and be whisked off in a limo.

The reception was at the Nations Bank building in downtown Dallas and was a blast. Mackenzie and her wedding party partner danced a couple of times, then she danced with Ken. He looked extremely well, Mackenzie thought to herself.

Knowing she had a flight the next day, Mackenzie left a little early because she wanted to get ready. She promised Ken they could have brunch before she left.

It was a very nice day. Nick and Tiphane were married and about to go on a month's vacation to the Cayman Islands. And Mackenzie knew she was okay because being alone wasn't as bad today as she thought it would be.

Mackenzie said her goodbyes to Aunt Cecile and the twins over the phone and promised she would be back soon. She camped out on Nick and Tiphane's couch and slept like a baby.

That Sunday morning, she packed and prepared to meet Ken at a little restaurant in Addison that served Sunday brunch for many of the athletes and industry people of Dallas.

The place was indeed packed with athletes and some celebrities, but she paid them no mind. She was really ready to eat and get to the airport. Ken was already there and sent a waiter to bring her over.

They hugged and commented on how well each of them looked, then sat and ordered their food. They talked for the next hour or so about the changes in their lives. Ken's fiancée was from West Texas and a pediatrician in Houston where they lived. They were going to get married in August, and he invited Mackenzie. "Three weddings in one year, I don't think so," she concluded with a laugh.

She told Ken that she was living in Atlanta and practicing law, still single, and probably moving back to Texas to practice here. They laughed some and promised they would keep in touch.

The waiter came over and cleared their plates, and Ken paid for their meals. She checked the time and realized she had only two hours before her flight.

Walking through the busy eatery to use the bathroom before she departed, she noted that the place was filled with tons of boob jobs, facials, and enlargements. Mackenzie went back over to the table and found Ken talking with some man who had his back towards her. Mackenzie excused herself when the man turned around.

It was Julian. The mood was awkward to say the least. Ken felt like he was in the middle. He shared a nervous glance with Mackenzie, with an apologetic half-smile as he shifted in his seat.

"Hello Julian," Mackenzie said, ignoring the need to faint or be rude. She took her seat like she was fine. Julian, a little lost for words, stared back at Mackenzie, then looked at Ken.

"Oh, I'm sorry, Ken, I didn't know you had company. How are you, Ms. Kennedy?" Julian, attempting to hide his discomfort and confusion, shook his head. "Well, I have to get back to my fiancée. It was nice seeing you guys." He excused himself before Ken could explain.

Ken apologized over and over and promised Mackenzie that he had been trying to get rid of him before she came back. She laughed it off and promised Ken that she was okay. Julian was her past. She wasn't bothered.

"I'm fine, Ken. Julian and I are no longer anything. Seeing him and his new fiancée is just how it is."

She looked good that day. So what that he was sitting with his fiancée? She was happy with her life and content being alone.

Ken never asked why they'd broken up, and she didn't offer any information.

They left, gave hugs, and she was on her way back to Atlanta.

Mackenzie slept the whole way back, picked up her car from the parking lot, and headed home so she could go to the gym.

At the gym, she did a power workout, a cycling class, aerobics, and then a cool down. When she finished, she showered there and decided she was going to eat out at the Cheesecake Factory and treat herself to some cheesecake.

Mackenzie sat outside and ate. She had a glass of Kendall Jackson and read a little of her book, *The Alchemist,* before leaving. On the way home, she stopped at the Publix on Ponce DeLeon, before going to the bookstore for a new book by Omar Tyree.

When she made it home, she had a message from Sam and quickly called him back. He told her about his wedding in a few weeks and made her promise she would be there.

She told him she wasn't working so she could spend a week there for his wedding. He caught her up on all of their old friends, their latest accomplishments, and his family, and then they hung up.

Mackenzie made her flight reservations through priceline.com, and then decided to call information to get Lauren's number. She felt bad that she had to call information to get her own sister's number. But all she could think of was Pat, all of her childhood mishaps, and Jun, and she knew why she had disassociated herself.

"Lauren, what you doing?"

"Mackenzie?"

"Yeah girl, it's me."

"Oh my God, I just talked with Aunt Cecile trying to get your number. Did she tell you I called?"

"No, I was just calling to tell you I would be in New York in two weeks."

"No Mackenzie. You need to come now. It's Daddy. He's sick. He just had a heart attack last week. He's still in the hospital. You need to come home."

Chapter Twenty-six

Mackenzie changed her flight and caught the next available flight out that Monday morning. She thought about her strained relationship with her father and how much she missed him. She had so much to tell him and knew that he would make it because he was tough. The entire plane ride she went over in her head what she would say. She looked through the clouds and ignored the turbulence that the plane was experiencing. She wanted Jun to know some things, like how hurt she'd been when he'd left Pat and the rest of them. How she'd pushed herself so hard because everyone had made her feel like she wouldn't amount to much, and how she'd always felt, *she loved him* although she didn't show it, and that he was probably one of her biggest fans. She remembered the one time he'd told her over the phone that she could do anything she put her mind to, and secretly that was what had pushed her to accomplish many of her goals. *"God, I hope he pulls through"*

She made it to New York by ten that morning and rushed to the Woodhull Hospital where she was meeting Lauren.

Parking her rental car on Broadway, she followed the instructions that Lauren had given her to find Jun. She went up to the ICU waiting area and found most of her brother's and sisters, her father's wife, and most of his family and close friends in the waiting area.

They all hugged and cried as they updated Mackenzie on Jun's condition. He had been diagnosed about a year ago with chronic heart failure and had been sick ever since. That hurt Mackenzie because it had been so many years since she'd seen Jun, and now she had to see him like this. She wasn't sure if she was ready, but after a nod from Lauren and the seriousness in her eyes, she knew she had to do it.

The doctors came out and told everyone, "He's in and out and it's possible that he may not remember any of you. I doubt that he can talk." This caused more fear because Mackenzie had been away for so long. What if he didn't remember her, then what?

But against her worries, fighting her tears, she and her brothers and sisters went in. She couldn't believe her eyes.

He was so frail and looked tired. He was still and had a ventilator to help him breathe. His room, decorated with flowers and cards, smelled like a funeral parlor and made Mackenzie's stomach turn.

They all gathered around his bedside and stood there until he opened his eyes.

"Daddy, Mackenzie's here." Lauren said.

He lifted his hand and reached out to her. She reached back and held his hand as she cried. She missed her blood so much, her heart physically ached.

"I'm doing good, Daddy. Real good. I've made something out of myself. I've been working really hard," Mackenzie said, trying to control her tears.

"I love you, Daddy. I always have. I remember you telling me I could do anything I put my mind to. If you'd never told me that," she said, holding his hand and placing a soft kiss on his face he closed his eyes again, "I would be nothing. You hear me, Daddy? I love you."

"Daddy, do you hear me? I love you. I understand now. Please don't leave me again. Daddy. Daddy."

Mackenzie began to frantically call out when she felt Jun squeeze her hand. She looked at him and he reopened his eyes. Looking at Mackenzie, he whispered, "Sorry."

She knew things were coming to an end. She let go as his eyes closed again and went outside to be alone. Mackenzie walked up Broadway with her arms folded and looking to the ground as trash moved slightly across the pavement. She looked up and thanked God for this day and making peace with her father.

She decided that she needed to be close to her family, so she headed back instead of being alone and running when she was hurting. There was plenty of love up in that hospital room with her family, and for the moment, she needed to bask in it even if it was hard to see him like that. But the image was too hard to handle.

She wanted to remember him in her own way, when Jun was still with her and Pat, bringing home Chips Ahoy cookies for them or laughing at one of his marine jokes. Or how he smelled before he left for work in the mornings and everything else about him before the drugs. She couldn't remember him being helpless like this.

So, instead of going back to the room, Mackenzie stopped at the store and bought a ginger ale and Platans potato chips, and then walked back to the hospital. She finished her food first, then went back upstairs and heard yells and her sister Erica screaming. She ran down the hall to the ICU waiting area as her heart beat fast and the sweat formed at her temples. She knew Jun was gone.

She grabbed her forehead and tried to take off running to get air, she was breathless, gasping for her own life. It seemed as though she was dying when Lauren grabbed her, held her tight, and let her cry into her arms.

Erica was distraught; her brothers held their heads down. They all cried and held each other as they saw the end of their only other parent.

Afterwards, they all went back to Lauren and Erica's apartment and sat discussing the funeral arrangements. Mackenzie met his wife Leticia for the first time and thanked her for caring for her father.

She met her many nieces, nephews, and extended family. They ate a good meal prepared by Erica his favorite meal, barbecue steak, cabbage, and rice. The scent filled the tiny apartment and all that stopped by either complimented the chef or partook in the meal. There was plenty of steak, cabbage, and rice to feed all that came by.

Erica was finally pulling herself together. Occasionally she would have to go to the bathroom and clean her face. After dinner, they all agreed on the funeral arrangements, drank coffee, and caught up with each other's lives.

Mackenzie was so happy to be home and saddened that she'd stayed away so long. She'd missed so many happy times and all of the love. All that she had searched the streets for was right here in Brooklyn with her family.

After everyone left and the kids went to sleep, Mackenzie and her sisters sat and talked in the tiny two-bedroom apartment, with wooden floors and bright white walls, about their Daddy and the old days.

They laughed about the times when they would perform talent shows or how they would dance to their grandfather's jukebox in upstate

New York in his trailer home. Her brothers would dance to "Flashlight" while Mackenzie, her sisters, and her cousins would perform "We are family."

And when their grandfather was busy entertaining the many patrons that stopped by to gamble on the weekends, they did errands to earn money so they, too, could gamble outside, away from the grownups.

"Come on, let's sing it. Let's sing, "We are family," Lauren asked her sisters, who were laughing as they reminisced about their summer vacations.

So, in between tears and laughter, they attempted to sing the song because no one could remember the words, just the "We are family. I got all my sisters with me." The three of them made up there own lyrics and sang like they used to do when they were younger.

They finally fell asleep in Erica's room and slept until noon the next day. Mackenzie woke up first and cleaned up the kitchen, then played with her niece and nephew.

The three of them cooked pancakes for Lauren and Erica and walked to the store for orange juice and candy. When they made it back, both Lauren and Erica were awake eating pancakes and drinking coffee.

They were off the rest of the week, so they decided to go out to New Jersey and put flowers on their mother's grave. The headstone that Mackenzie had bought last year with her first paycheck actually looked good.

They all took turns saying their words, cried a little, and then left, heading back to Brooklyn. They stopped at their Aunt Michelle's house in the back at the Cooper Projects and made sure she was holding up okay.

She fixed some pepper steak and rice, and they talked about going to get something to wear for the funeral. Her youngest brother Aaron showed up, and they all drove to Manhattan to get something to wear. Driving the streets of New York was a headache for Mackenzie. It was just as bad as Atlanta.

They paid to park and walked up and down Fifth Avenue in the hot, humid, summer temperatures looking for something to wear. Buying shoes was much easier, so they made sure to accomplish that first. Aaron wanted to go to 34th street to Macy's so they hailed a cab, piled in, and went to Macy's.

They all found something to wear in Macy's, so after all of the trying on and modeling around, they left and caught a cab back to her rental car. They dropped off their aunt and went back to Lauren and Erica's where they met up with Sean and Eric. They had gone shopping earlier, too, and were coming to show the Derby hats that they had bought.

Aaron wanted one, too, so they left and went to find him one as well. The funeral would be Thursday evening followed by the burial Friday morning.

Mackenzie called to let Sam know she was in town and what had happened, but she assured him that she would be there for him on his wedding day. He sent his regards to her family, and she told him she would catch up with him after all this was done.

On the day of the funeral, Mackenzie and her family all sat around and promised they would do better by keeping in touch. They exchanged information and made plans to meet up for Christmas.

Mackenzie apologized to her family through tears for being away. They all cried and said they were sorry they'd let her stay away so long.

They even made plans to visit their grandparents still living in the Marcy Projects.

The funeral was somber and filled with tears. Many of her father's old friends were there, along with their extended relatives from Connecticut. Her uncle did the eulogy, giving a family touch. Instead of the traditional funeral music, he played a CD of all of Jun's favorite music.

Mackenzie knew Jun would be smiling if he were here. He loved the O' Jay's and Frank Sinatra. The friends and family cried with smiles because they knew it, too. And as the sounds of Frank Sinatra singing "I Did It My Way" bellowed throughout the funeral home, there seemed to be peace throughout the family.

It was no secret that Jun had loved his lifestyle. And even in death, today there was a celebration of his life.

When the funeral was over, Mackenzie saw Aaron's sister, April, and his mother, who looked absolutely wonderful. Her skin was radiant and she sported long dreadlocks that were dyed blond. She smiled with a sense of peace now in her life. She was clean and living a new life. They talked for a moment, exchanged numbers, and everyone went back to Erica and Lauren's.

The house was filled with so many people and so much food. Mackenzie fixed herself a plate and went to Erica's room to take a nap. She slept for hours until her nephews finally woke her up, playing with thread on her face. She wrestled them both and played for a while until they were too tired to continue.

She took a shower and stayed up the rest of the night, finishing her book *The Alchemist*. It was made clear to her that she needed to go back home to Texas as soon as the book ended. She didn't want to admit that to herself, but the theme was so powerful in the book, she knew she had to do it.

She woke everyone up and they all got dressed for the burial. The hearse and the cars would be there by nine-thirty. This one time they couldn't be late. So, the house was filled with people rushing around as they shared the two bathrooms, the phone ringing off the hook, making cups of coffee, and her brothers and sisters chain smoking cigarettes.

Jun's wife and sisters were in one car, and her father's kids rode in the other. Mackenzie drove her nieces and nephews in her car and cracked up laughing at all of the funny stories they had.

"Aunt Macky, did you hear the story about Aunt Karen?" her youngest nephew asked, as he laughed.

"No. We have an Aunt Karen? Are you sure?"

With constant laughter filling the car, no one could answer the question of the hour.

With still more laughter, he asked again, "Did you hear the story about Aunt Karen?"

Laughing at the silliness of her nephew, Mackenzie replied, "No."

"Yeah, me either." He laughed in hysterics and blurted out as he held his side indicating that he was laughing too hard, "My mother wouldn't let me see it on the computer, but it sure was funny."

The entire car was filled with non-stop laughter as Mackenzie drove to the burial with her nieces and nephews.

It was what Mackenzie needed. She didn't ever want to ride in a funeral limousine again. She still had the image of being eleven in her first limousine to bury her mother.

After a small ceremony, they buried their father and said their goodbyes. Then they went to his wife's house for dinner and to look at old pictures. Mackenzie wasn't in any of them, just a few old school pictures that Lauren had given him. But she couldn't blame him. She could have kept in touch but it was just how it had to be.

And her mama dying so young had been God's plan, not her father's. She'd chosen to stay mad for all this time. She should have been better.

Mackenzie stayed with Erica and Lauren for a couple more days, then left to meet Sam on Long Island to prepare for his wedding.

Before leaving, she left her sisters with enough money to put down on a bigger place and promised she would call them before she left to go back to Atlanta.

Chapter Twenty-seven

Mackenzie drove up the northern expressway to the tip of Long Island not too far from the Hampton area to meet Sam and his fiancée Natalie.

She was just as Mackenzie imagined a beautiful, caramel complexioned, petite woman with long flowing hair and a body that wouldn't stop.

They had dinner at their new home, where they sat and talked about old times. His mother, sister, and grandparents came up later that evening, and they all sat around playing cards until Mackenzie had to retire.

She was physically tired and emotionally drained from the past week. Sam and her planned lunch for tomorrow, then she went to check in at the Day's Inn not too far from their home.

Mackenzie unpacked and took a quick shower, then fell fast asleep. Sam called to wake her up around ten that next morning and said he would be there to pick her up by noon for lunch.

Mackenzie jumped out of bed, did her crunch routine, a few push-ups, and showered before doing her hair and getting dressed.

By the time Sam made it to the hotel, she was finally dressed and ready to go.

They drove a ways to Manhattan, then went into BBQ's and sat and talked before eating.

Sam was now a marketing director for a men's fashion magazine, and his fiancée was and editor for a small publishing company.

They met his second year in college and had been together ever since. She was expecting their first child in March. Sam was so excited he didn't even recognize her uneasiness with all of his good news.

So, she told him about the women, drugs, Jay-Jay, and losing Julian. She cried on his shoulder, and he held her until she got herself together. That was actually the first time she'd cried for Julian since he'd left her on the floor of his apartment. She excused herself into the bathroom where she cleaned her face and touched up her makeup. She looked in the mirror and thought about little Jay-Jay, her skinny legs, and her curly red hair. Her hands that were long and skinny like Mackenzie's and she had their same smile and a mole at their lower neckline. She wondered what she was like now almost ten years old. She wondered if Julian had put two and two together and realized who Jay-Jay was.

She returned to the table with puffy eyes and a smile to let Sam know she was okay. As she sat in the filled restaurant, he grabbed her hand with eyes filled with tears and said, "Sweetie, you're going to be fine. You've always been a fighter and more importantly, a survivor. You haven't fallen apart, you've bounced back after each blow, each attack, and you're still standing. Baby, I know it's easy to say, but I promise you will get through this."

Sam ordered her some more iced tea and continued to hold her hand. And as usual, he put things in perspective in a spiritual manner.

She understood everything he said, and even believed it already. She just needed to let those tears fall for cleansing purposes. She told Sam that spiritually, she understood why things happened the way they did for her.

She had to go through those things in order to be where she was now, and not only that, her trials and triumphs would one day help a large group of women who'd also been through such ordeals. She had finally realized that God's plan was to use her.

And being with Julian was what she needed at the time to show her that she could love a man and be in a relationship, regardless of what she'd been through. "I had to let go of the fear that was controlling me for so long," she told Sam. This was much more than a junior high school crush, this was true love.

"It hurt what Julian did, and at times, I miss him; I miss him bad but I have to respect God's plan and purpose and move on." They talked about the firm she'd worked for, and he couldn't believe it. That was pretty much the response from anyone that she told.

After talking and listening to her good friend, they ordered barbecue chicken, fries, and coleslaw.

They walked through the village after dinner so she could pick up some vintage 502 Levi's and shoes. Then they drove to Bloomingdale's so she could buy Sam his cologne for losing the bet they'd made so many years ago. He was getting married first, so she had to oblige.

Sam took her to Tower Records and purchased her, his very own CD, which his choir had put out, and Mackenzie hugged him in excitement because his dreams were all coming true. She knew he deserved it. They drove back to Long Island and listened to it as Sam sung along.

After making it back to her hotel room, Mackenzie undressed and slipped on something comfortable. She flipped through the TV channels until she was tired enough to go to sleep.

That following day, she woke up, took a bath, did her nails, and gave herself a facial. She ironed her white linen sleeveless dress for that night's dinner and went out for something to eat, enjoying the cool air that Long Island morning's bring.

When she made it back after getting lost, there was a message from Sam. He wanted to make sure she was still coming tonight and to also make sure she had an off-white dress for the wedding. That was their color for the wedding.

Mackenzie forgot that Sam had told her about that yesterday, so she drove back into the city and went back to Bloomingdale's. She found an off-white Versace dress and some shoes to match. She thought she wouldn't have any luck because of the season, but then she remembered that fashion was changing. *People are wearing white in the winter.* She thought to herself.

Mackenzie found some accessories to match and bought some more Dulce and Gabanna perfume because she'd left hers at home, and then headed back to Long Island.

She made it back to Long Island around four, avoiding the rush hour traffic, put up her stuff, put on a mask, and then took an hour nap.

When she woke up, she called Sam to get the directions, then took her shower and started to get ready.

Mackenzie found the big, brick red restaurant with no problem and spotted Sam and Natalie as soon as she walked in.

She was glad that she'd come because Mishcah, Willie, and Red were all there. They hugged and commented on how age had treated them, then caught up with each other's lives.

Mishcah was married with two children, Willie was in the entertainment industry singing backup for various artists, and Red was an insurance executive for State Farm.

Life had been good to all of them. They'd survived the projects, the loss of their parents, and life's many blows.

Chapter Twenty-eight

By the time the wedding had arrived, Mackenzie was rejuvenated and anxious to get back to Atlanta. Since being up in New York, she hadn't worked out much except doing her crunches and jogging up to the store for orange juice twice. She felt the fat developing on her thighs.

She dressed for the wedding, packed her bags, and checked out. After the reception, she was heading to the airport and catching an early flight out. She enjoyed seeing everyone, but she was ready to go for the most part. She was dying to get to the gym.

The ceremony was being held at a church in Jamaica Queens that was absolutely flawless. The décor was Marble, with high ceilings, polished pews, and plush carpet. The wedding party all looked pristine in their off-white ensembles. The girls' dresses were low cut, sleeveless, chic dresses, while the groomsmen sported tailored, single-breasted suits with matching ties and shirts.

Sam and Natalie looked wonderful. Her train was about a mile long, and the cut of her fitted, sleeveless dress fit her perfectly. Sam was crisp as usual with a long suit coat and matching slacks, and the same matching shirt and tie as his groomsmen.

Mackenzie cried when they exchanged the vows that they'd written for each other and laughed when they kissed because she could tell that Sam was nervous.

Mackenzie, along with all of the other 300 guests or so, threw rice in the traditional manner, and then they all went into the city for the reception that was going to be held at one of the hotels there.

Mackenzie and all of her old friends sat together, and they sipped fine wine and ate fine foods. At least her friends did. Mackenzie was holding out for the fries she planned on getting once she left. It would be her last encounter with such high calorie food before returning to Atlanta and starting her workout routine.

She danced with Red and Willie and cracked up laughing at Mishcah because Sam's uncle kept trying to pick her up, feeding her decade-old pick-up lines even after she told him that she was happily married.

When the ceremony was over, Mackenzie said her goodbyes and drove high speed trying to catch her flight, which was leaving within the hour, after stopping for her McDonalds fries.

She hurried to the airport and turned in her rental car, lightly jogging down the corridor in her pumps trying to catch her flight.

By the grace of God, she made it just before they closed the doors. The stewardess said she was fortunate that this was an empty flight; otherwise, she would be waiting until tomorrow to leave out.

Mackenzie half-smiled and quickly took her seat in the first class section that she'd decided to bump herself up to after she'd made her reservations.

The stewardess was right. First class was actually fairly empty. Mackenzie wasn't sitting by anyone. She leaned back her chair after the signal went off and slept until it was time to land.

Dressed in her off-white dress and pumps, she moved through Hartsfield, quickly trying to get her luggage and hurry home.

When she didn't see her luggage, she was fuming. Mackenzie wasn't in the mood to hear that her luggage wasn't here. In fact, she wanted her luggage-period! The expression on her face was a dead giveaway of her demands.

She walked down the corridor and found the slightly overweight woman who came up to the counter as if she knew what she was going to say.

Mackenzie sighed, and then informed her that her luggage hadn't come off the plane. The woman shifted her body, and then asked for her name. Mackenzie told her "Mackenzie, Kennedy, and I just arrived on flight 727 from JFK airport."

She walked to the back, and Mackenzie stood there waiting for a good five minutes when she returned, speaking in her ghetto lingo. "Uh ma'am, yo' stuff is still up deh in J F K. It aint gon' get heay til dah mor'. Sorry." She shrugged, and Mackenzie just about lost it.

"What do you mean it won't be here until tomorrow? It should have gotten on the plane when I did."

"You checked din late doe, right? Yeah so, it didn't get on dat flight. And ain't no udder flights comin' in til tomor. Sorry."

She kept saying sorry like she meant it, which only pissed Mackenzie off more. She thanked her and asked when the flight would be in, trying not to seem too upset for fear that they might steal her luggage. The customer service rep walked to the back and then returned and said, "Eight ten in dah morning." Mackenzie thanked her again and walked off with her small carry-on.

She picked up her car in the parking area mad as hell. She threw her bag into the trunk, slammed it closed, opened the door, cranked up her Z3, and left Hartsfield in a hurry.

The sad thing was that she had to be back here tomorrow after church. Mackenzie drove down Camp Creek to 85S, picked up 20E, and headed downtown to her loft. The streets were busy as usual for a Saturday night, but she zipped in and out of lanes until she reached her exit.

When she made it home, it was too late to catch the gym, so she peeled off her dress from the wedding and reception to take a quick shower. She laid out a nice, black linen summer dress she'd purchased from Eddie Bauer with her ultra-sheer stockings and some sling-backs, then meditated for a few and went to sleep.

Mackenzie woke up at six the next morning and figured she would go to the seven-thirty service so she could get to the airport and pick up her luggage by ten at the latest. She dressed quickly, grabbed her workout bag, and headed to church.

Ironically, her pastor talked about the past and how every Christian has one. And without our past, we would have no future.

Mackenzie thought she was going to tear up the pews shouting because he was talking right! He went on to say how we also need to let go of that past as well, because if we didn't, it would hold us back.

And he was right. It was time to let go of her past drama-Julian included. For all that she had been through, she realized that it was part of God's plan. She knew she was hoping and praying that Julian would come back, but now it was time to let that go and get ready for her future.

After church, she drove back to the airport, made her way back to the customer service area that dealt with luggage, and waited for someone to assist her.

When no one came to the counter, she rung the little bell and waited patiently until her friend from yesterday came up front, wiping her eyes as if she'd awakened from a good dream. Mackenzie removed her shades and informed her that she was here for her luggage.

She spit out her ghetto language again and told her she would be right back. Seconds later, she emerged with her two Louis Vitianne bags. Mackenzie thanked her graciously and departed back to her car so she could get to the gym.

She made it to the gym in no time, changed, and went for overkill, slamming the weights and pumping her arms through rigorous sets. Mackenzie was letting out her anger towards Julian and how he'd left her, but after today it wouldn't even matter.

She ran on the treadmill for an hour like she was running to save her life. She wiped sweat and tears and ignored the pain in her legs, pushing it until she couldn't go anymore.

When she ran out of machines to use, she went to the showers and cleaned herself off. Mackenzie let the water run through her hair, down her back, and stood there for a while as her legs trembled. Today she was putting everything behind her. She was moving back to Texas when her lease was up.

She stepped out of the shower and dried off, noticing that she needed to shave again, and then got dressed.

On the way home, she stopped at Sylvia's for a dinner take-out, and then walked down to the Kroger to pick up some necessities.

As she was walking up the street, allowing her hair to dry in the sun, she felt like someone was watching her. She grabbed her purse and sped up. *"Now, I know Atlanta has its problems with wandering homeless, but as long as I've been here, I've never felt like someone was ever watching me,"* she thought.

Kroger was not too far from Sylvia's so if she had to, she would run. Mackenzie turned around but didn't see anyone, so she figured she was just tired from all of that working out and just being a bit paranoid.

She dipped into Kroger and picked up some razors, orange juice, fresh broccoli, and wheat bread. Mackenzie used the manual check out and walked back to her car. If someone was going to try something, they were going to get beat down with broccoli and a gallon of orange juice.

She made it home safely, put up her groceries, and then heated up her food in the microwave. Mackenzie changed out of her cover up sweats, took off her panties, and put on some scrubs Amos had given her. She snapped out of her bra, letting her titties breathe after having them strapped down in a sports bra for a couple of hours, and slipped on a fitted tank top.

She grabbed her food out of the microwave, poured a glass of lemonade, grabbed some napkins, and sat on her wooden floors in front of the TV to eat. She watched the weather channel for a sec, and then flipped it to UPN, which was showing the classic *Claudine*.

Mackenzie laughed in between taking bites of her dinner and cried, too, when James Earl Jones never showed up for the Father's Day party.

Her heart ached because she thought about Jay-Jay and how she'd let her go with Erasmus. She had missed so many of her birthday parties.

Claudine was definitely a movie about black love and the importance of family. Mackenzie wondered if she would ever see little Jay-Jay again.

Chapter Twenty-nine

Mackenzie watched the rest of *Claudine* and fell asleep on the floor until she heard the TV making that irritating sound that lets you know they are off the air.

Mackenzie cut off the TV, put up her mess, and cleaned up the kitchen. Realizing she had no work tomorrow, only decisions to make, she decided to finish reading the book of Genesis. She had been so fascinated with history after college that she'd promised herself that she would read Genesis to learn about the ancestry of black people.

Mackenzie wanted to know where she was from and about the covenant that God had with the true descendants of Israel. Deep into the thirty-second chapter, when Jacob was going to meet his brother Esau, her doorbell rang.

She looked in the kitchen at the clock on the microwave and it read 3:42. "Now, who would be at my door this late? Ernie knows to call first," she said aloud to herself.

Mackenzie walked to the door, declaring that she wasn't going to let fear get the best of her, and asked, "Who is it?"

"It's Julian, Mackenzie," the familiar voice replied.

"Julian who? I don't know a Julian," Mackenzie replied coldly.

"It's Julian. Julian Taylor."

Mackenzie unlatched the top lock and unlocked the bottom lock, then opened the door because part of her wanted to see him again.

"Hey," he said with a serious look on his face and a five o'clock shadow.

"Hey," she replied again, sounding cold, but her heart was beating fast and in contrast, she was warm all over.

Dressed in blue jeans that had the dirty look and a linen, short sleeve, cream-colored shirt showing a little of his chest hair, Julian asked if he could come in.

Mackenzie stepped back and opened the door enough so he could come in. She had definitely not been expecting this ever.

"What do you want, Julian?"

He looked around her loft, ignoring her question, then sat down at the dining table. "Why don't you have a seat?" Mackenzie said, trying to be funny. Her feelings were confusing her. Part of her was so angry with him, while another part was so happy to see him and to be near him again.

She stood by the wall, and it was quiet for a minute. "I'm sorry," Julian said, as he looked at her with those green eyes trying to peek into her soul.

"That's nice but sorry for what? Did you do something I need to know about? Because if you did, you don't have to apologize."

"I was wrong to let you go. I should have given you a chance to explain. I messed up."

She huffed and folded her arms, trying not to go off on him or grab him and hug him. "Julian, I have no idea what you're talking about, but it's about four in the morning, and I really need to get some sleep."

"I'm sorry about your dad."

"I beg your pardon?'

"I said I'm sorry about your dad."

"My dad? What do you know about dad?"

"I talked to Aunt Cecile. She told me you were in New York for your father's funeral. Is there anything I can do?"

"You can leave. That's what you can do."

Julian stood there and put his hands in his face, then pulled them across his baldhead and let out a sigh.

She watched him closely as he folded his hands on the top of his head for a moment. "Mackenzie, you can't just act like there was nothing between us. We need to talk. I'm here, and we need to talk."

"You mean *you* need to talk because I don't have anything to say. You want to let off some steam. I guess I can do the Christian thing and listen. Sure."

"All right, Mackenzie. This is it. I fucked up, okay. What else do you want me to say? I came all the way here so we could resolve what happened."

"You keep saying *WE,* and there's no *WE* here."

"Would you stop it with your smart-ass remarks? I'm not here to play games."

Mackenzie sighed again and walked into her room to the bathroom, trying to calm down. She counted to twenty. Julian was getting to her.

Mackenzie walked back out after splashing her face with cool water and lit into his ass. "Listen here, you no good, sorry excuse for a man. Don't you come in my house telling me about some games. Now when I wanted to talk to you to explain "my past" you walked out on me. Oh no, excuse me, you knocked me down and kicked the shit out of me, and then you walked. What makes you think I want to listen to anything you have to say?"

"You let me in. That means something."

"Yeah, you're right. It means I'm a bigger fool now than I was before for ever dealing with you."

"You mean that?"

"Yeah, I do," Mackenzie yelled, hoping that Julian would leave.

"You should have told me about your past instead of me having to hear it and see it from you and some ex-girlfriend."

"And you should have let me explain my past, which had nothing to do with you! It was also almost four years since I'd been living like that. Did you ever stop to think that maybe I didn't know how to tell you?"

Mackenzie shook her head at the situation. "My life was messed up back then. My child, my dumb ex-boyfriend had just assaulted me, and I was just confused. Not to mention the drugs, but it was my life and my choices at the time. There are no excuses; it is what it is."

"You still should have told me. And what child?"

"Why? You worried about some disease or something?" Mackenzie replied, ignoring his question about Jay-Jay.

"No, I was going to be your husband. Don't you think I should have been aware of such information? What if someone ever tried to blackmail you or something crazy like that? Then what, I'd be standing there looking stupid. And what child were you just referring to?"

"Is this what this is about? You looking stupid? Please. Julian, just go. You looked stupid leaving me there after someone gave you photos that you didn't bother to investigate. That's not what lawyers do! Is it?

What lawyer in his right mind would do that? Just go. There is nothing to discuss anymore."

"I'm not leaving until we get to the bottom of this, Mackenzie."

"And what would be the bottom? Me giving in to you? Fine, I give in. You were right. I was wrong, okay. Are you satisfied? Now you can leave."

Julian stood there and looked at her, just staring until she looked away. "I still want us to get married. I made"

"Before you even finish that statement, you need to know that I've moved on. I'm not interested in marrying you anymore. You're just not my type of man."

"So what Amarusus or Erasmus, whatever the hell her name is. Is she who you want to be with or"

Mackenzie walked over to the door, opened it, and held it until Julian walked over. "Get out. And for the record, if I wanted to be with a woman I could, but you don't see one here, do you?"

"I'm sorry. I was out of line."

Mackenzie looked out the door and ignored Julian.

"Get out, Julian." She knew eye contact would make this harder. He grabbed her free arm and pulled her into him, trying to hold onto the door. Julian grabbed her hand off the door and let it shut. "Julian, let go."

Julian pushed Mackenzie up against the wall, raising her arms and hands up and pushing his body into hers. He was determined to break her down.

"Julian, I said let go."

Julian responded by rubbing his face against hers, sending chills down her spine. He pressed against her harder, and she felt him grow in his crotch. Mackenzie pushed toward him, trying to get away, but the more she pushed the more he pushed. She tried to raise her knee, but he pressed in harder and let his tongue run across her earlobe like he would do when they were about to make love.

Mackenzie couldn't give into the ecstasy, allowing Julian to win. He'd hurt her and she couldn't take him back. *"I just can't,"* Mackenzie kept telling herself in her mind.

"I still love you," Julian whispered in her ear. "I still love you. I know you still love me," Julian whispered again, this time sucking on her earlobe, sending her over the edge because she couldn't fight it anymore. Mackenzie kissed the side of Julian's ear hard. Her body had been asleep for so long; she needed this.

They kissed, pulling off their shirts and tasting whatever flesh was showing. He pulled her hair down and ran his hand through it, then massaged her titties and sucked them like two popsicles. She wanted to come. Julian lifted her up against the wall as his pants fell to his ankles. In between kisses, Mackenzie straddled him as he pulled down her scrubs enough to slide inside.

They both let out sighs of ecstasy then moved with passion up against the wall. Mackenzie arched her back and he pulled her up and down until they exploded. They fell down to the floor, with her on top, shaking, and fell asleep in front of the door.

Mackenzie woke up the next morning in her bed with the bright sunlight in her eyes. She was dressed in only her scrub bottoms. Julian was staring down at her and stroking the side of her face. She rolled over and turned her back to him because she knew she had been wrong for letting this morning happen.

Julian moved in closer, placing his arm around her waist. "You feel like talking?"

"What do you want to talk about, Julian?" she asked, trying not to sound cold.

"About us and what happened."

She breathed a sigh of frustration and moved Julian's arm, stepping out of bed. Mackenzie ignored his comment and went into the bathroom to wash her face and brush her teeth.

Afterwards, she walked past Julian, sitting up in the bed, picked up her tank top, and put it back on. She went into the kitchen to get some orange juice when Julian walked across the living room in his boxers. His bare feet made squeaking sounds on the floor.

He walked over to the kitchen and stood in front of her. "You know, these forced antics of yours are not very becoming." Mackenzie says to him.

"Oh, I forced what happened with us this morning."

"Forget it, Julian. I have a bunch of errands to run this morning. If you would excuse me."

Julian grabbed her arm as she tried to walk by. "We need to talk about what happened this morning. I'm serious."

"Julian, we never had a problem with sex. We could do it at the drop of a hat. So don't go there."

"Don't go there?" Julian said with a raised voice. "Then where do you want me to go? You want me to tell you I understand that you used to mess with women before we fell in love? Tell you I understand about the drugs and the child I guess you lost? Fine. I understand. Okay, I'm sorry. I couldn't handle it at the time. I didn't know how to react. I was wrong."

She yanked her arm away from Julian and glared in his eyes before walking into her bedroom. Julian followed behind her. "So, what are you saying? You want that instead of me?"

She shook her head at Julian, furious.

"You know, I'm not even going to answer that. It would be a waste of breath. You don't listen, Julian. What I experienced with Erasmus and other women some seven or eight years ago is my past. It means absolutely nothing to me. It's my past, and it's now my fortune; without it, I wouldn't be the woman I am today. I wouldn't have been able to love a man like you. So, don't go throwing my past around like you know what you're talking about. If you would have gave me a chance to explain back then, we wouldn't be standing here right now. You didn't trust me enough to listen. You just walked out, and you still want me to marry you? I don't think so, Mr. Julian Taylor.

"And as far as Jay-Jay is concerned, she's my daughter. Erasmus took her when she left. I was so messed up I didn't bother to fight or try to find her. I didn't know how. I was so ashamed I don't think I wanted her until I became sober."

The dining area was quiet for a moment as the two searched for something to look at besides each other, realizing that the love they'd shared should have been stronger.

"Jay-Jay is yours?" Why didn't you tell me, Mackenzie?"

"Julian, no one knows about her. I've been so ashamed I couldn't even tell my dying father. No one knows but Erasmus, myself, and her family and my best friend Sam. I don't even have any pictures of her. Can you believe that? My own daughter.

"Erasmus bought her back because they needed help. I was trying to be a mother and help them out. That's all it was." Mackenzie began to cry.

"Wait a sec, don't do this to yourself. If I'm understanding this correctly you were in no position to take care of her, right?"

Mackenzie sighed, trying to forget about Jay-Jay and Erasmus. For all she knew, Erasmus's family had probably adopted Jay-Jay, making it even harder to get her back. It would definitely be a process. Right now, Mackenzie had to deal with Julian.

"Julian, this morning should not have happened. I'm sorry I lost control. But we're through. That's all behind me."

Julian looked at her in amazement. "Help me understand because I don't. We loved each other deeply. We were connected, a team. I don't understand."

"You know, at first I didn't understand either, but after I accepted you walking out on me, without giving me a chance, I let go. You didn't even try to hear that God delivered me from all of that and even if I wanted to go back, I couldn't. You didn't even give me a chance or anything. I was trying to help my family. There was nothing romantic going on." Mackenzie convinced herself a long time ago that the last sexual encounter between she and Erasmus was a mistake it was like it never happened.

"I know, and I struggled with that this last year."

"Yeah, I'm sure, by getting engaged, right?" Julian looked away for a second.

"Yeah, what would she say if she knew you were here? No one likes being made a fool of or being second, Julian. You're the one who needs to stop playing games."

Julian sighed and shook his head. "Why are you being so tough? This is not like you. It's Julian. Your friend, your lover, your future husband."

Mackenzie rolled her eyes at his comforting words.

"I ended it with Celeste the moment I saw you in Dallas with Ken. I've been trying to find you. I called Aunt Cecile. She told me about your father and where I could find you. I didn't want to call. I just wanted to find you so we could fix things. Mackenzie, I want to fix things."

Mackenzie fought back her tears as usual, determined not to show any signs of weakness, and asked, "Julian can you please leave." She went into the bathroom and started the shower. She took her time showering, shaving her legs, and washing her hair.

When she finished, Mackenzie wrapped a towel around her hair and another around her body and came out of the bathroom. Julian was sitting on her bed, fully dressed, waiting on her. The scent of her fresh body made him move in his seat a little, but she didn't care. He needed to see what he'd left behind. "You still here?"

"I made reservations for St. Croix. Our flight leaves tomorrow at noon. I'll be back to pick you up at ten in the morning. I'm stepping out on faith. I just want to know if you're going to do the same."

"Take care of yourself, Julian," she said without looking at him.

Julian walked out of the room to the front door and let himself out. She waited for a few moments, then locked the door. Mackenzie sat on her couch massaging her temples and searched for the phone to call Lauren.

"Wake up," Mackenzie said, "I need to talk." After much fussing and fixing a cup of coffee, Lauren listened attentively as she told her the entire story about her and Julian, including Erasmus and Jay-Jay.

"Wait a minute…I have a little niece? What does she look like? How old is she?"

"Believe it or not, just like Erasmus, but mixed the last time I saw her."

"Stop lying. Oh my god."

"I wish I was. She's my color, skinny with red air, ringlets, and light brown eyes. She's a big girl now almost ten."

"Wow. A lot has happened. Why didn't you tell us?"

"Scared."

"Mackenzie, you should have told us; we would have understood."

"I know that now, but it was too late, when Daddy died, and I didn't have the energy to explain all of this. It was too hard."

 "Well, little sister, let me give you some advice."

"Wait a minute, why aren't you at work?" she asked Lauren.

Lauren chimed, "Vacation."

"Be at LaGuardia by noon. If it's going to be a later flight, I will call you back; otherwise, be there by noon."

"Uh. Mackenzie, just for the record, Mr. Julian has you whipped. You do know that, right? That's why you can't sleep. You miss having him breathe on your ass! And we will discus my niece when I see you."

They talked for a few more moments, then Mackenzie told her, "Hurry up, and do not be late. No family traditions today or CPT."

She got online and made reservations for Lauren. There was a flight out at 1:15 in the afternoon.

Lauren made it in around four that afternoon, and they went straight to Sylvia's to eat and talk some more about Mackenzie and Julian and Jay-Jay. Lauren told her younger sister she had a plan, and she had better listen closely. Mackenzie did.

Afterwards, the two went to the mall and did a little shopping, buying shoes, of course, and some leather pants that were on sale at Armani Exchange.

They sashayed through the mall as vanilla and caramel, catching stares from the men and dirty looks from the women because they were walking on cloud nine, heads high up in the air.

That night, they did Lauren's hair and their nails and cracked up laughing watching *Blue Streak* on pay per view. They finally fell asleep in her bed talking about growing up and the fun times they all shared.

"You know we have to find Miss Jay-Jay. I mean, if Erasmus's folks are as hell bent on keeping her as you say we need to find her fast. Do you have all of her stuff, like birth certificates, social security card and what about the father? Does he know?" Lauren asked, ending the laughter.

"Well, I had it but after I came out of the hospital, my stuff at the apartment was ransacked. But when I saw Erasmus last she said she had it all. She's has been in jail for the last year for some crazy stuff and Jay-Jay's been with her folks. I just hope that Erasmus will do what's right and bring her back to me."

"Is she okay, what about the father? You left that part out."

"She was fine when we were separated again. Smart, lady-like , skinny as a rail, loves basketball, and just as friendly and happy as she wanted to be.

"The father, I don't want to even talk about him. He made me swear that I wouldn't have it."

"Obviously you lied," Lauren states, trying to make light of the situation. "Jay-Jay has your athleticism, huh?"

"Yeah, she does. I did lie, huh? I miss Jay-Jay so much. Sometimes I have to catch myself with my tears. How do you explain sudden tears in a sheer moment of laughter? God, I made the wrong choice; I know I did. I have to find her."

"Well, let's get through this and we will."

"You promise? Because I can't do it alone."

"I promise, little sister. I promise."

They hugged wiping away tears and retired for an early morning.

That morning, she awoke early and left Lauren sleeping to do some running at the gym. She hit the treadmill for about thirty minutes, and then stopped at Kroger to pick up some bagels and cream cheese.

Mackenzie made it home, and Lauren was awake cleaning up their mess from last night and listening to her *Best of Sade* CD.

Mackenzie hummed a little to the sounds of *Sade*, let Lauren clean up, and went to find something to wear and take a shower. After her shower, she had her bagel and cream cheese and slipped on some blue jeans and a Gap tank top with her Timberland sandals.

Mackenzie picked up her Bible, trying to get back into the story of Jacob and Esau. Lauren finished her shower and was sitting at the table doing a puzzle when the doorbell rang. She looked at her clock; it was ten o' clock on the dot. Mackenzie looked at Lauren, then headed to the bedroom. Lauren shot Mackenzie a naughty girl smirk before answering the door.

"Hi, Julian. How are you? I'm Lauren, Mackenzie's older sister. The caramel version of Mackenzie, as she likes to put it."

"Hello. How are you?"

"Doing fine. It's just too damn hot in Atlanta. Come on in and have a seat. I'll go get Mackenzie."

Lauren walked into the bedroom, giving Mackenzie her naughty girl grin again.

Julian stood up when Mackenzie walked out of the room, adjusted his pants, and placed his hand in his pockets.

"So, you're back?" Mackenzie said, shaking her head.

"Yeah, I'm back.

"Listen Mackenzie. I need you to know something. I'm here because I love you more than anything. Being without you is something I don't ever want to experience again. I need you, and I want you. I want you to be Mrs. Julian Taylor. And if you say no today, I'll just keep rescheduling our trip to St. Croix until you say yes."

Mackenzie stared at Julian, and then looked away before speaking softly. "What you said was very nice, and I know it wasn't easy to come here after how rude I've been. But what you did to me last year hurt real bad."

"I know, and I'm sorry."

"Let me finish, Julian. I'm in a place in my life in which I'm not putting anyone ahead of me. I've been to hell and back and finally, I'm free; no chains are holding me anymore. If you want to marry me, you have to understand that my past does not control me, nor does it mean that I can't ever find true love and make it work. I gave you the best love a person could receive. If you don't plan to stay for a lifetime, you need to leave right now, because love doesn't walk out or quit. It's supposed to have some resiliency, Julian."

Julian walked over to her, pulling his hands out of his pockets. "So what are you saying, Mackenzie? Are we going to St. Croix?" Mackenzie paused momentarily, looking away, still hiding those tears.

When Lauren walked out of the room, teary-eyed, she blurted out, "Yeah we're going to St. Croix. Now hug his ass so we can catch this plane."

Mackenzie reached out and hugged Julian. They embraced before sharing a wet kiss. Then the three of them shared a group hug filled with tears and lots of love.

The End...

If you enjoyed *When the Drama Has Ceased* you won't want to miss J. Monique's sexy, sassy, and sizzlin' sequel with a twist you won't forget! Turn the page for a special preview of *Something about Ginger*~coming soon to a bookstore near you.

Chapter One

"Honey, you know, I had the strangest dream last night," Mackenzie told Julian, as they sat closely on the airplane returning from their month-long honeymoon in St. Croix.

"Really? What about? You know, we only had a couple of hours of sleep," Julian replied, touching the bottom of her lip.

She smiled back at Julian with a flirtatious grin. "I know, but I was still able to dream what seemed like a series of dreams. I woke up at one point but didn't bother to wake you. You seemed to be sleeping soundly, kind of breathing in and out, in a rhythm."

Mackenzie mimicked him for a moment and Julian laughed. Shaking his head, he said, "Who, me?"

They kissed in between laughs and Mackenzie, startled, looked at the flight attendant, who had an obvious, worried look, on her face. Julian, who sensed Mackenzie's concern, followed her gaze to the flight attendant, who had begun to fanning herself,

The tall, fair-complexioned flight attendant with the crop cut was flustered as she reached for the microphone, to give an announcement.

But, before she could get a word out, she was whisked away by another short, full-figured flight attendant, and they vanished into the corridor. They talked in what sounded like muffled whispers and sobs.

"Something's wrong," Mackenzie said.

"I think you're right. I'd better go ask what's going on."

Julian began to unfasten his seat belt and excused himself. He proceeded to find the flight attendants while the other first class patrons either sipped on fine wine, played with their laptops, or dosed off into Never-Never Land.

He reached the corridor of the plane, next to the pilots' section, and saw that the two flight attendants were wiping their eyes.

"Umm, excuse me, but uh, my wife and I were wondering if everything is okay. Is there something we need to know? Like if this plane is going to land safely," he asked, with a puzzled look on his face.

The two flight attendants looked at each other, and then looked at Julian.

"Sir," the tall one said, as she cleared her throat, "there seems to be a state of emergency nationwide. The FAA is asking that we not land this plane but divert to Canada. That's all I can tell you."

"Wait a minute. What do you mean national security? What's going on?" Julian asked. He was looking for answers and not some drummed up speech they were going to concoct.

With a look of empathy, the tall flight attendant spoke earnestly. "Sir we can't give out any more information because we are unsure. They have informed the pilot that we cannot land on U.S. soil until given clearance. I'm sorry, sir."

Julian looked at the two women who offered support to one another by holding hands and asked that they keep him posted. They agreed.

Flustered, he went back to his seat.

"You're right, hon, something is wrong, but they're not saying. All they told me was that they can't land the plane on U.S. soil." Julian knew not to tell Mackenzie about the state of emergency for fear that Mackenzie would become worried. He knew that that kind of information had better come with explicit details, and he had none to give.

They can't land the plane. That's not good. What about the fuel? We may run out," Mackenzie said, trying not to sound worried.

In the back of her mind, her dreams were coming clear to her.

"So, what did you dream about?" Julian asked, trying to get her mind off their situation.

"Oh, well it was weird. Sam and Red were both in it but then just disappeared when we were at church. I kept looking all over for them but it was like I was going around in circles. Then Lauren finds me at the church, and she's crying telling me she was worried about me."

Was I in it?" Julian asked quizzically.

"We were together at first, then I leave—that's when I meet up with Sam and Red at the church, and by the way, we are talking, but I have no idea what was said. I'm telling you, it was weird. But very graphic."

Julian looked attentively at Mackenzie and grabbed her hand.

"It does sound weird, but I'm sure everything is okay. We can call Lauren as soon as we land."

Mackenzie held Julian's hand and turned to the window. She realized that worry would be her worst enemy. She decided to catch up on her rest. She and Julian had tons of things to do as a married couple. First and foremost, they had to find a new home in California now that Julian had decided to team up with his old friend and Mackenzie's old flame,

Ken, to start up a firm in San Francisco. But just as she began to fall asleep, the pilot began making an announcement.

"Good morning, ladies and gentlemen," the mild-spoken, unseen pilot said before clearing his throat. "American Airlines would like to thank you for choosing our airline, and we welcome you to fl y again with us in the very near future. We would like to bring to your attention that the FAA has issued a warning and request that we land in Canada. While we cannot give any specifics, we would like to assure you that there aren't any safety issues with this plane. Please do not be alarmed; we assure you that THERE ARE NO PROBLEMS WITH THE PLANE.

This was just sent to us from the FAA. Once again, this flight will be headed to Canada; we will not be landing at John F. Kennedy airport.

Thank you, and thanks for flying American Airlines."

The first class passengers began to sit upright, visibly concerned.

There was an older guy with a deep Italian accent that asked, "Uh, wat do ya mean? This is insane. My wife is supposed to pick me up from the airport at noon. What's going on here?"

"Sir, we are sorry for the inconvenience, but with all the news going on, I'm sure your wife will know that your plane won't be landing in New York at noon," the shorter flight attendant said.

The slightly balding man was agitated but at a lost for words. He, along with the other passengers, looked around in search of more information or group cohesiveness to get to the bottom of their ordeal.

Julian and Mackenzie continued to hold hands and wait for further word.

Mackenzie knew something was terribly wrong—something that involved her loved ones, something that made her knees weak—and she thought of using the restroom, but she decided to wait so she wouldn't miss anything.

Julian couldn't wait. He excused himself as Mackenzie sat quietly and prayed; trying to put her dreams out of her mind.

Sam was married to Natalie now, and they had been expecting their first child. Maybe the dream had something to do with Natalie having the baby sooner than she thought, and Sam had to leave in a hurry—or Lauren was worried about leaving Mackenzie in St. Croix with Julian.

After all, the two of us back together and deciding to get married on a whim would make anyone worry after they found out why we broke up in the first place, Mackenzie thought to herself.

Julian returned to his seat and grabbed Mackenzie's hand. She turned back to the window and forced herself to catch up on her sleep. She knew getting back to the States meant doing a lot of work. She had to arrange to get her things from Atlanta; and Julian had to arrange to sub-lease his condo in Dallas. Then there was Jay-Jay—she still had to get her back.

Mackenzie was ready for a change and used that energy to forget what was going on now. And although she and Ken had shared a brief kiss so many years ago, she was delighted that he and Julian would be working together. This was going to give her a chance to do some independent work as well.

She pictured the four of them all newly weds, new to the area, and ready to take San Francisco by storm. She drifted off to sleep in anticipation of her new life.